MY DAR

I

It was a simply fabulous summer—the one when I was fifteen—the best ever. Lazing on beaches, eating divine food, messing about with lots of kids of all nationalities and even doing a bit of water-skiing.

Dad, who's an actor, was completely relaxed for once, safe in the knowledge that his television series was due to go on more or less into infinity, and that he'd been "promoted"—the rather stuffed-shirt army officer he played had been given another star or pip or stripe or whatever they get because the actor who had been playing the lead had left the cast (lots of actors' jokes about "deserted", "shot trying to escape" etc.). So Dad was able to lie on the beach, turning a tasty shade of lobster, moaning comfortably about the extra heavy rehearsal schedule he'd have to face back in England; meanwhile Mum, who is always pretty easy-going, sat beside him and mused aloud about the things we could buy with the extra money he'd get.

I remarked to my older brother Alastair once, after we'd been sitting with them, "The things Dad finds to grumble about! Do you remember the last out-of-work patch when he was ready to put his head in the oven?"

"That was before they stopped the gas being poisonous. I don't know what out-of-work actors with large families and big mortgages do these days," said Alastair, idly watching the hot sand trickle through his fingers.

"I wouldn't go back to that for anything," I said with a shudder.

"Amazing you remember it. You were only ten or something."

"Eleven. It was the year I took the eleven-plus and got into Lady Mary."

I stopped talking. Did Alastair hate to be reminded that he had not passed his eleven-plus three years before that? He didn't say anything, just lay as before with his hat over his eyes. I looked at him critically. He's big and muscly and quite good-looking too, and at seventeen I thought he should be going after some of the gorgeous girls-of-all-nations who kept sauntering past, giving him the come-on. But he was positively retarded on the subject of girls. It was with the greatest difficulty that I managed to drag him off with me in the evenings to the local taverna-discos (without him, Dad wouldn't have let me go) in the hope of getting a glimpse of an Italian I had noticed. Actually that was as far as it went, and I was quite relieved when I observed his goings-on with older girls. Learn to walk before you run, I say, and whenever I looked into those great black come-to-bed Sicilian eyes I realized I was hardly out of my push-chair.

As for Bruce, my younger brother, he fell in with some local urchins and took off. We scarcely saw him except at meals for the whole fortnight. Even Mum had a real rest, and we all came home looking as if we'd spent six weeks in the Bahamas (which was just what my arch-enemy at school, the dreaded Pamela Wilton, *had* done). Dad had to use a much lighter make-up for the officer to lighten his tan, when he began—with a great show of reluctance—to rehearse for the new series.

Alastair had, for the moment, finished school. He'd dragged himself through the last couple of years, longing with all his heart to leave, and no sooner were we back home from the holiday than he joyfully started what he claimed was a temporary job at the local garage.

Dad, who'd been hinting all summer that he wanted Alastair to go back to school and take some A-levels, was driven back on saying, "Won't hurt as a filler till we make some proper decisions." Al said nothing. He folded his new overalls into a carrier-bag, took his lunch-box from Mum, kissed her, winked at me, and sauntered off to his first day's work.

A day or two later Bruce, with everything in place just for once because of a brand-new uniform, set off for *his* first day at his new school, Willcox.

His getting into this very good school had been an occasion of great rejoicing. It was the climax of a long and, at times, bitter struggle in Dad's life. Every time one of us had to transfer from the local primary school the household would enter a ghastly period of stress, soul-searching and general uproar. The worst time was with Alastair.

The whole vexed subject of secondary education is all mixed up, in our house, with the even more vexed subject of politics.

Now I happen to be very interested in politics, something most of my girl-friends think is freaky. But I don't see how anyone could grow up in our family and *not* take some interest. Dad is Labour and Mum Tory and they argue continuously so I get both sides flung at me and of course I haven't made up my mind yet. But one thing I am sure of, and that is that it's a bit silly to have principles which are so high you can't live up to them.

What I mean, for instance, is this. Being a Socialist, Dad isn't supposed to try to get a "privileged" education for his children. So when Alastair failed the eleven-plus, as I've mentioned, Dad shouldn't have minded the idea of his going to the local secondary mod, which, after all, was a good democratic school where everybody sent their kids if they didn't get into a grammar. Or did they? Well, in our district the truth was nobody did anything of the sort. Instead, they somehow scraped the fees together, coached their little dimwits like mad and squeezed them willy-nilly through the entrance exam to some more or less posh private school.

That naturally meant that the local secondary mod was left with a pretty ropy reputation for, shall we say, roughness. At the time Dad was trying to resign himself to sending Al to it, horror-stories were reaching him daily about universal smoking from the age of twelve, teachers being assaulted, girls pushed off the pavements (and into the bushes) and in general nothing being learnt that could land a boy in any higher sphere of life than jug.

Well, on top of this poor old Dad and his principles were being fired at by shot and shell at home. Mum's ideas were simple. You did your best for your own kids. If you could help others on the way, fine, but nobody could convince her that throwing her son into a sink-school was going to raise the general standard of education and manners there.

Then there was Grandad, Mum's father, a retired colonel. He and Dad could hardly be said to get along. Their every thought and word struck sparks from each other. Grandad stamped in one day at the height of the crisis and boomed that he'd rather see his grandson dead at his feet than going to school with a bunch of "oafs". "One sound apple in a barrel of rotten ones won't keep firm long!" he roared. "As for doing anything about the bad 'uns—"

I don't remember anything else about the row, but I remember that. I think it was the first political idea that had ever penetrated my head.

I hope you won't think too badly of Dad's will-power when you hear how it all ended. He was overpowered, and not just by Mum and Grandad but his own reluctance to send Alastair to that grotty school. He not only stifled his conscience, but let Grandad pay the first year's fees to Burnfield Court. He paid him back later, when the army serial got under way; but at the time it was a total defeat, both for Dad and for socialism. It was years before I really noticed how much it had hurt him. It was as if he'd been pulled in half, and had stuck himself back together again not quite straight.

I think it was when I realized this that I decided to take a serious interest in politics. It seemed to me so extraordinary that a thing like school should be able to damage a marvellous man like Dad. And there are a lot of other things that seemed very wrong to me, not least the fact that most people think it's somehow not done to even mention the word "class".

One day I found a book lying around the house called *Noblesse Oblige* by Nancy Mitford. Mum saw me at it and said, "Oh, you've got hold of that thing! You won't understand it. All that's a thing of the past now, but we thought it a scream when it first came out."

I didn't think it was a scream. I wasn't so sure it was a thing of the past, either. It was mostly about the way people talk, and how you can tell whether they're upper, middle or lower class from the words they use for different things. "Toilet" and "loo" for instance. We always called it a toilet at school but a loo at home. I'd never realized it before. Same with "dinner" and "lunch". Whoever heard of a "lunch-lady" at school? Was it all a joke, as Mum said, an anachronism, or did it mean something?

It wasn't till that year when I was fifteen that I found out how important all that was going to be *to me*.

2

The day Bruce started at Willcox Dad drove him to the station with me in the back seat. The school was two stops down the line, and Bruce insisted on going the rest of the way alone. He's a perfect little fiend, my brother Bruce, but I will say that for him, he's got plenty of bottle and can cope with life pretty well for his age.

Dad and I saw him on to the train. There were a couple of other boys in Willcox blazers which put Dad's mind at rest about the longish walk at the other end. Dad's mind must have been altogether easier now than for a long time. Alastair had struggled through Burnfield Court somehow or other; I was safely and happily at Lady Mary Engels, a very good girls' school where I was being paid for by the Council, and now Bruce was off to the second-best boys' school in West London, also paid for by the Council. (The last lot that were, as it turned out. The Labour Government put a stop to all that right after Bruce's lot got in. Willcox has gone independent now.)

Ironic that there should have been no school fees now that at last we were comfortably off. The army serial on TV showed no signs of ever ending. Dad was bored bananas with his part as the officer and we tried to sympathize but we were really hypocrites. The truth was, we liked having enough money and having Dad just normally bad-tempered, not suicidal like he was when he was "resting" for nearly a year.

Dad gave a contented sigh as the train disappeared, put his arm round me and led me back to the car.

"I've got time to run you to school," he said.

"Don't make yourself late for rehearsal," I said. "I can get the bus."

He shook his head and helped me into the front seat, doing up the seat-belt for me. On the way he said, "It was nice, the holiday—wasn't it?"

"Absolutely fabulous," I replied.

"You were all so good. Pure delight." After a moment he added, "Did you and Alastair get up to any mischief, those evenings you were out together?"

"Depends what you call mischief."

"Came in pretty late sometimes."

"Oh, it was all kid-stuff. You know Al. He hasn't much devil in him."

Dad frowned. "But you have."

"If so, it hasn't showed itself yet."

"Hm. I sometimes wonder when it will."

At the school gate, just as I was getting out, he suddenly said, "Kate. Don't run Alastair down."

I was flummoxed for a minute, thinking he meant run him down on my bike or something. Then I got it, and said in surprise, "I don't. Why should I?"

"Well—" he hesitated. "You and Bruce—you're so—bright, quick-witted. *You* know. And Alastair's a different type altogether. Sometimes I suspect that you in particular tend to bank on his good nature—make use of him, just because he lacks the confidence you have, the—"

"What *are* you nattering on about, Dad? You make me sound like a wicked capitalist exploiter, and Al like a downtrodden worker!"

Dad was embarrassed.

"Oh, never mind. Forget it. Run now, or you'll be late."

I leant into the car and kissed him. He had to wear his hair ridiculously short for the officer, and it was ages before I could learn to love the military moustache that also went with the part, but now I did. He's lovely looking, is my Dad—not tall, but straight and well-built and with these fierce but kind eyes. Suddenly I gave him a second, bigger kiss and said, "I like old Al now, actually. I haven't had a fight with him for ages."

"That wasn't quite what I meant," said Dad.

It was great to be back at school. Our French teacher, Jammy Jamieson, had gathered venom in Bognor and I could see her squaring up for a nice juicy term-long battle with me. That day we just sparred a little, but enough to make my best friend Emma Jocelyn say under her breath, "Look out, Kate! She's sharpening her knife for you."

Seeing Emma again was one of the best bits of being back. She and our other friends, Abby, Kath and Tina, flung themselves on my and each other's necks, and festooned together we exchanged shrieks and an occasional coherent sentence about our holidays. It would be days before we all caught up with the news, and weeks before we got fed up with inviting each other home at weekends. That is one disadvantage of going to a non-local school, you can't really see your friends much because of homework and the fact that you're all so scattered. Emma lives *miles* from me, it's practically an excursion to visit her.

The dreaded Pamela Wilton kept aloof from our ecstatic reunion, eyeing us patronizingly from a distance. Tina nudged me and indicated her with her eyebrows.

"Boy-friend," she hissed (if you can hiss, with no s's).

This was intriguing. "Oh? What sort?"

"How should I know? She let fall she had one, that's all. He goes to Willcox."

"My kid brother goes there now," I said. "Find out his name and I'll set my spy on him."

Tina thought this an excellent plan, and before the day was out had passed me a note which contained the words, "Geoffrey Gordon".

That evening when the family forgathered round the supper table, all except Al who was working late at the garage, I asked Bruce if he'd keep an eye out for a chap called Geoffrey Gordon.

"He's not in my class," Bruce said. Trust him to know the names of all his classmates after one day.

"I never said he was, dumbhead. He's much older than you, probably in the sixth form."

"Oh, I shan't have anything to do with him then. We're dirt to all that lot. Why, anyhow?"

"He's the boy-friend of my worst enemy at school. I want to know what he's like."

Bruce gave me one of his brief, assessing stares and then put another large piece of chop in his mouth.

"The weird sister," he remarked.

Dad was fidgeting. He wanted to retire to his little attic study and start learning his lines for the next day's rehearsal. But he didn't want to go till Alastair got home.

"This is a bit much," he burst out at last to Mum. "From nine in the morning till this hour? It's sweated labour! The damn place shut two hours ago!"

"They go on working on rush-jobs till after eight sometimes," said Bruce. "He told me."

"Well, but that's the mechanics, the proper ones I mean. Alastair's only supposed to be helping round the place."

"He's learning."

"Codswallop. Learning what, for God's sake? He's not going to be there long enough to learn anything worthwhile."

"He knows how to change a tyre already."

"I should hope he knew that before!"

"A *tyre*, Dad. Not just a wheel. Any fool can do that, even you."

Dad flew off the handle. Well, it was a bit strong.

"You mind your tongue, my little lad, or you'll get a thick ear!"

"Sorry then."

"I should think so."

Mum created a diversion, something she's very good at.

"Quick, it's nearly time for the programme! Take your fruit-salad into the living-room."

It was a ceremony rather like family prayers. Every member of the family who was at home, and casual visitors as well, had to sit in front of the box for twenty-six minutes twice a week for the current episode of Dad's series. Yes, twice a week—it was repeated, and we were expected to watch it both times. I don't say we always did—homework, for one thing, was considered a good enough excuse, and of course if we were out we were out, though it was rather frowned on to *be* out at that sacred hour. Not that I minded. I enjoyed the silly thing, it had "got" me (along with umpteen million others all over Britain) and I wouldn't have wanted to miss it even if Dad hadn't been in it.

Tonight he had a goodish chunk. The story was about a regiment in the last war, and Dad was the second in command. It was ironic in a way. His own father had been a lance-corporal in the First World War, and Dad, who'd been just about old enough to join up at the end of the Second, had only got as far as being a private. He claimed to have been the most inefficient private in the service at that. Yet here he was, moustache bristling, ordering everyone about, "as to the manner born" (whatever that may mean, it's one of Grandad's pet expressions). Knowing Dad as well as we did, it was rather hard to keep a straight face sometimes, especially when his character got a bit high-handed and shrill. My Dad's got an awful temper in real life, but when he's angry he roars and swears and stamps, he doesn't get pinch-lipped and quivery and neurotic like the officer.

The person in the family who enjoys the programme most is Dad's brother Steve. Whenever we see him—mostly only at Christmas because all Dad's relations live up north—Uncle Steve tells us how he simply rolls about every time he watches because the officer is so totally unlike Dad's real self. "It's the posh Sandhurst accent that gets me!" he says, in his own Lancashire one. Dad used to talk broad Lancashire until he went to R.A.D.A. and had it beaten out of him, and he can still put it on when he likes. It gives me a funny feeling, talking to Uncle Steve and Dad's other brother Joe. Dad isn't like their brother, he doesn't even look like them. They're tremendous fun—we get on very well with our cousins too—but they're both working men and proud of it, and Dad's come away from them, socially as well as geographically. They tease him rotten about it. I'm never sure whether he minds this or not.

So we watched the programme and told Dad how good he was in his big scene (which was true, but we would have said it anyway—it's part of the ritual) and then I went up to my room to do my homework and Bruce went out to kick a ball around the next-door kids' garden. It's a bit bigger than ours with more open space and their father isn't so fussy about his flower-beds.

I love my room. It's quite small and all neatly fitted out like a ship's cabin. Dad did most of it, even including the bunk-bed of pine which has a sort of alcove underneath it containing my dressing-table. This had once been a desk, but when I started (about four years ago) taking some sort of passing interest in my appearance, Mum transformed it into a dressing-table, with little drawers and the right sort of light, and for my fifteenth birthday in March she gave me a starter make-up kit—nothing gaudy, you understand, just a couple of fairly innocuous pinkish lipsticks and some eye-shadow (practically invisible in use) and brush-on mascara in the lightest of light browns, to darken my too-pale lashes.

These have been driving me mad ever since I noticed at the age of twelve that no one but me ever *would* notice them. The first time I sneaked some of Mum's mascara (a week after this awful discovery) I knew I would not rest until I had some of my own which I could wear all day, and all night too if possible—it upset me to think of those pasty stubby little hairs, like albino spiders' legs, lying on my cheeks, even in sleep. But it was ages before Mum and Dad would hear of make-up, and in Lady Mary, if you can believe it, girls are forbidden to wear any until their senior year. Of course we all do; Tina was tarting her eyes up like mad when she was barely fourteen—and being told sharply by Jammy to go and wash it off. One thing about this idiotic, antiquated prohibition—it teaches you to be subtle about applying the stuff. Anything at all obvious gets you sent straight to the washroom, and in extreme cases Jammy's been known to lend a hand with the corner of a rough towel, well drenched in liquid soap. Once you've had soapy mascara rubbed into your eyes by that witchy claw, as I did the day after I got my birthday-present and rather overdid it in my joy, you tend to use a very light hand with the old brush afterwards.

Anyway I resisted the inevitable temptation to go straight to my dressing-table this evening and start a few experiments because, first day of school notwithstanding, all the teachers had fairly lumbered us with work, especially Jammy of course. (I often wondered if she'd have hated me so much, or me her, if instead of French she'd been teaching me English or Economics or one of the things I'm good at.) All I did was switch the lights on for just a moment and check that I looked reasonable in *case* the doorbell suddenly rang. Not that it was likely to at that hour, but sometimes Rebecca Daniels from next door would come in for a chat and occasionally she'd bring a boy with her.

I rather dreaded Rebecca, though not like Pamela Wilton of course. I'm honest enough to admit that my dread of Rebecca, *unlike* my dread of Pamela, was caused entirely by jealousy and was no fault of hers at all. (Pamela on the other hand was just a ghastly stuck-up affected silly creep who deserved to be dreaded.) Rebecca, after all, can't help being so pretty and having had boys flocking round her from the age of approximately three and a half. It's all on account of her Jewish blood. *God*, how I wish I had a bit of exotic blood in me somewhere! Even if it didn't provide me with foot-long sooty eyelashes and curly black hair and incredible liquid eyes like the sexy Sicilian's, it would give me a *feeling* of being something other than a plain old doughy English girl with all this stupid straight fair hair and blue eyes and—well, I mustn't be a bore about my eyelashes but they really are the curse of my life. Of course there is one nice thing about Rebecca which is that she has to watch her figure, and that she will, despite watching it, inevitably one day be as fat as her mother. I am size ten and my mother is as slim as a rail though we both eat like pigs. I get a good deal of quiet consolation out of this whenever I'm with Rebecca, even when she has a boy in tow gazing at her as if having the bust of a mature woman at the age of fifteen is entirely normal and very desirable (which perhaps from his point of view it is).

She didn't come that night, though, and I was able to get on with my work. I had to skimp on something, so I skimped on French. Well, I was dead beat by nine o'clock and anyway, Jammy wouldn't be satisfied, so I left most of it, though my conscience wasn't easy.

At nine I knocked off and got undressed. I felt like a long, hot, lazy bath with loads of bubble-maker and my new book, which Kath had lent me saying it was absolutely smashing and had made her cry. *Of course* she had taken the edge off it by *telling* me the girl dies in the end, for which I could have shot her, but nevertheless I was looking forward to it.

So I was somewhat annoyed (shall we say) when I arrived at the bathroom door to find it locked, and bathy sounds coming out.

"Who on earth's having a bath at this hour?" I shouted, banging. It was *my* hour and everyone in the family should know it.

"Me," said Alastair.

"You stinker! You've used all the hot water!"

"Can't help it. I'm filthy," he said smugly. "You should see me. Grease to the elbows, sweaty feet—"

"All right, I get the message."

I stamped downstairs in a huff.

"I do wish to God we had another bathroom!" I exclaimed as I burst into the living-room where Mum was sitting alone, mending in front of the telly, very cosy and Mum-like.

"Don't take God's name in vain," she said automatically.

"You believe in him," I accused her. She claims to be an agnostic like Daddy (they never argue about religion) but I always suspect she is nothing of the sort.

"I don't."

"Then why do you mind my taking his name in vain?"

"It doesn't sound good. It's a sort of swearing."

"Daddy swears like fifty navvies."

Mum looked annoyed. "Daddy is *grown-up*."

"Then he should be *better* than us, not worse. More controlled, more—"

It was the old, old argument. We all three agree it's not fair to be expected to stick to rules our parents can't stick to.

"Listen, Kate! Your father has spent his entire adult life either in the army or in the theatre. Soldiers are well-known for using swear-words whenever possible, and actors are very little better. Your father has inevitably picked up bad language as a habit, a speech-mannerism, and it's a very hard habit to break."

"Well if he picked it up when he was already a man, how can he expect a little girl like me not to pick it up from him?"

"You haven't got as many worries and stresses as he has."

"Well I've got one now! Alastair's grabbed off the bathroom and all the hot water."

"I should think so. You should have seen him when he got in! Grease to the elbows—"

"And smelly feet. He told me all about it. Well I haven't been lying under a car all day but I did play horrible hockey and I dare say I'm a bit niffy myself—"

"Kate, don't be *coarse*," said Mum primly. She's not really prim, but sometimes she puts it on. "You can use the basin in our room and have a good wash."

"I don't *want* a good wash! I want a lovely long soak, I was looking forward to it! Why can't we have another bathroom? Rebecca's family's got *three*, and their house is just like ours in reverse—"

"They're six in the family, not to mention their *au pair*. Besides, their downstairs bathroom is just where my glory-hole is and I'm not sacrificing *that*, not to have the cleanest children in London."

"You're just selfish," I said, only half joking.

"Yup," said Mum, being Bruce, and bit off her thread. "Go to bed."

So I did, and lay awake for a while dreaming of being Rebecca, including her Jewish blood and her house which I have to admit is twenty times nicer than ours with its converted-loft playroom and huge plate-glass windows and luxury kitchen and furniture. It's all so modern it's like something out of "2001 A.D." The thing I like best is a fireplace built *in the middle of the room* with a dimpled copper hood-thing for a chimney. This weird arrangement goes right up through the middle of the house, making the most exotic hot square pillar through Rebecca's bedroom and on up through the attic playroom. Rebecca's decorated her bit of it with mosaic, copying designs from ancient Greece. She *would*. They look absolutely stunningly classical in that wildly *avant-garde* room. Of course Leo, her gorgeous older brother who's going to be an archaeologist, did most of it though he lets her take the credit.

While I was at it I let myself have a little mini-dream about Leo, too. Even though I knew it was completely pointless. He was twenty-two to begin with, and hence would never so much as glance in my direction even if I were as beautiful as Delilah. Nevertheless I'd had this crush on him for simply ages. I confessed about it to Mum once, when Dad was away filming in Manchester and I slept in her bed. I do that sometimes. It's fun—we really talk then, in the dark, and it's as if we were sisters. When I confessed about Leo, she just said, "Well of course I don't blame you, he is divine, only don't break your heart over him because you haven't a hope."

"Why not?" I asked (then. I was only thirteen or something.) "As I grow up the age-difference won't be so terrible. When I'm nineteen, he'll be twenty-six—"

"And married. Or digging up tombs in Egypt. Or most probably both."

"He won't be able to go to Egypt because he's a Jew and they won't have him." We were just learning about the Middle East at school and, besides, there happened to be a war going on out there at that very time.

"Well, that's another thing," said Mum slowly.

"What?"

"Him being Jewish. Not that Daddy or I would care, but *his* parents might."

I hadn't the remotest idea what she meant, and she had a tough time explaining it to me. I still don't get it, if you want to know the truth, but I've written it off as one of those extraordinary warps in the adult world that you just have to accept. In a way, now, I was glad. Every time I saw him, which I did very often of course, kicking about in the garden with his twin brothers or waiting for a bus or getting into his little car in our joint drive, my heart gave a corny lurch and I sort of went to pieces in various other ways, and it helped a bit to be able to say to myself very firmly, "There is *absolutely nothing doing* so forget it." Because I'd since confirmed what Mum told me. When I asked Rebecca (in connection with herself, of course, not mentioning Leo) if she'd marry a non-Jew, she said all she hoped was that she never wanted to because if she did there'd be the most alarming outcry at home. Well, I wouldn't want to come between the man I loved and his family. Not that I *loved* Leo exactly, I mean I wasn't too sure what love was but I didn't see how you could call something love when the other person was scarcely aware of your existence. That was just a crush—infatuation—puppy-love. Calling my feeling by all those scornful baby-names helped me to keep it under control.

That's why it was a mini-dream and I timed it—five minutes dead, just long enough for us to be on an archaeological dig together and for me to fall into an excavation and break my leg and for all the other workers to go back to camp, forgetting about me, and for it to get dark, and for him to come looking for me and carry me out. The part where he picked me up and I gritted my teeth so as not to worry him by yelling from the pain in my broken leg was so exciting that I was quite relieved when I glanced at the luminous clock-face and saw that my five minutes was up. I didn't cheat as I might have done (I'd picked up a tremendously rare shard in the bottom of the excavation and had it clutched in my hand, ready to give to him) but rolled over in my bunk. My last thought before going to sleep was nothing to do with Leo. It was, "Maybe if I get up the minute Mum calls me, I'll have time to do a bit more French after all."

3

It was October before Bruce finally bothered to find out something about this Geoffrey that the dreaded Pamela was keen on.

She hadn't gone off him or anything in the meantime. In fact she was on him stronger than ever, and talked about him *ad nauseam* until the rest of us were ready to scream. Tina had also raked up some kind of boy-friend by this time. She was keeping him rather dark, but at least we'd seen him. His father used to pick her up after school in his car occasionally, with the boy-friend Tony huddled furtively in the back seat. We all tried to peer at him without being too rude about it, but it's just about as hard to peer *politely* into the back of a car as it is to peer politely up a Scotsman's kilt, and for the same reason—you have to bend down too far to let it be casual. We were always urging Tina to make him get out so we could get a good look, but she went all silly. She wouldn't even describe him, but from what we could see by peering he was quite presentable, I mean not spotty or anything. His hair was awful, almost short-back-and-sides, but that was because he went to an absolutely anti-progressive school where, among other barbarities, they still kept a cane. It was the sort of place a boy goes to who isn't strong-minded enough to survive a comprehensive or clever enough for a really good school. Nevertheless he was a boy, and even though he was only sixteen, and so not to be taken seriously, I must admit I envied Tina a bit.

But the mystery of Geoffrey (known as the dreaded Geoffrey by association) remained, and I determined to solve it, so I gave Bruce no peace till at last he said one day at tea,

"That chap you're interested in, Geoffrey Gordon, is a villain."

"Oh *good*!" I said delightedly.

"Eh?" asked Alastair, home early for once. "Why good if you're interested in him?"

I brushed him aside. "I don't even know him. Tell more, Brucekins."

"If you call me Brucekins I'll bash you in and not tell you another word."

"It's a term of affection."

"It's a damn silly term."

"Oy," said Dad mildly from behind his script. (The officer was so built up these days poor Dad even had to learn lines at mealtimes.)

"Anyway, do go on."

"Well, he plays squash, I'll give him that. That's how I know him." Bruce is a pretty good squash-player for his age, and had lost no time in getting stuck into it at school where they had smashing courts. "I played him yesterday."

"Did he beat you?"

"Of course. He's three times my size and donkeys' years older."

"Is that why he's a villain—because he beat you?"

"Of *course* not, what do you think? One of the others bet me I wouldn't dare ask him for a game. He's a villain because he runs around with a villainous crowd. Bullies."

"Who do they bully?"

"Me, for one. Only I don't take much notice. You know, shoving in the corridors, making idiotic remarks, that sort of thing. They tease you rotten if they find out you're in any way different."

"How are you different?" asked Alastair, who was listening more closely than usual.

"Oh well, Dad being an actor doesn't help." Despite the completely careless way Bruce said this, Dad instantly looked up, and Mum did too. He had our complete attention, but he didn't seem to notice and just went on tucking in to his tea. "Can I have another Penguin, Mum?"

"Yes. Go on."

Bruce took the Penguin and unwrapped it.

"Your mother meant, go on with what you were saying."

"What?—Oh, the creeps. Well, it's nothing much, they just sort of *strut* when they see me coming."

Dad sat up straight. "Strut? What do you mean, strut?"

"Like you in the programme. That special walk you do, with your back very stiff and your legs sort of flicking out slowly one by one."

"You make me sound like a peg-legged centipede," said Dad. But he looked upset. "Why the hell should they do that?—What else do they do?"

"Oh, nothing really. They salute me sometimes and then fall about laughing at their own brilliance."

Dad got up from the table and went to the window with his script dangling from his hand. He muttered something that sounded like "little bastards".

"Oh, they are," Bruce assured him quite cheerfully. "*I* don't mind it, but you should see what they do to some of the others."

"What like?"

"Well, there's a boy in our class called Jeremy Benthall. He's slightly brain-damaged. It hasn't affected his mind, he's brilliant as it happens, but he walks a bit jerkily and his speech is odd. We don't notice it any more, but you can imagine what Geoffrey Gordon and his mates make of *him*."

Mum had gone funny-looking. "What?" she asked tightly.

Bruce shrugged. "Oh, imitations, hobbling about, pawing the air and gibbering... There's one of them, chap called Mark Collins, who every time he sees Jeremy does his famous Hunchback of Notre Dame bit." Bruce did Mark Collins doing the Hunchback, a hideous grotesque with a twisted face.

"And this boy does this in front of the brain-damaged one?" asked Alastair. He'd gone funny-looking too. If there's one thing Alastair never could stand, it's cruelty. One of my earliest memories is seeing him, absolutely white with rage, fling himself on to a big boy on the common who we came on, crouched behind some blackberry bushes doing things to a bird.

"Yup. And there's another boy who talks really posh—you know, I-say-jolly-good-ever-so, and the other day I saw them all round him in the playground. They had him sort of backed against the railings and they were egging him on to say things like 'house' and 'horrors' and 'heavens'—words with aitches. He was crying."

"And what did you do?" asked Alastair tensely.

"*Me?*" Bruce looked up in great surprise. "Nothing! Who do you think I am, Batman? There were five of them, great big—" He indicated giants of eight feet by three.

"You could have told a teacher!" exclaimed Mum.

Bruce looked at me and rolled his eyes.

"He couldn't very well do *that*," I said.

"Anyway there were only the dinner-ladies on at that point, and they're useless."

Dad turned round from the window.

"And this is supposed to be the best boys' school in West London," he said. "Of all the scandalous, disgusting—"

"Second-best," said Bruce, getting up from the table. "But I bet it goes on in the best one, too. There are always bullies, in every school. Well, I'm off." It was his Scouts night.

"Done your homework?" Dad asked automatically.

"More or less. Bye, Mum, bye, Dad."

There was a heavy silence round the table when he'd gone. Finally Dad stirred.

"I suppose we have to be thankful that Bruce knows how to let it roll off him," he said. "Thank heaven he's no poor vulnerable kid... But it hurts to think they use my bloody mannerisms to taunt him with."

"Be glad he hasn't any of his own," said Mum, getting up to clear, "like Jeremy Benthall."

I would like to be able to say that I kept the evil news about Pamela's boy-friend tactfully to myself. I didn't. I spilled the entire beans in the first break the following day. Emma, Tina, Kath and Abby stood round me agog.

"Incredible!" said Emma at last. "He's obviously an erk. What does she see in him?"

"She's an erk herself," said Abby.

"Not an *erk*," said Emma.

We were silent. We all knew what she meant, but it's not a thing you can say.

"Maybe he's gorgeous," said Kath.

We looked at each other doubtfully. Can any amount of gorgeousness outweigh being an erk and a bully? Apparently it can.

"But what about all the things she said? How generous and kind he is, how good-mannered—"

"Maybe to *her*—"

"I don't believe it! He's practically in the Mafia."

"We've only got Kate's brother's word for that."

"Well," said Tina, "there's only one thing for it." We all looked at her expectantly. She's really the pace-setter for our bunch, she gets all the ideas and leads the way. "We've got to meet him."

"How?"

"We'll have to give a party and invite her. And him."

Sensation!

"A party? With boys?"

"Why not?"

"You're all right, you've got a boy-friend. What about us?"

"Oh, you'll dig up someone. Bring your brothers and we'll swop around."

"I haven't got a brother!" wailed Emma.

"You can have Alastair," I whispered to her comfortingly. That cheered her up at once.

"But *where* can we have it?" was the next question.

We looked at Tina. "Not at my place," she said instantly. "It's *minute*, and besides, Mum'd have a fit."

"We've all got Mums," Abby pointed out.

"But not fit-having ones like mine," said Tina firmly. This was typical of her. She threw up brilliant ideas which somehow landed on the heads of the rest of us.

We talked about it at length during the lunch-break. There were three possible houses we could hold it in—Emma's, Kath's or mine (Abby's Mum was actually on the verge of having another baby by her second husband). Neither Emma nor Kath were keen. I guessed why in each case. Kath's parents were fearfully grand and her house was full of valuable ornaments and antique furniture. Heaven knows it was big enough for a party involving half our school, but her parents were old and square and the surroundings might daunt us all. Emma's case was the opposite. *Her* parents were both struggling artists and they lived in a little terrace house in a rather humble district, miles away. It was a lovely place to visit because you felt so much at home there, and it, too, had nice things, mostly painted or made by her parents. We'd be welcome to have our party there, Emma said, and I knew it was true; but it was awfully small. We wouldn't be able to dance or anything.

So in the end, it came down to Muggins.

"I'll ask," I conceded finally.

"Don't just ask—*beg*," said Tina as we separated.

I didn't have to beg. Surprisingly, Mum agreed quite readily.

"You've earned a party," she said, which pleased me because I didn't know I had, but when pressed for details of my virtues she turned vague and said, "Well, you occasionally help round the house. You work hard at school. And you could have given us a lot more worry than you have." I thought of Rebecca, whose goings-on with boys worry her mother *sick* apparently, and a couple of other girls I knew, who do much worse, and thought that maybe I had been rather good in a negative kind of way.

Dad was more cautious.

"How many guests?"

"Twelve—six boys and six girls," I said promptly.

"And that's really all?—no waifs and strays?"

"Gosh, no!"

"I'll want to know who they all are."

Here was a slight problem. The conversation about the dreaded Geoffrey was too recent. I couldn't tell Dad *he* was coming.

"Well, it's just us five, plus a girl called Pamela Wilton and a boy each."

"It's the boys I'm worrying about. Who are they?"

"I'm inviting Alastair."

"Incest! Who else?"

"Tina's bringing her boy-friend Tony Beynton, his father's a company director, and—"

"Did I ask what their blasted fathers do?" shouted Dad. "I don't care about their incomes or their class credentials! I just want to know their names. Go on."

"Abby's bringing *her* older brother Ian—"

"How old?"

"Seventeen. And Kath said she'd try to bring a boy called William something. She's known him for ages, he's all right. Emma hasn't got anybody yet. I thought maybe Alastair would invite a friend." I stopped.

Dad was keeping count. "That's only five. Who's the sixth?"

"Pamela's boy-friend," I said innocently.

"What's *his* name?"

"I don't know how it helps you to know their names," said Mum at the critical moment. Funny how often she does that, like an instinct.

"I suppose not," muttered Dad.

"So can we?"

"When?"

"We thought . . . Hallowe'en. Thirty-first of October."

"Oh crikey! Fancy-dress and all that?"

"Of *course* not, we're not infants!" I said scornfully.

"Oh well . . . If you behave yourselves . . . After all, what harm can twelve of you do? Only just keep in mind that your mother and I are going to be right here all the time."

4

"Staying *in*?"

Tina put every morsel of her considerable scorn into her voice.

"What do your parents think we're going to do—wreck the place?"

"They probably think we need chaperoning," I said with a giggle, thinking of Alastair and this William of Kath's whom she'd privately told me was about as sexy as a currant bun. "Anyway it's their house. We can't expect them to just walk out and hope for the best."

"I suppose that means no drink," said Tina in disgust.

I was taken aback. I hadn't figured on there being any drink anyway. Emma caught my eye, and, seeing I suppose that I was startled too, ventured to ask, "What kind of drink were you thinking about?"

"Well it's perfectly obvious we can't have a proper party without wine."

I relaxed. I'd drunk wine in Italy, and at home sometimes too, when there were people for dinner. For one awful moment I'd thought she meant whisky and gin.

"I don't think they'd mind the odd bottle of vino," I said carelessly.

"Well, Tony will certainly bring some *automatically* unless he's told not to, in which case he won't bother coming," said Tina loftily.

Not a word of thanks about getting a place to have it. That was just like Tina. Later Emma said, "I think it's jolly nice of your parents to let us. And if her Tony can't enjoy himself without getting sloshed, I hope he *doesn't* come."

Feeling very warm towards her, I asked her to stay the night of the party. I knew her father doesn't have a car and I didn't know how she'd get home.

"Who's going to ask *her*?" Kath hissed after school.

"I will," said Tina boldly.

"What if she says no? Then it'll all be for nothing."

"She won't say no. There aren't *that* many parties, even in her exotic life."

Far from saying no, Pamela simply fell about with excitement. Having treated us with the utmost scorn for years past, hardly speaking to anyone but Tina whom she considered her equal in cleverness if not in social rank, she now came simpering over to us.

"What an entirely splendid idea to throw a do," she said. "I'd adore to come." She honestly said that. She really was quite unspeakable. I often wondered how she got like that. Actually I think I know, more or less. Her parents are real jet-set types, constantly whisking about the globe—her father's "in oil". "Up to the neck, and boiling, I hope," as Abby once said when we were especially sick of her. She never had anything ordinary, not even holidays—she went to places like Bahrain. She lived with her aunt and uncle, jetsetty too by inclination, but apparently a bit past it now. I'd seen them a couple of times at school functions. The aunt looked like Hermione Gingold playing Miss Haversham, if she ever did—a bizarre sort of doll, gaudy but dusty somehow. I'd have felt sorry for anyone but the dreaded Pamela who had to live with her. The parents we never caught a glimpse of.

Now I was facing her and looking into those languid eyes, it seemed more incredible than ever that she would have looked twice at an erk like this Geoffrey sounded. My curiosity burned me.

"And you'll bring Geoffrey?" Tina was saying.

"But of course, if he's free," said Pamela.

"And a bottle?"

"Oh, *severial*!" That was her idea of a joke. "What *fun*! A party where there are no boring adults." This was her way of letting us know that she normally only went to terribly sophisticated grown-up parties. "And imagine you all asking *me*," she added, her eyes suddenly languid no longer but surprisingly beady. I wondered uneasily if she knew we detested her.

There's a lot more to giving a party in your home than I'd thought. I found this out as the day of the great event drew nigh and Mum started to fuss.

"We can leave the furniture till the last minute," she said, "but things like ordering glasses and food will have to be done in advance."

"Ordering *glasses*?"

"Well, I'm not about to risk mine. We'll get in some wine on sale-or-return. The wine merchant will then supply glasses."

"What if they get broken?" Alastair, ever practical, asked.

"Then our hostess, here, will have to pay for them out of pocket-money."

"Of course they won't get broken!" I scoffed.

Little did I know.

We were having it on a Saturday, naturally. On the Friday when I came home from school the hall seemed to be full of groceries. There was a whole crate of wine.

"Surely we won't need all this?"

"I should hope not indeed," said Mum, who was bustling about. "I had to order that much to get the glasses. I'll make a punch out of a bottleful or maybe two and lots of fruit-juice. Surely that'll be enough. I don't really see why you need alcohol at all—we never used to need drink to enjoy ourselves."

"And what about all this food?"

"Oh, you'll need *that*. I don't mind that at all."

In the kitchen, a sort of creative culinary chaos met my gaze.

"Mum, you shouldn't! It's not necessary to do all this. A few sandwiches and bowls of crisps—"

"Rot," she said tartly. "Your first party? Sandwiches and crisps? Put the salad things away, we can do that tomorrow afternoon. These cooked dishes must be got out of the way this evening."

I felt very pleased. Mum was laying things on with as much care as for a grown-up do. I pitched in eagerly and helped as much as I could. The family got short rations that night because Mum was entangled with patés and risottos. We all found places to sit somehow round the edge of the crowded kitchen table with mugs of tinned soup and hunks of bread and butter.

Alastair said it was all very hard on a poor working man. He'd been standing over a hot carburettor all day and he wanted some real food. It was like "water water everywhere and not a drop to drink".

"*Nor any* drop to drink," said Dad testily. "If you must quote clichés, get them right." He was also fed up about no proper dinner, it seemed. Or maybe it was Alastair's obvious relish for his job that was eating him.

"What's this affair in aid of, anyway?" Alastair inquired. He hadn't exactly agreed to come yet, and had flatly refused to oblige by bringing anybody, so he wasn't the most popular brother I had just then.

"It's just a party," I said. "You know, one of those teenage orgies you read about—nothing to get in a twist about." I left out the knickers part in deference to Mum. That expression drives her absolutely up the pole.

"I know what it's in aid of," said Bruce from behind his comic. He was unashamedly reading at table because, as he said, we weren't really "at table" in any polite sense.

"What?" said Alastair. I looked at Bruce nervously.

"They want to see what each other's boy-friends are like."

My blood ran cold. Did he know about Geoffrey? Would he announce that he was coming? But he didn't.

"Ah," said Alastair after a moment. But later when we were washing up together he said, "Isn't there a less expensive way to see each other's boy-friends?"

"We couldn't see Pamela's without inviting her," I said unwarily.

"Who's Pamela? I haven't met her, have I?"

"Of course not. She's dreaded."

"Not *that* Pamela?"

"Yes."

He gazed at me, dishcloth poised. "You mean you're throwing a party just to get a look at the boy-friend of a girl you can't stand? What on earth for?"

I opened my mouth to give him the obvious answer, and then discovered there wasn't one.

"Oh, you wouldn't understand," I said. A stock reply, I realize, but I hadn't another handy. It did seem a bit odd, now I thought about it. Why *were* we so curious?

"Are you asking Rebecca?" Alastair unexpectedly inquired.

"No. The others don't know her. It's just from our school."

"Won't she hear the noise and be hurt?"

I hadn't thought of that.

"Well . . . maybe we could ask her. I'll see."

Tina wasn't keen, but nobody else minded. In the end Tina said, "We won't have to find a boy for her, will we?"

"She'll find a few for us if we need them."

"We need them!" said Emma fervently.

This was on the Saturday morning. All the girls (except Pamela) had come over to help, which was nice of them, especially Emma who'd had all those miles to come. We were terribly excited and nervous, which made us giggly, and if it hadn't been for Mum organizing us like mad we wouldn't have got much done. As it was, she had Kath and Abby on the fruit-salad, Emma and me polishing the silver, while she and Tina plied to and fro from the dining-room arranging the buffet. There were tall candles, a big bowl of fruit, knives and forks rolled up in napkins, and the beginnings of a royal feast accumulating on our best white linen cloth. Dad, who mercifully had the day off (he often rehearses at weekends), was busy pushing back the chairs and sofas in the double-ended living-room and getting the rugs rolled up. Even Bruce was sorting out the best records, though I had to re-sort them later to get rid of the Rolf Harrises.

Well, so I nipped out of the back door and across to the back door of the Daniels' house which adjoins ours. Mrs Daniels answered. She's very elegant despite the fat and never looks hot or untidy as Mum tends to when she's cooking. I should think she has her hair done about every other day virtually. Anyway she had this *au pair* to help, a French girl called Marie-Noelle. She was in the kitchen now, grating potatoes, which seemed strange, but the Daniels have odd things to eat sometimes. She was a nice girl, in a lumpy, uncommunicative way—at least Mum was always saying she was nice and urging me to make her feel welcome in England.

"Rebecca's practising. Please don't interrupt her for long," said Mrs Daniels, after pressing a kiss on my cheek.

Rebecca was learning the 'cello. She was hard at work, sawing away on it in the attic playroom. I could sometimes hear her right through the wall from my bedroom when there weren't too many aeroplanes roaring overhead. She looked glad to stop when I walked in.

"We're having a party tonight," I said. "Would you like to come?"

She perked up like a squirrel, then drooped again over her 'cello. It's such a lugubrious-looking instrument; you can't play it without looking tragic, especially when you've got long black hair and these great melancholy eyes.

"I'm not allowed to. I got in late again last night."

Suddenly I wanted her to come. It would be good to have someone from outside our tight-knit little gang. Besides, there was the question of boys. She'd bring at least two, and my secret fear, that Alastair would flee at the last moment, *might* be eased if she were coming. Not that he was gone on her or anything, but he did like her.

"If I persuade your Mum, will you come? And bring some boys?" The "some" slipped out. I had meant to say "a".

"I'd love to!"

On the way downstairs I revised my plan and decided to ask my Mum to ask her Mum. And it worked—but at a price.

"I had to ask Marie-Noelle too," said Mum. Then, looking at our faces, "I *had* to, she looked so left out, it would have been too mean not to include her."

"Mum, how could you! You've ruined everything! She's *years* older than we are—"

"All of *two* years—"

"And she's another girl!" wailed Tina. "She'll throw out the numbers!"

"Rebecca's bringing two boys, and I asked Leo to drop round too," said Mum with a touch of defiance.

That silenced me. It nearly killed me, as a matter of fact.

Tina was scribbling on our kitchen telephone pad.

"Let's see. Girls: us five, Pamela, Rebecca and this Thingie-Noelle. Boys: Tony, William—he *is* coming, Kath?—Ian, Alastair, Geoffrey, Rebecca's two, plus Leo—well, it's just about okay, as long as no one drops out. What's this Leo like?"

Emma, who'd seen him around, swooned into one of the pushed-back armchairs. Then she sat up and said, "But ancient. Father-figure stuff."

"How old?"

Emma looked at me. I was feeling almost too overwhelmed at the prospect to speak, but I managed to croak out, "Twenty-two".

"Wow," whispered Tina, awed.

"What made him agree to come?" I asked.

"Marie-Noelle said she was too shy. Her English is still a bit sketchy. So he offered to bring her and settle her in."

I felt a sort of wave of love buffet against me. (I mean, of infatuation.) Kind, kind Leo! Just the sort of thing he would do, offer to bring a lumpy French *au pair* to a kids' party so she wouldn't be left out. Emma must have seen me go all glassy-eyed (she spotted ages ago that I had a thing about Leo) and gave me a sharp nudge to pull myself together before Tina noticed. Tina's very quick, and rather insensitive, about things like that.

I must say Mum and Dad were marvellous before it all began. Apart from the work they both did (Mum especially) they were wonderfully *free*, I mean apart from a brief and inevitable word about not drinking too much punch and being careful not to tread food into the carpet, they didn't lecture me at all. Dad did ask how long it was all likely to go on for, and when I said I thought not past midnight, he said, "That's okay, but I'm rehearsing in the morning and we have got neighbours, so please keep it down to a mild roar after eleven." Mum said, "Is it all right if I pop down every so often, just to see if you need any help?" I was privately quite relieved that she wanted to do this. To be honest, the prospect, now it was so close, terrified me. I was so glad Tina was coming. She was the only one of us with any experience of this sort of party, and she was full of good advice when she arrived, half-an-hour early, with Tony in tow.

"Let me taste the punch." She sipped from the ladle. "Hm, nice. We must watch out that nobody slips anything extra into it." Before I could ask what she meant, she went on, "We must post Alastair at the door to keep off gatecrashers until at least nine-thirty."

"What gatecrashers?"

"Oh," she said airily, "there are always a few kids who hear there's a party going on and try to bust in." I said nothing. This must be what Dad had meant when he asked about "waifs and strays"—I had thought he meant poor things like Marie-Noelle.

"How do you keep them out?" asked Emma.

"Well, you can't always. You just have to try to discourage them."

"Dad said, only twelve guests."

"It's sixteen already," said Tina cheerfully. "Don't worry. Come and see what we brought for decorations."

Tony was opening some plastic shopping-bags he'd come laden with. They turned out to contain no fewer than three bottles of red wine, some Hallowe'en masks, some orange and black balloons and a stack of witches' hats.

"Where did these come from?" cried Emma, trying on a hat and a Charles-de-Gaulle nose.

"I bought them," said Tony modestly. I hadn't had much chance to look at him yet, and indeed he wasn't much to look at—rather weedy and unpulled-together, I would have thought, for Tina especially. But perhaps she liked him for being bossable—she is a bit of a bossyboots, and Tony didn't look as if he'd resent that. "I bet she told him to buy them," Emma whispered as we ran upstairs to finish getting ready. On the way I knocked loudly on Alastair's door. "Hurry up!" I called.

Emma and I sat side by side at my dressing-table and did our eyes in concentrated silence. Tina and Tony were trying out records downstairs. All the lights and candles were on, although it wasn't yet perfectly dark, and the smell of the food and the punch drifting upstairs, mingling with dabs of our mothers' scent, filled us with a rare excitement. We turned to each other at the same moment and peered critically at each other's eye make-up.

"Yours is lovely! I love the silvery stuff in the corners."

"I like yours better. The shine's *wild.*"

"But it wears off."

We were both keyed up and Emma's hands shook as she gripped mine.

"I wish I'd been going to parties since I was twelve, like Pamela! Then I wouldn't be so nervous."

"Do you think there'll really be gatecrashers?" I asked.

"I hope not!" Emma said. "—Although," she added practically, "that was how Tina met Tony. *He* gatecrashed a party she was at."

The bell rang. We rushed downstairs. Alastair, looking amazingly self-possessed, was just opening the door. Outside were Kath, Abby and her brother Ian. I'd met him before, at her place. Nothing wonderful, but nice, like her. Their parents were divorced about five years ago and that made Abby and Ian very close to each other. I didn't know Abby then, but she came to school just afterwards. *Wrecked.* I swear I don't know how *any*body gets over a thing like that. I've told Dad and Mum, often. If they ever get divorced, I'll die.

Well, Emma and I rushed forward and welcomed Abby and Kath (just as if we hadn't seen them in the morning) and Ian shook hands with Alastair, and then, wouldn't you know it, the two boys immediately disappeared up to Alastair's bedroom to look at some stupid car-magazine Alastair was idiot enough to mention. Honestly, Ian hardly had his coat off! That left the five of us—and Tony, who looked seriously outnumbered, but I must say he coped very well. He presented us all with witches' hats and masks and Tina led a sort of *danse macabre* round the room, which warmed us all up.

Then Tony said, "What about some booze?" I'd forgotten all about the punch and my duties as hostess—I'd been counting on Alastair to dish it out—and before I knew quite what was happening, Tony had produced a corkscrew (Dad had deliberately put ours away) and uncorked one of his bottles, and was pouring out very full glasses for everyone.

"We're supposed to drink this," I said feebly, pointing to the punch in its nice cut-glass bowl. It had loads of cut-up fruit floating in it. Tony pulled out a silver ladleful and let it trickle back with the fruit making little sploshes.

"Very pretty," he said, "aesthetically speaking. But as a drinking man, I must say I prefer mine straight."

I tried to catch Tina's eye, but she was gazing at Tony with a soppy look on her face and I couldn't signal to her. I was just wondering whether I had courage enough to insist on at least having punch myself, when darling Emma said, "Punch for me, I don't like the taste of this." She tipped her wine into the punch, swirled the ladle round and doled out a glassful. Gratefully I did the same.

Then there was a silence. None of us knew what to say. I could have throttled Alastair. What would it be like if they stayed up there all evening? What would we do if nobody thought of anything to say, ever? But thank heaven, the doorbell rang again at that moment, and we all raced to see who it was.

Outside was William, Kath's friend. I purposely don't say boy-friend, because he wasn't, just the son of some family friends, and rather stodgy she always said, so I was pleasantly surprised. I thought straight away that he was very nice-looking. Not tall, but *nice*-looking, friendly-looking—typical sort of boy-next-door look, a good stand-by for occasions like this. Nice manners, too. No question of *his* disappearing, though he must have felt a bit embarrassed when he saw how few there were on the male team. He didn't let himself be pushed by Tony into having wine, either, and in fact actually asked for Coke. Tina had laughed at Mum's crate of Cokes, stored tactfully under the table, and I couldn't help smirking at Tina a little when this nice William asked for one.

"Well? And where is the guest of honour?" asked Tony. He'd evidently been let in on the root-cause of the party.

Abby was at the front window. "Somebody's coming, but it isn't them."

Gatecrashers! I thought instantly, in panic. But it wasn't.

It was Rebecca. She looked *stunning*, so stunning that even Tina goggled. Our group had all agreed to wear jeans and nice tops, and we all had, though Tina had pushed out the boat a bit with an off-the-shoulder job. But Rebecca had not been a party to this agreement. She was wearing a Laura Ashley number in sort of mulberry-and-cream cotton, with a heavenly oriental-looking silk embroidered shawl-thing *flung* round it and a marvellous big silver ornament on a chain round her neck that looked like something out of a North African bazaar. Neither Tony nor William had ever seen her before of course, and the moment she walked in I knew that Tina, at least, would never forgive me for asking her.

Trailing adoringly in her wake came two boys from our neighbourhood called Adam Scobie and Dominic Heywood. Unpromising as they were (both sixteen—I don't think Dominic was even that much—and hopelessly adolescent) they were boys and we needed them, so I hurried to give them drinks. They glanced for guidance at Tony, and plumped for the wine. Rebecca asked for punch, and stood with the glass twinkling in her hand and the candlelight touching her hair in all the right places, looking like some kind of gorgeous odelisk or obelisk or whatever they're called. The four boys couldn't take their eyes off her.

Tony, who had appeared to be in a trance, suddenly broke out of it and said abruptly, "What about a dance?"

All the boys except William made an instinctive jerk towards Rebecca, but Tony got there first, and the other three were obliged to look dismally round to see what else was on offer. There was only us. Adam took Emma, who was the smallest (Adam is practically a *dwarf*, he's actually shorter than me) and Dominic grabbed Abby. William, unlike Tony, did not forget who had invited him and danced off with Kath. That left Tina and me.

We pretended to be making small adjustments to the tablecloth and Tina muttered savagely, "How *could* you? I could kill you." I looked at her, startled, because she sounded as if she really meant it. Her small, cat-like face was scarlet and she looked as if she might cry. I opened my mouth to ask what was the matter—after all, one dance! But then I realized that, never having had a boy-friend, I didn't really know what she was feeling. Supposing by some miracle I had gone to a party with Leo and some gorgeous obelisk—And speaking, or rather thinking, of Leo, the doorbell rang. The *back* doorbell this time.

"That'll be Leo and Marie-Noelle!" I cried in shameful relief, and ran through into the kitchen, abandoning poor Tina completely to her new role of cabbage.

It was not, however, Leo and Marie-Noelle, after all. It was the first gatecrashers.

There were three of them, two boys and a girl, all complete strangers, all armed with bottles. One of the bottles was gin—only a small bottle, but still, the sight of it panicked me somehow almost more than them just being there, looking as if they had no doubt at all about being allowed in.

"Hi! Is this where the party is?" asked the girl brightly.

"Who are you?"

"Friends of the girl who's giving it."

"I'm the girl who's giving it."

They exchanged lightning glances, and the tallest boy, who looked about eighteen, said quickly, "She means the other girl."

"Which?"

There was a fractional pause, and then the same boy said, "Well, can we come in?"

"No. Only the ones who're invited," I said, feeling perfectly feeble, and made that feeling worse by adding, "My father won't let me ask anyone in who we don't know."

I noticed the other boy, a short, stocky kid about a year younger than the first one and with very long hair, was sort of edging round the door, which I was holding just ajar. I moved into his way, and he stopped, but said wheedlingly, "Couldn't we just come in for a bit? We've brought our own booze."

"No," I said. "Sorry. Would you go away now?"

"But we're friends of—" began the girl, and almost pushed into me. The boys were right behind her. I turned my head desperately, though I wouldn't have had the nerve to call for help, and there, like a miracle, standing in the kitchen doorway was Daddy.

"What's the problem, Kate?" he asked.

"These kids want to come in—"

"Very sorry, nothing doing. Off you go," said Dad. And in one minute he had more or less swept them off the back doorstep, through the gate to the front (which he bolted) and had closed the door behind them.

"Oh, Daddy! Thank goodness!" I said, throwing myself round his neck.

"Think nothing of it. You know what, I think I'll hang around until things get under way. Will you introduce me to everyone?"

When we went back together to the living-room, some of the lights had been switched off.

"Oy," said Dad, and switched them on again firmly. The couples stopped dancing. I looked round quickly—no sign of Pamela and Geoffrey yet. How ironic, I thought, if after all our trouble they didn't come!

"This is my father," I said rather awkwardly.

The great thing about actors is that even if they're secretly rather embarrassed, they know how to carry off almost any situation. He shook hands all round, served drinks, and handed round some pre-supper food which I'd forgotten to do. He chatted comfortably to everybody and I could see the boys liked him. After a few minutes of this he said, "Well, I'm off upstairs. But I'm around if you need anything." He beckoned me out into the hall and whispered, in quite a different tone, "Where the hell is Alastair?"

"Up in his room talking motors with Abby's brother Ian."

Dad looked decidedly annoyed.

"Don't you want him down here?"

"Of course I do!"

"I'll winkle him out, leave it to me." He started upstairs, and then stopped and said, "And listen, Kate. The slightest trouble—no matter what—you come and get me. Okay?" I nodded. "Were those boys drinking plain wine?"

"Tony brought it—I couldn't do anything."

"Well, watch out. Don't let them overdo it."

He went on up before I could ask him how to stop them.

5

The next hour or so was fun. Alastair and Ian came down two minutes after Dad had gone up. They looked rather sheepish, and Alastair muttered something to me about not realizing things had got started. After that he did his duty "in an exemplary fashion" as Grandad would say, in fact I was quite surprised. Two months of being out on his own, I mean working instead of at school, seemed to have done wonders. As I watched him chatting up my girl-friends and bringing them things to eat, and even dancing, I remembered his gauche behaviour of the summer and was amazed.

Ian, who was older but still at school, wasn't a patch on my brother for—well, *savoir-faire*. He couldn't seem to talk to any girl except his sister, and kind of hung round Alastair, ill-at-ease and silent. Nothing anyone could do, even Abby, could persuade him to dance, so he was pretty much of a dead loss.

But even without him things were going well, and when Leo finally arrived with Marie-Noelle (who had apparently lost her nerve at the last minute) I was in the seventh heaven. I'd been terrified that Leo, as an older man among all us silly babies (as we must seem to him), would be patronizing or aloof, but of course, being Leo, he wasn't at all. He was just quiet and well-mannered and perfect. He danced with all us girls in turn, and with Marie-Noelle in between.

But he didn't have to worry about her for long. William had been to France for his first without-the-family holiday that summer and was dying to show off his French. Before long he and Marie-Noelle (who didn't look nearly so lumpish in one of those terribly *simple* French kaftans) were off in a corner with a bowl of Japanese crackers, gassing on and on and every now and then whooping with Gallic laughter. If Leo hadn't been there to focus on, I might have been a little upset about this because I had rather fancied William when he'd arrived.

Rebecca was still being a honeypot, but Tina had managed to grab Tony back for a dance or two and was looking happier. Emma and Adam Scobie seemed to have hit it off, and Dominic danced with Abby whenever Rebecca was otherwise engaged.

Kath wasn't exactly overjoyed about William and Marie-Noelle, but Leo, seeing the situation, concentrated on her, which naturally put William clean out of her head.

So that left Ian, sitting on the sofa like a bump on a log, and me. I tried to talk to him, but it was hopeless. So I sat and tried not to watch Leo dancing with Kath, found I couldn't help it, and finally went out to the kitchen to put the garlic-rolls into the oven and fish the salads out of the fridge. I wasn't miserable because I *had* been dancing until a few minutes ago, and with Leo actually in the house and bound to dance with me for a second time soon I could hardly help being happy. The first dance had been so marvellous I wasn't even thinking about it now. I was saving it to go over when I wasn't so busy, like tonight in bed, when it was all over.

Mum came creeping down while I was in the kitchen.

"Everything all right?"

"Perfect, thanks, Mum!"

"Need any help?"

"No thanks, you've done nearly everything."

"Daddy wants to know if everybody's sober."

"So far, but it's amazing how the wine's disappearing. Tony's three bottles are almost gone already."

"Is everybody here?"

"All except the dreaded Pamela." I giggled. "I don't care. She's probably flown out to the Seychelles for the evening."

She hadn't, though.

At about eleven o'clock we'd all eaten and were sitting about listening to records in a bloated stupor. I, at least, was feeling very satisfied with my first effort at party-giving—not that much of the credit belonged to me, but I pretended it did. Leo happened to be sitting next to me for the time being. Not touching or anything, but he was right next to me on the floor with our backs to the big armchair. I had a glass of punch that he had brought me. It was mainly bits of rather brown-looking fruit by now. I must have drunk about six glasses of it, but it hadn't had the slightest effect—trust Mum. The boys who had been drinking plain wine looked a bit flushed and hectic, but nothing to worry about. Daddy had been down twice more and eventually said he was going to bed since we were obviously all so well able to take care of ourselves. "You *will* clear up and not leave a mess for Mum in the morning," he mentioned to me, and I had promised that Emma and I would deal with everything before we turned in. I was beginning to feel a bit tired, in a contented way, and was almost looking forward to them all going home so Emma and I could mull over the evening.

I leant over to Emma, who was sitting near me choosing the next record.

"I do wonder what happened to—"

At that moment there was a knock on the front door.

We all sat up and looked at each other.

"Pamela!" we all shrieked. "I'll go," I added, and scrambling to my feet went out into the hall.

As I approached the door I could hear voices outside. Pamela was there, I could hear her shrill laugh, but there certainly seemed to be more than one person with her. Still, I wasn't expecting what I saw when I opened the door. There she was, in knee-length velvet trousers and boots and one of those droopy satin blouses partly covered by a floor-length Welsh-tweed cloak. Surrounding her virtually on all sides were no fewer than *five* boys, and there were two other girls as well.

I gaped at her.

"Hal*lo*, Kate! Here we are at last. Dreadfully sorry to be so late but we've been to another party on the way! Hope you don't mind my bringing a few friends along, we've brought our own supplies."

Like some kind of chorus in a musical, all the boys simultaneously waved bottles in the air and gave a cheer. A drunken cheer. I looked at their flushed faces and dishevelled hair and unfocused eyes and felt frightened. I didn't know what to do. And Dad had gone to bed. I would have to cope with this somehow on my own.

"Well Pamela, the thing is, the party's practically over."

"Then we'll start it going again, won't we, Geoff?" she said gaily, turning to the boy on her right. I looked at him. So this was Geoffrey.

He *was* rather gorgeous I suppose, if you like that type—big and well-built and shaggy-haired. My *very* first reaction to him, to be honest, was that he was about the malest young man I'd ever seen. At the same moment I realized that not many boys of seventeen or so that one meets in a social way—no, come on, I must use the right words, what I mean is *boys of my own class*—not many of them *are* noticeably "male" until they are much older. It's hard to explain exactly what I mean. It's not their looks so much, but there's something lacking in the way they hold themselves, the way they behave around girls, even the way they look at you... That masculine something doesn't seem to happen to our boys until they're about twenty or even older. Until they're confident. Until they're *experienced*. Perhaps that's the real point, and here let me be quite frank in the interests of Science—until they've actually had sex with a girl, or more than one girl, they don't have that male look that Geoffrey had.

Most of us long for boy-friends. We need them, to go to parties with and maybe kiss and so on—boy-friends basically to give us status with our friends, confidence in ourselves as attractive girls. We feel incomplete without them. But I'd already noticed that girls like Rebecca and Tina who managed to get boy-friends of around their own age, while they put on airs about them and showed them off to the rest of us, didn't seem to be very satisfied with them as companions or partners. Tina pretended to be quite gone on Tony and maybe she thought she was, but she never mentioned the word "love" in connection with him—I mean, she'd never even dream about marrying him. The idea was absurd. He was just a sort of playmate, a status-symbol, a one-up-man for her, and I've often seen her aggravated with him for being "unreliable" or "dumb"—in a word, *immature*.

Even though I'd never so much as had five minutes' conversation alone with Leo, I honestly think I felt more love for him in the grown-up meaning of the word than Tina did for Tony, or Rebecca for any of her "swains" (as Daddy called them). Those girls had a sort of underlying contempt for their boy-friends. You can't love someone you have contempt for. And when I looked at Geoffrey, just looked at him standing on the porch with a bottle in his hand staring at me, I knew that a girl could be frightened of him or even hate him, but she could never have that kind of contempt for him, because, whatever else he was, he was already a man. Good or bad, he wasn't a boy any longer. And in that moment I knew why Pamela was keen on him—keen enough so that the class difference didn't matter, or at least not enough to put her off.

Meanwhile, what to do about this invasion?

Because they weren't exactly gatecrashers. They were friends of a friend (or an enemy), and no matter how little we liked Pamela we had invited her. If I turned her friends away but let her in, it would be very rude—anyway I couldn't think of the words to do it. So after a moment I stood reluctantly aside, and in they all damn well came.

The whole of our quite large hall was suddenly like a rush-hour railway-station, a seething noisy mass of bodies. They flung off their coats and slung them on to the newel-post at the foot of the stairs till it looked like a great hairy monster. I tried to tell them my parents were asleep and beg them to keep their voices down, but they weren't bothered. I don't think they heard me. I glanced despairingly upstairs, half-hoping, half-dreading that Daddy would hear and come to my rescue. But he must have been sound asleep.

The newcomers surged through into the living-room, laughing and talking, quite ignoring me. I had a glimpse from behind them of the other kids standing up, almost huddling together it seemed, gazing at this horde bearing down on them. I caught sight of Leo and felt momentarily reassured. *He* would be a match for all these uncouth giants, I felt sure.

Pamela greeted the girls airily and introduced them, and me, to her friends. Apart from Geoffrey, there was Dave, Moti (a coloured boy, I think Pakistani or something), Vernon—and Mark Collins. I remembered *that* name all right.

The two girls were called Denise and Claudia. They were about our age but somehow quite different, and this wasn't a matter of class (though Denise talked Cockney). They were different the way the boys were different from Ian and William and Alastair. For the same reason, perhaps—more experience—more confidence—but it was more than that. They were bold, cocky, indifferent. Snide. After looking us up and down, mainly to see what we were wearing, they took no further notice of us. They looked our boys over in the same sort of way, whispered and nudged a bit and curled their lips in scorn before turning back to their own. Only towards Leo did they show any interest. One of them—Claudia, a tall girl with an Afro-like mass of yellow curls like an untrimmed poodle and a sexy figure—sauntered over to him and tried to get off with him, but he simply stood there looking down at her calmly and showing his disinterest so clearly that she soon drifted back to her own crowd.

They had gone into the dining-room, and were now busy scoffing the rest of the food and making a new punch. If you could call that horrible mixture punch. It certainly had nothing more than its name in common with what we'd been drinking. Into the cut-glass bowl went the contents of all their bottles, and they weren't all wine. I arrived in time to see a bottle of whisky gurgling into a witch's brew of goodness knows what else—there was an empty Guinness bottle and one of Merrydown cider. I was appalled. Daddy often says it's fatal to mix your drinks.

As they drank, some of the boys started fooling around, pushing each other. One of them got shoved against the table, just as another was ladling the "punch" into a glass. The ladle fell back into the bowl, the red stuff flew in the air and landed in a great splash, like a bloodstain, on Mum's beautiful white table-cloth.

"Oh, do look out!" I cried.

"The blood of the vampires," said the boy with a grin. It was the one they called Vernon, a strapping lout with lank black hair. He was wearing a Willcox blazer over an American university tee-shirt, flared trousers and platform shoes. "Blame Mark, he pushed me," he added, giving Mark Collins a heavy shove which nearly knocked him down. It did knock him right into Pamela, who fell backwards into Geoffrey's arms.

Geoffrey let himself sink on to the carpet with Pamela sprawled across his knees. "Thanks, mate," he said to Mark. Then he kissed her very hard on the mouth.

While he was still doing it I turned hastily and went back into the living-room. The others were standing around looking subdued and anxious. I went up to Alastair who was talking to Rebecca.

"We've got to get rid of them," I said.

He looked at me helplessly. "How?"

"Couldn't you just tell them to go?"

Alastair glanced at Rebecca and then round the room.

"I could try, I suppose."

"Go in there and just ask them politely to leave," I urged.

He started bravely out of the room, but before he reached the door it opened and in they all came again. They all had full glasses and platefuls of food, which I noticed was getting scattered all over the carpet. Geoffrey had his arm round Pamela and she was laughing up at him, her hair mussed.

"Can we dance?" asked the dark boy, Moti, and without waiting for an answer crossed straight to the record-player and switched it on. Then he looked round, picked out Rebecca as the prettiest and said, "Want to dance?"

I think if he hadn't been coloured she might have said "no", but she has this thing about coloured people. She was so determined to show she wasn't prejudiced that she couldn't treat them as if they were ordinary—I'd noticed it with the few dark-skinned kids at the local primary, she simply fell over backwards to be nice to them. She threw one despairing look at Alastair, who seemed to have shrunk since these other boys arrived, and let Moti grab her and start dancing with her.

That was a signal for the others. They all left their own girls (except Geoffrey) and made for us. Vernon grabbed Tina; Dave, Abby. And when I turned to make my escape, there was Mark Collins blocking my way.

"Let's dance."

"No, thanks."

"Why not?"

Ridiculous as it seems, I couldn't find an answer. Except, "Because you're an erk and I don't dance with erks." Maybe I should have said that. But all my life I had seen my father and mother behaving with perfect politeness to everyone who came to our house. They were even polite to the awful men who came to ask for our television licence (we had it all the time), and to the angry father who came to complain that Bruce had knocked his son off his bicycle (a lie) and even to the vicar, whom Dad afterwards described as an oily antediluvian old hypocrite. Well, maybe Dad himself was the hypocrite, for welcoming the old fellow to his face and being rude behind his back; but I'd got the idea that the important thing was courtesy, especially in one's own house, and because of that I was too inhibited to tell Mark Collins to get lost. So I danced with him.

He danced very well. You could say he was an expert. I'm crazy about dancing and very few boys I know really can. We danced apart, facing each other, and he fixed his eyes on mine in a strange way I wasn't used to—our boys don't look at you when they dance. His eyes were odd, somehow. We were moving quite slowly to the music and after a few moments he said, "You dance great."

"Thanks," I said shortly.

"Nice party."

"Glad you like it," I said sarcastically.

"I hope you didn't mind us barging in uninvited."

"Do you do it often?"

He grinned. "We go where the action is."

"And do you always get let in?"

He shrugged. "Sometimes—sometimes not. If they shut the front door we usually creep round at the back. We mostly get in somehow." I was silent, and he added, "I suppose you disapprove."

That's an awful sort of Mrs Whitehouse word, although it more or less exactly described what I was thinking. So I said, "Well, it does seem a bit of a cheek."

"It's only for kicks. Where's the harm?" He waved his arm at the others, who were nearly all dancing now. "Look. Your party was half-dead when we arrived, everyone sitting around. Now the scene's jumping. You ought to be pleased."

"My mother's not going to be pleased when she sees her best white tablecloth."

"Oh—that. Yeah, I'm sorry about that."

"What was the idea, fighting?"

"*Fighting*? We weren't fighting. Just messing about."

"Like that? At a party? In a strange house?"

He looked surprised. "You think that's so bad?"

"I think it's bad-mannered."

Now it was his turn to find nothing to say. He just looked at me as we jigged around; I couldn't read his expression. It might have been sheepish, or scornful, or curious. He had a strange face, kind of sinister; you couldn't tell what he was thinking. He was dark, with collar-length hair, slightly wavy and clean, not lank and greasy-looking like Vernon's, and these odd eyes. One was a bit bigger than the other, or maybe he just had a trick of opening one wider. It gave him a lopsided look, like two different half-faces stuck together, and his mouth helped that look by turning up at one side. When I'd first seen it I'd thought it was a sort of permanent sneer. Now I wasn't sure. Neither of his eyes was sneering now, yet the mouth kept that twisted-up look at one end. Ugly, almost. Rather like . . . Suddenly I heard myself saying,

"Do the hunchback."

He stopped dancing.

"What?"

"Aren't you the one who can do the Hunchback of Notre Dame?"

He gave me the weirdest look now, cold as ice, and said in a matching tone, "I don't have to do him. Don't I look enough like him already?"

And he walked away from me, right in the middle of the record.

Well, who cared? I was glad to get rid of him. I looked round. The scene was indeed jumping, and jumping pretty high at that. It was now getting on for midnight, and there hadn't been half this much noise all evening. I was amazed Mum and Dad could sleep through it. The lights had gone out, all except one dim corner one, and because of this I couldn't at first spot the person I was looking for, who was Leo. Then I did spot him. He was sitting by himself in a far corner of the living-room, just watching the fracas.

I made my way to him. It wasn't so easy. There were dancing kids everywhere, and, I noticed abruptly, a lot of smoke. Tony had smoked earlier, but none of the rest of us are such idiots, even Tina who might have started just because it's frowned on decided against it after those films they showed at school of all the syrupy black tar in your lungs. But either they don't show those films at Willcox or all these boys decided they *wanted* lungs like inky sponges because they were all puffing away, at least most of them were, and the air was thick with smoke and drink-fumes. You don't get many fumes with wine, but whisky really reeks, and by this time (I noticed) even our "own" boys had been drinking some of that awful muck they'd mixed up.

I reached Leo and bent over him. He looked up at me with his dark eyes, quite as beautiful and Jewish as Rebecca's. "Leo—"

"Yes?"

I hesitated. "Where's Marie-Noelle?"

"She went home. Not her scene."

"Nor yours."

"No, well—I thought you'd like me to stay."

I gazed at him. "Leo—" I began again.

"I know what you want. And I can't do it."

"Why not?"

"It's too late, for one thing. I should have come to the door with you. Now they're well stuck in, you'll never get them out."

"But then what'll I do?"

"There are three alternatives. You can go and wake your father. You can call the police. Or you can just let it ride till they leave by themselves."

I viewed these three possibilities bleakly. Then I said, "Which would you do, if you were me?"

"If I were *you*, Kate Dunhill, I shouldn't have invited Pamela Whatsit to my party in the first place."

"Well, but I did. Now what?"

He looked round thoughtfully.

"I think on balance I'd let matters take their course. Meanwhile I'd dance with me."

We danced, but I couldn't enjoy it as I had the first time. He held me lightly and I tried to have that exciting awareness of his arm round me and our hands holding that had thrilled me before, but now all I could think of was how dark it was and what Dad would think if he came down now. I wanted him desperately, but I hoped he wouldn't—the thought of his anger, and my shame, was too much.

Suddenly there was a scuffle in the darkness, and a small crash.

"There goes the first glass," said Leo quietly.

I left him at once and rushed to the light-switch by the door. But the second I switched it on, there was a groan from what sounded like everybody and at once Dave materialized beside me, switched off, and before I could switch on again, started dancing with me. He held me far too close; I could smell the whisky on his breath. I pulled away.

"Don't be a spoil-sport," he muttered.

"What got broken?"

"Just a glass or something. We'll clear it up later."

"Excuse me, I don't want to dance just now. I must—"

"Then let's not dance," he said, and tried to kiss me. I smelt his mouth coming and ducked and it landed on my neck. Now I really did pull away. I wanted to hit him but I didn't, of course. I just dodged clear and ran through into the kitchen.

Vernon and Denise were in there. They were doing what the Americans call raiding the fridge. They'd actually got out the joint we were supposed to eat for tomorrow's lunch and Vernon was carving great raw slices off it, while Denise was hacking at a fresh loaf taken from our bread-bin.

"What on earth are you doing?" I asked, aghast.

"We're going to cook up some steak," said Vernon cheerfully.

"We're starving," said Denise. "There wasn't much nosh left by the time we came, you lot had scoffed it all."

"Where's the marg?" asked Vernon, reaching for a frying-pan.

I started forward and snatched the shattered joint out of his hand. "Stop that!" I almost shouted. He looked flabbergasted.

"What's up with you, then?"

"Leave our meat alone! Nobody asked you to come. If you're hungry go somewhere else. Home, for instance." I was so angry I could hardly speak clearly. Denise stared at me, breadknife in hand, and then burst out laughing.

"What do you think we go out for?" she said. "We can't have fun at home. Listen, is this a B and B party?"

"A what?"

She smirked knowingly. "If you don't know, then it isn't. Come on, Vern. She'll be crying in a minute."

She tossed her head and went out and he went after her. She was right. I was very nearly crying, from sheer rage and bewilderment. People don't behave like that, and when they do you feel as if the whole world had gone crazy. When I looked at the cold, wet, slippery meat in my hand, dripping on my jeans, I felt so outraged I wanted to kill somebody. If people just do as they like and you can't even talk to them about it, everything seems to fall to pieces and get messy and scary and out of control.

I leant over the table, dropping tears on the meat as I stupidly tried to pile the slices back together again. I felt completely alone. Even Leo had somehow failed me. I don't know what he could have done, but I felt he should have *tried*. And I had the awful feeling that if people could take your Sunday joint out of your fridge and cut it up and not even feel ashamed when you caught them at it, anything was possible. When I thought of that, I really began to cry.

I shoved the meat back in the fridge and looked at myself in the mirror Mum keeps over the sink. I looked a fright. All my eye make-up had run. I must pull myself together! I decided to go upstairs and do something about my face, and while I was there maybe I'd get up courage to wake Dad. Anyway I just had to get away from it all for a few minutes.

I sneaked through the other door into the hall. The row from the living-room was awful, but the dining-room was empty, the candles burning low. Some wax had spilt on the table-cloth too. I blew them out and went on upstairs, drying my eyes on a paper napkin and giving my nose a good blow.

It was dark and relatively quiet on the landing. I went into the bathroom to wash my face, and stopped. Someone had been sick in the basin. At first I was horrified and then I thought, well I have to be thankful they bothered to make it to the bathroom I suppose. I swished the water in hard and managed to get rid of the worst. I knew being sick if you've drunk too much is something that can happen to anyone. It might have been one of my own friends—Ian, maybe, he was swigging away at that so-called punch last time I'd seen him, the silly twit. I tried to be charitable and think that it was his mother's and father's fault for getting a divorce and arresting his development. Somehow I preferred to blame poor Ian. Thinking it might be one of the invaders would have made me too furious and disgusted.

I washed my face (using the bathtaps), and then went along to my own room to repair my make-up. I thought of it as putting on fresh armour for the fray. I had to pass Dad's and Mum's bedroom and I paused for a moment and thought, "I'm not really alone. Leo wasn't my last resort—*they* are, even if they do sleep like logs." I felt better for being so near to them, and opened my bedroom door with quite a jaunty air.

It was my evening for entering rooms all unsuspecting and stopping dead in the doorway. There was somebody on my bunk.

Some *bodies*.

I snapped on the light, and something rolled off the edge and landed feet first on the floor. It was Geoffrey, and still on the bed was Pamela. She wasn't undressed—there hadn't been time, but she was pretty unpulled-together and I won't describe Geoffrey's clothes too closely. Luckily he did have some decent instincts left and turned his back on me.

I went hot and cold. I tried to say "Get out" but I couldn't speak.

"Is this your room?" asked Pamela coolly, peering down from the bunk.

I nodded. I could actually feel my forehead prickling—it's not the back of your neck that prickles, it's your forehead and top lip where the perspiration breaks out in moments of intense feeling.

She gave a tinkly little nervous laugh.

"We opened your parents' door first," she said. "Lucky they sleep well. We thought it was a B and B party—you don't mind, do you?"

Now I found my voice. I wanted to scream at them but I managed not to. "Get out of my room," I hissed. "Get out of the house."

Something in the way I said it must have got through to her at last. Her cool smile dropped off and she sat up, trying to smooth her hair.

"Listen, sorry if you mind—we were only snogging—"

"Out."

They looked at each other. Then Pamela rolled over and lowered herself ungracefully to the ground backwards. Geoffrey lent a hand, but he was eyeing me anxiously as if he thought I might do something violent. I was shaking all over. They went out past me without speaking or looking at me. Pamela was not quite so brazen as Denise and obviously felt shattered at being caught, however she might hide it. Her nose was in the air but her face was puce-coloured. I stood in the passage and watched them go downstairs. Then I went back into my room, sat down at my dressing-table, put my head on it and howled.

6

Just as I was deciding I *must* go down again, I heard light footsteps running along the passage and Emma burst in.

"Oh, Kate! It's so awful—wait till you see the mess in the dining-room—I tried to stop them but they wouldn't take any notice—do come!"

My blood ran cold all over again. I felt like a deserter, hearing the war has started while he's been running away. I rushed downstairs and into the now candleless dining-room.

There was some kind of free-for-all going on. Moti, Dave, Ian—yes, bump-on-a-log Ian—Claudia and *Tina* were having a bread-fight. And not only bits of roll, but anything they could lay their hands on. Crumpled-up table-napkins and candle-ends were just the most harmless of the things they were throwing at each other. I saw wine-corks, cigarette-butts, match-boxes, and of course olives, gherkins and other gobbets of food hurtling through the air. Some connected with people's heads, but most of them hit the walls, leaving little wet or greasy or dirty marks. The floor was littered.

I stood paralysed for about three seconds. Then I simply let fly.

"*Stop* it, *stop* it!" I screamed. I rushed into the midst of it, catching a wet gherkin on my cheek, and grabbed Tina, who seemed to be quite beyond herself with excitement and was jumping up and down like a little girl flinging whatever she could lay her hands on. I pulled her arms down to her sides and shook her, hard. "Tina, stop that! Have you gone crazy? Stop, stop!"

She looked at me, this sort of zany grin still on her face, and then seemed to come back to herself. She went all white and started to sway, her mouth open. "Gosh, Kate—I'm sorry—" she gasped, and then said in quite a different voice, "I'm going to throw up."

"In the loo," I said, and pushed her through into the hall cloakroom. Then I rushed back. There was a lull. The bread-fighters were standing around, panting and half-laughing and looking sort of dazed and silly. Ian was leaning against the wall with his eyes closed. Claudia lifted her hand to throw the last soggy bit of punch-fruit at Moti, but I had lost all my inhibitions by this time and just knocked it out of her fingers.

"Pigs!" I burst out. "You're pigs, all of you! Look at the carpet—look at the table—look at yourselves! You're no better than—" But I couldn't think of anything bad enough. Emma was standing in the archway with her hands over her mouth and her eyes enormous. Behind her I suddenly saw the living-room door open across the hall and Leo and Alastair coming out.

"Good God!" exclaimed Leo in horror when he saw the mess. Alastair didn't say anything. He must have felt as sick as I did, and for exactly the same reason.

At that moment we all heard a door close upstairs and the next moment Dad's sleepy voice calling, "What's going on down there?"

Then there really was a panic. Like a stampeding herd, the gatecrashers sprang into the hall, fought for their coats off the newel-post, and bolted from the house. From the kitchen and living-room, like scared rats, ran Denise, Vernon, Geoffrey and Pamela. *Their* coats had been knocked to the floor, but they grabbed them up any old how and fled, leaving the front door swinging. To do her justice (not that she deserves it), Pamela did have enough decency to come back just long enough to say brightly, "Sorry if we've overstepped the—" But then her eyes snapped up towards the head of the stairs and in a flash she'd disappeared after the others.

We looked up, too. Dad had appeared in his dressing-gown, his hair standing on end—as well it might. He paused and looked down at us, his bleary eyes suddenly sharpening. Others had come into the hall by now, and were standing in a huddle, looking up fearfully as if Dad were some Greek Nemesis descending on them. He came slowly down the stairs and we all made way for him. His eyes were fixed on Alastair with a look that made him quail. I knew that sooner or later that look would be turned on me.

I prayed that he would not turn right into the dining-room but of course he did. He switched on the light and stood in the archway with his back to us. There was a gasp from Kath and the others who hadn't seen the fight, but apart from that, the most deadly silence. Then Dad, slowly and terribly, turned round.

I've seen Dad in a rage many times. I grew up with his rages and they long ago lost the power really to frighten me. It just seems to be something he needs to do every now and then, a letting-off of steam. Occasionally he takes a swipe at Bruce, but beyond that he's not really dangerous, it's all bark and no bite. But this was different.

"Alastair," he said, with horrible quietness, "explain."

"I can't, Dad. It just—happened."

"Who made this unspeakably filthy mess?"

Alastair looked round desperately.

Little as I wanted to draw Dad's attention to myself, I had to help.

"None of us, Dad, honestly. It was the gatecrashers."

"Gatecrashers!"

"Yes. They—"

He didn't listen to more, but strode across the hall, scattering us left and right, and went into the living-room, switching on the lights there. Again we saw him standing with his back to us, and beyond in the suddenly lit-up room I could see a horrid mess of a different sort—all the sofa-cushions on the floor, the air filled with smoke, a wine-stain down near the skirting-board. As Dad stepped in, his slipper crunched on some broken glass. He looked down as if he couldn't believe it. Then he took one quick look round that room and turned again.

This time we all fell back before his expression, which was one of absolutely speechless outrage.

If he had ever looked that way as the officer, I swear the entire cast might have taken to their heels in sheer terror. Emma let out a little whimper. I reached behind me and she clutched my hand so hard it hurt.

"This—pigsty", said Dad in tones of iron, "is to be cleaned up, *now*, until it approximates as nearly as possible to my home as it was when you entered it this evening."

We stood for a moment as if frozen. Then for the first time he raised his voice.

"I said *now*!"

We jumped. And suddenly I found myself in charge.

"Yes, come on, let's clean it up! Tony, Alastair, William, you go and clear up the living-room. Emma, you know where the dust-pan and brush are, the stiff brush, bring them into the dining-room and get the stuff off the floor. Kath and Abby, clear the table. I'll help you. Tina—" I glanced round. Then, remembering where she was, I hurriedly added, "I mean, Leo—would you mind helping the boys—open the windows at the garden end and let the smoke out—" I marvelled at myself, giving him orders, but he simply nodded and followed the others.

Rebecca had sunk into the hall chair and was sobbing her eyes out.

"Horrible—beastly—I want to go home!" she blubbed.

"Well you're not going home yet," I said sharply. "Get up and find an apron and help Kath and Abby with the dishes."

Ian was still leaning, like a two-by-four plank, against the dining-room wall. I shook him briskly. "Ian, you go and—"

He didn't open his eyes, but slid gently to the floor where he lay in a crumpled heap. I left him. Rebecca's "swains", Adam and Dominic, came skulking out of the kitchen.

"It's time we were going," muttered one of them.

"Not till this is all cleaned up."

"But we didn't do it—"

"I don't care about that. You've got to help."

But they wouldn't, the little wets. As soon as my back was turned they'd gone skiving off.

I helped Emma with the carpet-sweeping, picking up all the dry bits by hand and putting them in a waste-paper basket. I worked like a fury—it helped to ease the rage and misery that was burning inside me. Nobody said anything. All you could hear through the three rooms were the subdued sounds of work. Dad had vanished. All I could find to be thankful for now (apart from the worst being over) was that Mum hadn't seen her lovely, cared-for home in that state.

She wouldn't have been angry, not Mum; she'd just have burst into tears, which would have been a million billion times worse.

When the waste-paper basket was full to the brim I gathered up the ruined table-cloth and went through into the kitchen. Kath and Abby were putting things away in the fridge and piling dirty glasses and dishes by the sink. Rebecca was rather inefficiently poking about the floor with a broom, sniffing occasionally. And manning the sink itself was an unfamiliar back. The elbows were flapping and steam was rising from the washing-up bowl in a very business-like fashion. I went to see who it was.

Of all the surprises I had had that evening, none was more shattering than the discovery that it was Mark Collins.

I just gawped at him through the steam.

"What on *earth* are you doing still here!" I finally exclaimed.

"Washing up," he said blandly, plying his Scotchbrite with a practised hand.

"Why didn't you go with the others?"

"Couldn't very well leave you with all this."

"*They* did—your mates."

"Well, they hadn't much option. Caught with their knickers properly down. Luckily I was out here having a smoke when your old man came down like a wolf on the fold."

I didn't know what to say. I was utterly flabbergasted. I just left him to get on with it and went to see how the living-room work-party was getting on.

Things looked so much better in there that one might almost have thought nothing had happened. The sofa-cushions were restored, the broken glass swept up, the spilt wine wiped away. Luckily we have a sort of William Morris wallpaper, dark flower pattern, and the carpet is chocolate brown, so the marks didn't show. The worst was cigarette burns. Leo drew me over to the polished occasional table and showed me no fewer than three, where there'd been an ashtray. The cigarettes had just been left on it to burn down and drop off on to the table-top.

"And there's another on the mantelpiece, and two holes in the carpet."

I felt myself getting mad all over again. Leo put his hands on my shoulders and looked down at me.

"Now don't cry," he said gently. "It wasn't your fault, you know."

Suddenly I felt overwhelmed by tiredness. I sort of swayed forwards and leant against him. He put one arm round me like a brother.

"Oh, Leo—"

"It was my fault if it was anybody's. I'm afraid I was just as out of my depth as you were. I gave you damned bad advice. I should have made you call your father right at the outset."

"How could you know it would all get so much worse?"

William came up to us.

"Excuse me, but is there anything else we can do? Because I think I ought to take Kath home—it's terribly late."

"No. You go. Thanks a lot, William," I said, standing away from Leo and doing my best to smile at him. For a few minutes I had hated all of them, all "our" boys, for not stopping the hooligans somehow, but I was beginning to realize that if they'd tried there'd have been a real fight and things would have been ten times worse. Ultimately Alastair and I were responsible, and in a way even he wasn't because he hadn't had any part in inviting that dreaded, dreaded Pamela, in fact he'd as good as told me not to. So it was quite fair that I should have to face what I had to face, if not tonight then certainly tomorrow —Dad's fury and Mum's unhappiness and the disappointment of both of them in me.

I collected up the others who were just finishing off their appointed tasks, fetched their coats from Bruce's room (he was staying overnight with the Daniels twins next door) and eventually saw them all off. They were all very subdued indeed, especially Tina who looked like a ghost and for once in her life hadn't one word to say for herself. *She* hadn't even the conscience-easing of having helped to clear up—she'd just sat on the floor in the loo all the time feeling rotten, till I came to tell her it was time to go.

They'd all had permission to call mini-cabs to go home in, which they did, and at long last the door shut behind the last of them (even Ian was lugged out somehow by Abby and William), leaving only

Alastair, Leo, Rebecca and Emma, who was staying the night. We didn't say much, just trailed into the kitchen and slumped into chairs round the table. We all looked and felt pretty frightful, me the worst needless to say, but I think Leo felt next-worst.

At last Leo seemed to pull himself together. He stood up and hoiked Rebecca to her feet.

"I'll be round in the morning to talk to your mother," he said.

"You needn't bother."

"Oh yes I need."

They left through the back door which I rebolted after them. I had never thought of locking our doors before, but now I wanted to. Somehow the house didn't seem the same safe place any more as it always had.

Alastair said, "What a night."

I shuddered. "Never again. I swear it. I will never give another party as long as I live."

"I keep thinking what *my* mother and father would have thought if it had happened at our place," said Emma. "What'll your father say in the morning? Will he murder you?"

"I wouldn't blame him if he murdered both of us," said Alastair glumly. "Who'd like some hot chocolate?"

"Oh, don't let's mess up the kitchen again!" I begged.

"I'll wash up," said Alastair, and got out the milk.

"Speaking of washing up," I said, "what happened to Mark Collins?"

"Oh, he took off about ten minutes before the others. He's got his own transport—a motorbike."

"So that's what that roaring noise was."

"Fancy him staying like that," said Emma. "He washed every dish and glass."

"Were there any glasses left?" asked Alastair cynically.

I got up and went to look in the partitioned crate they'd come in. I counted. "We lost five. How much do you think they cost?"

"Lord knows. Twenty or thirty p. a-piece, at least."

I said one of Daddy's most navvy-ish words.

"I'll split it with you," said Alastair. "No, I won't, I'll pay all of it."

"You needn't—"

"I know, but I'm going to."

I didn't argue. I hadn't strength. Five thirties are one pound fifty which is three weeks' pocket-money. But I did rather love old Alastair all of a sudden.

We carried our cocoa up to bed. Emma was meant to be sleeping in Bruce's bed but she looked so pathetic somehow (and I didn't fancy being alone either) I said she could bunk in with me, tops to tails. We got undressed and clambered up the ladder. I was absolutely dead beat, but not too tired to clamber down again and fetch a clean pillow-case out of the linen-cupboard when I saw Pamela's disgusting lipstick all over mine.

I told Emma about that.

"Ugh! How sordid! How could she, and with that ape-man?" Emma whispered. You may imagine we were keeping our voices right down, what with Daddy being next door and still awake from the sound of it. I heard his door open and close—probably going down to see what sort of sight would meet Mum's eyes when she went down in the morning. Again I thanked heaven she is such a heavy sleeper.

"Is that what you thought of him?"

"Isn't it what *you* did?"

"I don't know. In a way."

"They all were. Just like apes out of a jungle."

"Did you like Adam?"

"Sort of . . . He's little and gentle . . . I don't like these big hairy types, they scare me."

"It's because you're so little yourself," I teased.

"Yes. When I looked at Geoffrey—and that Mark, too, all of them really—I sort of saw myself like that girl on the King-Kong posters, being carried in one huge shaggy paw through a forest of sky-scrapers. You know, hair hanging down. Screaming."

I giggled. It did me so much good. She giggled too.

"Well, don't worry, at least Adam will never pick you up in one shaggy paw, or even two."

"He couldn't lift me with a pulley!" she said, her whisper breaking out into a kind of thin choked shriek of laughter. She buried her face in my spare pillow until she'd muffled her giggles, and then asked, "Who did you like—apart from Leo?"

"No one," I said quickly. Then we were both quiet. I was just about to drift off to sleep when I thought of something.

"Emma."

"Hm?"

"What's a B and B party?"

She was silent for a moment, then she said, "Bed and breakfast."

"How did you know?"

"Tina told me, ages ago. Some girls at school give them. When their parents are away. Then their boy-friends stay the night."

"Oh," I said. What else was there to say?

7

I woke the next morning (late) with a sense of doom.

Emma's feet were lying, like two strange bed-toys, on my pillow. I tickled one idly and she woke up with a jerk.

"What'll happen? Had I better go home straight away?"

"Oh no, don't! Stay with me. Anyway Dad's rehearsing."

The house was ominously quiet. I looked at my clock—it was nearly eleven. We got up, moving stealthily and talking in whispers. When we were dressed and there was no further excuse for staying in my room we crept guiltily down. My heart was thumping. I peeped into Alastair's room on the way but it was empty. Whatever he'd had to face, he'd got it over with. I envied him.

I had a quick look into the dining-room and living-room. Everything looked normal—more normal than last night. Mum had worked her experienced magic and removed the last traces of debauchery, other than the burns and stains which one had to search for. Perhaps things weren't so bad.

The kitchen was empty too. I looked through the window and saw Mum in the garden, cutting some late roses. She didn't look too devastated, but she was quite far away. Tentatively I put on a kettle for tea and reached for the Alpen.

The back door burst open, giving me heart-failure. It was Bruce.

"Well, so your do was an orgy, after all! What I missed!"

I tried to look dignified and remote, and said nothing. Emma and I sat down at the table to eat.

"Actually we didn't altogether miss it. I bet you didn't know we crept over in our pyjamas at about eleven to have a squint at you all capering about. We came round the back and peeped through the curtains."

"Who, you and the twins?"

"Only me and Neville. Rudy was asleep, the poor twerp. *Cor!*" he said with wicked relish, picking a raisin out of my cereal with his *mucky* little fingers. "Snogging away, you all were—lights out—wait till I tell Dad—"

"If the lights were out you can't have seen what we were doing," I retorted coolly. Whatever sort of little monster he is, he's not a tell-tale, so I wasn't worried and anyway he was making it up.

Nevertheless I suddenly decided, on impulse, not to wait till Mum got in from the garden. I put down my spoon and went out through the back door and down the path to where she was. She'd started on the chrysanths now—Dad's pride. She must have heard me coming but she didn't look round. My heart simply sank.

I stood by her while she snipped and snipped with the cutters.

"Mum."

She looked round at me. I had been wrong. She *was* angry after all.

"Well?"

"Mum. I'm terribly sorry. We couldn't help it—honestly."

"I believe you." But still she stood there looking angry.

"Did—did Leo come?"

"Yes."

"What did he say?"

"He took the blame. He said he realizes now he should have woken us. And so he should—if *you* hadn't sense enough to."

I hung my head.

"Two things stick in my throat," she went on. "No, three. The main one is that you were too frightened, or too silly, or *something*, to come and call us when things got out of hand. The second thing is that you invited that Geoffrey Gordon, *knowing* what he was like, just out of idle curiosity."

My head came right up at that. "How did you know?"

"Never mind." But I did mind, because they could only have found out from Alastair. Wait till I laid hands on him!

"And what's the third thing?"

"The third thing is the damage. I feel as if the house had been vandalized."

"*I* feel that, too. Honestly, Mum. I feel really ghastly about it."

"But you don't know everything. Did you know they were not only vandals, but thieves?"

"*What?*"

"Oh, yes! My two little alabaster eggs, Daddy's table-lighter, *three* ashtrays, the guest-towel from the downstairs cloakroom, and probably a few more things we haven't missed yet."

Now I *was* shocked. I had thought I couldn't be shocked any more, but now I was really, really shocked. Wildness and drunkenness is one thing—a horrible thing, as I'd discovered. But *stealing*!

"I didn't think they were *criminals*," I said—and burst into tears.

Mum put the flowers and cutter on the path and put her arms round me.

"Poor darling, poor old Katie," she said. "Mummy's poor! What a shame. Never mind, it's all done with." She soothed and petted me as if I'd been about four years old, and that's about how old I felt. It's funny how you can feel you're really growing up and getting control of things, and then suddenly it all vanishes and you feel as helpless and needing of comfort as when you were little.

She led me into the house through the french windows and sat me down in the living-room to cry it out. She went through to the kitchen and soon brought me in a fresh hot cup of tea and a box of tissues to blow my nose on. Then she left me alone. After a bit Bruce came in and stood looking at me with his hands in his pockets. I was just sniffing and gulping a bit by that time, drinking my tea.

"I told you they were creeps," he said.

"Oh, shut up!" I said.

"I'm not crowing. I'm telling you. He's a villain, that Geoffrey. The whole school knows it."

"But how did a boy like that get into a good school in the first place?"

Bruce laughed uproariously.

"They don't test them for behaviour, you know! He's clever enough."

"And the others? Dave, Moti—that awful Vernon? Mark Collins?"

"They're bright. Moti's Dad's got a chain of shops, he's as sharp as a tack—carpets, Indian food, goodness knows what. Geoffrey's Dad's a policeman, believe it or not. Mark's got a terrific brain."

I looked up. "Has he?"

"Yup. Nearly top of his class. When he bothers. But he's too busy bunking off most of the time."

"What does *his* father do?"

"Dunno. I don't keep files on them all."

"Bruce."

"What?"

"You know that story you told us—about Mark doing the Hunchback in front of Jeremy Thing."

"Yup."

"Well . . . did he, really? I mean, did you see him do it?"

"No, *I* didn't. But Neville did." The Daniels twins also go to Willcox. And Neville is famous for his vivid imagination (shall we say).

"Then you can't be absolutely sure?"

"What do you care?" asked Bruce, getting beady.

"Oh, I don't of course. But I think it's wrong to go about spreading rumours about people without being sure. I mean, if he *did* do that in front of someone with a disability it would be so absolutely *filthy* rotten that he'd have to be the lowest of the low."

"Which now you've met him you don't think he is."

To which of course I could only retort "Shut up" again, which was feeble but I was tired of the subject. Besides, I realized I'd left Emma on her own far too long. So, now the crisis was over more or less, I borrowed Mum's bike for Emma and we went off for a ride on the common.

When we came back there'd been two phone calls. One was from Emma's Mum to ask when, if ever, she planned to come home and wanting to know all about the party. The other was some boy, for me. He'd left his number but no name.

Naturally I was extremely curious but I had to let Emma use the phone first and she gassed on for hours to her Mum, telling her all, just as if it couldn't have waited till she got home, while I tried not to dance up and down with impatience. Finally she got off the line and I rushed up to Dad's and Mum's bedroom with the bit of paper to phone in privacy.

"Hallo."

"Hallo—this is Kate Dunhill."

"Hallo."

"Who is it?"

"Me. Mark Collins."

There was a silence. I swallowed hard.

"Oh. Hallo," I said, yet again, for lack of some inspiration.

"Hallo. Well. How are you this morning?"

"I'm okay, thanks," I said shortly. The fact was I didn't know how to behave. I didn't know what I *felt*. I *would* have known, except for his having stayed to wash up. That threw me.

"I thought I'd ring you up to see that your parents had left you in one piece." His voice over the phone was deep and not so Cockney as it sounded face to face, or rather, mouth to ear.

"They've been very nice about everything," I said defensively.

"Your old man's quite a guy."

"What do you mean?"

"Well—I mean he's tough. He's tougher in real life than he is on the box. Was he really an officer in the army?"

"No. A private."

"Mine was a sergeant, so my Dad's better than your Dad, so there."

I couldn't help smiling, but I managed not to laugh aloud.

"It was nice of you to stay and help," I said.

"Washing dishes is second nature to me."

"Oh?"

"I hope you don't think it's poofy?"

"Of course not! Dad does it all the time."

"And there's nothing poofy about him, as I saw for myself. Funny. I always thought actors were all poofs."

"What a silly thing to think."

"Yeah, I see that now. He scared me rigid. That's why I stayed, really. I thought he might hunt us all down with his troops. No safe hiding-place."

"It's a good idea, in the case of all your mates. I'll suggest it to him."

"Am I on the blacklist?"

"No," I said after a moment.

"Because of my skill at the sink?"

"Well, and because you didn't go sneaking into bedrooms or throw food about, or break any glasses."

There was a pause, and then he said, "Well, I did break one as a matter of fact."

"Then you owe me thirty p."

"When can I give it to you?"

I felt a little breathless. Did he mean what I thought he meant?

"You can give it to my brother Bruce at school tomorrow."

"I'd rather give it to you direct."

I couldn't think of an answer to that so I kept quiet. Just at that moment Emma came in and signalled to me that she had to go. I tried to wave her away but of course she pretended not to get it, and drifted closer.

"Well, what do you say?" Mark was asking.

"What about?"

"Us meeting."

"When?"

"Where do you go to school?"

"Lady Mary Engels."

"Oh, yeah. Well you get on the train your end and I'll get on it at mine, and we'll meet in the middle." He named a station. "Let's say four-thirty. I'll bring the money. Then maybe we can do something."

"Do something?"

Emma pricked up her ears and opened her eyes till they were quite round.

"Yeah. A flick or something."

"When's this supposed to be?"

"Tomorrow."

"A film on a week-night? You're crazy. My parents'd have fits."

"Can't you do your homework after?"

"No, I can't! It takes me hours and I have to go to bed at nine-thirty."

"At nine-thirty!" he echoed incredulously. "Hell, I don't get to bed *ever* before eleven!"

"How on earth can you work the next day?"

"I dunno. I just do. I don't need much sleep at all."

I remembered reading somewhere that very bright kids don't need as much sleep as others. I'd always thought it was rubbish because I'm not stupid but I need hours and hours of sleep, more than ever recently.

"Well anyway, I can't possibly. I'd never get permission."

"What about Friday then?"

"I'll have to ask."

"You *are* hung up on your parents, aren't you?"

I felt myself getting mad at him again.

"Well if you were a bit more hung up on yours, maybe you wouldn't go around gatecrashing other people's parties!" And I banged down the phone.

"Wow! Who *was* that?" asked Emma.

I told her. She goggled more than ever.

"Did he ask you out?"

"Yes. Tomorrow. Can you believe it? He must think I live a life of complete freedom. Come on, I'll walk you to the bus."

When we were half-way down the stairs the phone rang. I took it in the hall.

"It's me again. We were cut off."

"No, we weren't."

"You mean you hung up on me?"

"Yes."

"Well don't, it's rude."

"Look who's talking!"

"You're the one who's so fussy about manners. And to answer your previous charge, I plead guilty to gatecrashing but I must point out that if I hadn't we wouldn't have met."

"That's no excuse."

Emma was pointing urgently at her watch.

"I must go," I said.

"Hey, hang on, we haven't settled anything yet! What about Friday?"

"I'll have to ask, as I said, because of being hung up on parents and rules and being a good little girl and all that. And I doubt very much whether I'll be allowed. Now I'm going to hang up again, so goodbye."

And I did. I couldn't help feeling I'd handled him rather well.

8

At school the next day I managed to forget all about Mark (except during French of course, when I had nothing else to think about). We were in a ferment all day, and when whispering in class proved inadequate we passed notes. Abby got caught and sent out. That calmed us down a bit, but only till break, and that wasn't long enough, so we all skived off hockey and sat in the changing rooms, shivering.

Pamela hadn't come to school.

"Early bout of flu?" suggested Kath.

"Late bout of funk," retorted Tina.

Tina was right back on form. She had had, she triumphantly reported, a shattering hangover the day before—"My first and my last—never again will I drink another drop!"—but was completely recovered and seemed blandly unaware of having misbehaved. When Emma said (cattily for her), "I think we ought to make you captain of netball, you're so good at *throwing*," Tina just looked at her as if she'd gone round the bend.

Abby, however, was embarrassingly ashamed of Ian's lapse, and went on and on about how sorry he was about it, how he'd never been drunk before, how shy he normally was, what a stupid, repressive school he went to which made him liable to break out etc. etc. We got quite tired of telling her over and over again that it didn't matter.

They were all full of questions about Rebecca, Leo and Marie-Noelle. Kath said William was very struck on this *femme fatale* and had almost sulked after she went home early. He'd actually had the cheek to ask Kath to get her phone number from me.

"I know he's not my boy-friend or anything, but still I think that's a bit thick. I'm not his sister either, and I did invite him."

"Oh, let him ring her up," I said. "If he sees her without that kaftan on, I mean in her ordinary day-clothes, he'll have another think, I bet. She's got an awful figure."

"That pretty hair, though." Marie-Noelle had this admittedly rather attractive longish reddish hair.

"Speaking of hair," said Tina grimly, "I could have pulled all that black wool off Rebecca's head by hand. She looked like Hedy Lamarr in that awful film of Samson and Delilah I saw the other night on TV. Sickening. Tony didn't stop all the way home. He kept asking why I don't grow mine long. As if it could look like *that* if I grew it for a million years." And she drew forward a limp mousy lock and surveyed it dismally.

Kath said, "If William gets off with Marie-Noelle, I'm going to get off with Leo. He danced more with me than with anyone." We all laughed at this, and Abby asked, "Seriously, has he got a girl-friend?"

"If so, I've never seen her," I said, wondering as I said it why my heart didn't do its normal little leaps and plungings. Although I'd long ago faced the hopelessness of my "passion" for Leo, I had never been able to contemplate his being in love with anyone else. Now I was able to wonder about it quite calmly.

"Find out and tell us," said Tina.

"I think we've let our female curiosity get us into enough bother," I said.

"And after all, we never solved our little problem. What *does* the posh Pamela see in the erk Geoffrey?"

Everyone shuddered exaggeratedly. Everyone except me. Of course Emma caught me not shuddering and gave me a beady look. While we were getting into our coats after school she edged me into a corner of the cloakroom and said, "Have you asked your Dad about Friday?"

"No."

"Why not?"

I shrugged moodily. "It's a waste of time. He'll never let me."

"Because it's a boy, or because it's *that* boy?"

"He never saw Mark, but he'll remember the name. Bruce said something about him once. Something grotty. I don't think now that it's true, but Dad thinks it is. He won't understand me even considering going out with him."

"But," said Emma thoughtfully, "although he has an awful voice and is rough-looking, a bit, I thought right away he was nicer than the others."

"He gangs around with them. He does all the same things."

"He wasn't as bad as them on Saturday, not nearly."

"I know what Dad'll say, that you judge a man by the company he keeps."

"Ask him if he'd like to be judged by some of his friends. *My* Dad's friends are all the most outlandish people, one of his favourite men-friends is a great shambling pot-bellied Irish sculptor who's never sober. He comes banging on our door at two in the morning sometimes, shouting and sobbing and throwing his arms round everybody, and borrowing money. Dad says he's a genius and he just loves him. And he has a woman friend who's a Lesbian."

"*Really?*" I asked, intrigued. My Dad had some homosexual actor friends, but no Lesbians had ever crossed my path. "Is she a genius too?"

"No. She is a painter, but a very bad one. Daddy likes her because he says she's got the most penetrating mind he's ever known. They went to art school together. As a matter of fact she's my godmother."

"A Lesbian godmother? How exotic! Why didn't you tell me?"

"Oh well, she's not much use. She never gives presents. But sometimes she takes me out to dinner parties with her. They're nothing like parties really, they're sort of intellectual gatherings. Everyone sits about discussing philosophy and art and things like world government. I can hardly understand a word and I'm usually bored, but Mum says it's good for me. She always feeds me first so I won't eat all the peanuts, because that and olives are all there ever are. Extra-brainy people don't seem to need food."

We'd drifted right off the track of my date with Mark. I was so intrigued with what Emma was saying that again I'd entirely stopped thinking about him, so I naturally got a shock when, arriving at the school gate, I saw him leaning against it.

He stopped leaning as I came up.

"Hi," he said carelessly. "Here's your thirty p." And he gave it to me. It was warm from being held in his hand.

"How did you get here so quickly?"

"On my bike. But it wasn't quick, I got stuck in traffic."

"So quickly after school, I mean."

"Oh, I didn't go to school today."

"Why not?"

"Didn't feel like it. I went swimming instead."

I looked round for Emma but she'd taken off. Fine friend. I looked back at Mark helplessly.

"I must go home."

"How do you go?"

"By bus."

"Come on the back of the bike?"

He pointed to a great black hairy-looking contraption propped against the kerb.

"I don't think I'd better."

"Has your father specifically forbidden you to ride pillion?"

"No, but—"

"Then come on."

Before I quite knew what was happening I found myself, with a helmet clapped on my head, perched on the back seat of his bike with my school skirt rucked up and my school bag stuffed between his back and my stomach. He kicked the starter. The whole thing bounded forward like some kind of panther leaping on its prey, and we were off.

I had the satisfaction of catching a quick glimpse of Tina's and Abby's faces as they came down to the gate and saw me whirl away in a cloud of exhaust and dead leaves. Then we were roaring down the road. The wind whipped my front hair and rushed up my skirt. I tried to hold everything in place, until we hurtled round the first sharp bend. Then I saw the kerb coming up on my left to meet me and I simply shut my eyes tight and hung on to Mark's jacket with all my might.

I've always hated motorbikes. In theory. I think I caught it from Mum. Mum hardly ever gets worked up, but she rivals Dad when it comes to what she calls "unnecessary noise". The jets which zoom over our house, sometimes at one-minute intervals, on their way to London Airport, can reduce her to such a state that I've seen her rush outside and shake both fists at them. But motorbikes get her most of all. In calm, rational moments, she can be brought to see that planes have to fly people to and fro and that to make them silent would be too expensive. But who needs motorbikes, and above all, who needs them to be so noisy? She practically goes mad every time one roars by.

She also hates them because she says they kill more young men than any other form of transport. For years she's been saying that her worst dreads, the things she has nightmares about, are that Bruce will get his front teeth knocked out in football, that I will want to be an actress, and that Alastair will get a motorbike.

Well, all I can say is that she can never have ridden on one.

For the first few minutes of my first ride I admit I was terrified. I just hung on with my eyes closed and waited for the crash. But after a few moments of this I thought, how do I know where he's taking me? So I forced my eyelids open and, through a haze of tears (the wind, not terror), I managed to look around.

When I'd reassured myself that we were on the way to my house all right, I relaxed a little. I don't know how I managed this, since we were zooming in and out of the traffic along the main road, with our knees barely scraping past cars and buses; I knew perfectly well Mark was showing off like crazy and going far faster than he ought to, but somehow I felt safe. He drove the way he danced—expertly. And the noise had a strange effect too. It sort of deadened some area of my brain that should have been warning me of the danger. In fact it shut out the world around us as if with a wall. Nothing could touch us! I felt a wild surge of excitement as we rounded the bend into our road, again practically lying out on our sides. By the time we drew up outside our gate every part of me felt more alive, more aware, than ever before in my life. Speed! Noise! Wind! Who can describe it? As I clambered off, breathless with excitement, I knew that I would never be able to share Mum's hatred of motorbikes again.

My legs were shaking and would hardly hold me up. Mark kicked the foot down (to stop the bike toppling over), turned round to me, saw the state I was in, and grinned.

"Like it?"

"Fabulous," I managed to croak.

He handed me an oily hanky with which I wiped my eyes.

"I'll get you a pair of goggles for next time."

We stood looking at each other. He looked different by daylight. Less sinister somehow, despite the twisted face. No, that's not true, it wasn't *twisted*, but it wasn't symmetrical. Nor was it at all handsome. But it was a strong face. And if you looked at one eye at a time, you saw that there was one kind one and one—well, kind of cynical. Narrow. I couldn't find the right adjective. Angry?

"Cup of tea for the driver?" he asked.

I hesitated. Dad wouldn't be back yet, nor would Bruce or Alastair.

"Okay then."

I took him in round the side. It felt funny to be home so early. It usually took at least half an hour by bus. Mum looked up in astonishment as I came in through the back door.

"Good grief, did you come by rocket?"

I gulped. Get it over! "No, by motorbike," I said bravely.

Mum turned pale. Honestly. She clutched the sink.

"Mum, this is Mark Collins," I went on hastily.

She offered him a limp hand, staring at him as if he were a bat out of hell. Then she turned back to me.

"You mean to tell me you—"

"Mark picked me up after school and rode me home on his—" I decided it would be better not to mention the dreaded word again so I quickly interrupted myself. "Could we have some tea, Mum?"

Mum moved to put the kettle on in a sort of daze. This was her nightmare come true in a distorted way. It was as if *Alastair* had lost his front teeth, or *Bruce* had said he was going on the stage. I felt a giggle coming. "Sit down," I said to Mark, and hurriedly put some digestives on a plate.

Silence.

Mum made the tea, put it before us, took off her apron and left the kitchen.

"She hates me," said Mark.

"It's not you. It's the bike." And I explained about Mum's phobia.

"Oh, hell," he said, glumly stirring his tea.

"Doesn't *your* Mum mind?"

"My Mum has four sons, two of them older than me. She used up all her protests when *they* got bikes and old bangers and that. By the time it was my turn, she hadn't much energy left."

I suddenly knew I was bursting with questions. I wanted to know all about him, where he lived, what his brothers' names were, what his Mum was like, what his Dad did for a living. I especially wanted to know that, I didn't stop to ask myself why. So I asked that first.

"What does your Dad do?"

He looked at me over his teacup. I was startled, because it seemed as if only his cynical eye was fixed on me. The kind one had sort of gone to sleep.

"Are you a snob?" he asked.

"Of course not!" I cried. "Of course I'm not."

"Don't overdo it." He bit into a biscuit. "Okay, let's test you." And he began to sing. " 'My old man's a dustman—he wears a dustman's hat—he wears gorblimey trousers AND he lives in a council flat!' "

I laughed. I felt embarrassed. "No, really."

"You don't believe me?"

"No."

"Because dustmen's kids don't go to Willcox?"

"No . . . Not because of that. I'm sure some do."

"Precious few, believe me. So is it because, although I talk gorblimey and gatecrash, I don't throw food about or take girls into other girls' bedrooms?"

I fairly blushed now. "Did Geoffrey tell you?"

"I saw him going up."

I said nothing.

"Let's get back to the little matter of the professions of fathers.

Geoffrey's Dad's a copper. Quite high up in the force, too. Doesn't fit your scheme of things either, does it?"

"I haven't got a *scheme* of things," I said, getting mad again. "I think maybe *you* have. You think because I'm—middle-class, I take up attitudes. Well, I don't, so don't stuff me in a pigeon-hole and think you know what I think about everything."

"Okay then. Supposing I told you my Dad's a bank manager."

"I might believe that."

"Oh?" he said in surprise, sitting up straight.

I pounced.

"Aha! You're pleased."

"Pleased?"

"Pleased that I could believe it. It flatters you to think you could pass yourself off as a bank manager's son. *You're* the snob if you ask me."

For a moment he looked all stiff around the mouth. Then he relaxed, laughed, and put his hand over his face.

"Maybe we're all snobs in a way," he said.

That was the moment, looking back on it, when I began to like him, seriously. But I wasn't aware of it then. We were sparring. I realized he'd given way to me a little, had let me know that I'd caught him out and scored a point, and I thought, "That's nice of him, not many boys would admit it."

"Well, anyway I don't really care about your Dad. I only asked because—"

"Because your Mum will ask the minute I've gone."

I thought. "Maybe. If she doesn't, she'll be holding herself back."

"I wish for her sake he *was* a bank manager."

"But then my Dad would disapprove. He absolutely despises bank managers. Especially his own."

Now we both roared with laughter and it was our first laugh together.

"Anyway," I said thoughtlessly, "you don't have to worry about my Dad. He's a Socialist."

"The worst class-snobs of all, believe me," he said.

"What's that supposed to mean?"

"My Dad also votes Labour. He actually preaches class-warfare. He hates your lot like poison. I tell you, if you ever come around our house, you'll have to put on a good Cockney accent or I'll never hear the end of it from Dad."

I gazed at him in astonishment.

"You mean he'd object to you going out with a middle-class girl?"

"So we are going out?"

That brought me up short.

"Well, you did ask me."

"I don't remember you saying you'd come."

"I'll have to ask Dad," I said again, to gain time.

"You said I didn't have to worry about your Dad, him being so keen on the workers and that."

"It's nothing to do with the workers. It's to do with you being a boy."

"Ah! Sex rears its ugly head. Well, but you'll have to tell him he's got nothing to worry about. I know me place." He started to act. "To me, a middle-class girl is a princess. Pure. Sacred. Untouchable. At least by the likes of me. I only want to be treated as dust under your feet. Your humble slave . . . If, just occasionally like, you'd extend your dainty hand and let me press it reverently to my coarse lips—that is all the reward I seek."

"Reward for what?" I got out between giggles.

"Taking you to the odd flick."

"Oh, you are stupid! All right, I'll tell him all that. He'll think I've got mixed up with a lunatic."

"So you are mixed up with me?"

"No, I'm not! Now I've got homework to do. I went to school today even if you didn't."

He got up reluctantly and put on his helmet.

"I'll wheel the bike round the corner before I start it," he said.

I went out to see him off. I was standing at the kerb chatting to him while he sat across the bike when Bruce and the twins came dawdling down the road, bashing each other with their schoolbags. When he saw me Bruce stopped dead and did the most *rude* goggling act at Mark.

"Don't stare," I said to him pretty sharply.

He pulled a face at me and he and the twins shambled into our house, nudging and glancing back at us, grinning.

"Is that your brother?" asked Mark in surprise. "Geoff says he's a good squash-player but a sight too cheeky. He wants to watch it with Geoff, you know. Old Geoff can come it a bit strong when he thinks one of the little twerps is getting above himself."

"Why do you like Geoffrey?"

"He's good for a giggle."

"He's horrible."

"He's all right."

"Well, *I* think he's horrible."

"Why?"

"He's a bully. You've just said so."

"Oh, go on. You can't let the first-years get too cheeky. In the public schools they keep them in their places by beating them and making them fag."

"That's all over long ago."

"*Is* it? Believe me it's not! Anyway, we never lay hands on them."

"What about the boy you backed up against the school railings and made him show off his aitches?"

He stared at me, then laughed. "MI5 isn't in it with you! I can see we'll have to watch our step."

"Well? Why did you do that? Wasn't that cruel?"

"Listen. That little twerp just begs for it. Every time he passes some kid who doesn't talk the Queen's English he says, 'There goes one of the guttersnipes.' Or else he says, 'Where were *you* brought up? In a barn?' "

"Yes, but which came first? You mocking him for his posh accent or him mocking you for your unposh one?"

Mark frowned. "Look, it doesn't matter. The fact is, him and us are sort of natural enemies."

"So your Dad would say. But even if I thought you were right, which I don't, you're older and bigger than him and you shouldn't stoop to ganging up. That's bullying."

"We had to put up with it when we were their age. It's the name of the game. When I started at Willcox there were some boys in the upper school who made my life a bloody misery."

"Posh ones, I suppose?" I asked sarcastically.

"You bet your life! They used to strut round the place as if they owned it. No question of *them* keeping their hands to themselves. Or their feet. They used to mix in when we were playing games, stick their legs out and that. Many's the time I've gone home with a bloody nose and the wind half knocked out of me—"

"But there's no need to hand it on now you're big."

"We don't. Not like that."

"But you make their lives a misery in a different way. Why when you know what it feels like do you do it to them?"

Mark looked at me. A stubborn, almost stupid look had come over his face. The kind eye was almost closed, and his accent had gone broad Cockney—defiant Cockney. "That's life. Do as you was done by. That's the golden rule these days."

"Well, I think it's a stinking rule!" I said, suddenly really furious.

He went on looking at me for a moment. All the nice feeling between us had just evaporated into thin air. We stared at each other like—well, like enemies. Class enemies? Culture enemies? I didn't stop to think until later.

Abruptly he kicked his motorbike to life, slammed down his visor-thing over his face, and roared away without another word.

9

Well, I thought that was that, and at that moment I wasn't sorry. It's odd how you can put unpleasant facts right out of your mind when it doesn't suit you to think about them. While I'd been talking to Mark over tea I'd allowed myself to forget all about the gang and the bullying and all that, but then Bruce appeared and it all rushed back. I don't know if there was any connection, but although I really thought I didn't care about Mark, I had a particularly vicious row with Bruce that evening which ended up with me cuffing him on the head, something I haven't done for years. Of course he retaliated, giving me a nasty kick on my shin, and the end of it was we were both sent to our rooms in disgrace. I was all upset and got no homework done at all, which in turn led to more trouble at school the next day.

It didn't improve matters that the girls were bursting with curiosity about me and Mark and I had to tell them I'd given him the push. Tina had to come over all smart and say she was going to submit it to the *Guinness Book of Records* as the shortest romance in history. Emma, needless to relate, was nicer, and to her alone I told the whole story. She said I was quite right to chuck him, that going out with him could only have ended in disaster.

Nevertheless as Friday approached I couldn't help feeling a bit miserable. When you've never really been out with a boy and then you nearly do but don't, it's bound to be a bit of a let-down. The row at home had, of course, completely blown over. We were all being nice to each other again. So naturally everyone noticed that I was in a mood (shall we say). I knew Mum must've reported to Dad about Mark so I wasn't too surprised when he came knocking on my bedroom door on Thursday evening after supper.

"What's up with you?" he asked, after a few preliminaries about homework etc. A bit abrupt, but that's Dad's way.

It couldn't hurt to tell him now, so I did, and with a lot less discretion than if I *had* wanted to get his permission to go out with Mark the next day. Dad was very quiet and let me get it all off my chest. (That's another thing about actors. They're trained to be good listeners. As long as you're not another actor talking about your recent parts, of course—no actor will sit quiet for that.)

At last he stirred and looked up at me with a funny wry look.

"Well! So he's taken himself off. Luckily for me, eh?"

"How do you mean, Dad?"

"Would have put my principles properly to the test."

I do like that about Dad. He tries so hard to be honest with himself.

"Would you have agreed to me going out with him?"

After a little thought he said, "Yes, I think so. But I'd have had to meet him first. Honestly, Kate—it's the bullying that prejudices me against the lad, not his background. I'd feel just the same about one of those well-spoken young louts he was telling you about who used to bully *him*."

"And you don't hold the party against him?"

"Maybe a bit. I do think stamping into other people's houses uninvited is absolutely *grotesque*."

That night after homework, at about nine o'clock, I strolled next door to visit Rebecca. I felt I needed taking out of myself. She was up in the playroom in her dressing-gown watching television (fancy having a colour set just for the children!). But she was obviously not very gripped because she switched off the moment I came in.

I think I've mentioned that Rebecca goes to a different school. I hadn't had a chance to mull over the party with her. I think she felt a bit pallid about it; anyway she didn't seem to want to discuss it much.

"It wasn't your fault at all, Kate, but it was a pretty grotty party, *I* thought."

"Yes, well, it certainly was at the end. I liked the beginning part though, didn't you?"

"I can never remember nice beginnings if there were bad endings."

I thought this a rather interesting remark. Messy endings do tend to swamp what went before them, but I thought one had to try and remember *anything* that was good and not allow it to be spoilt. But she didn't agree.

"Take Adam. I used to think he was very sweet and we had some nice conversations—I even let him kiss me once. (We were sitting down, of course, he couldn't have reached otherwise.) But now I shall never speak to him again."

"Why ever not? What's he done?"

She stared at me with her great black-fringed eyes.

"Don't you *know*? He's gone off with your friend Emma Jocelyn."

"*What*?"

"Yes. Dominic told me. He phoned her up the night after the party and he's taking her to a disco tomorrow."

"Cor!" I breathed, like Bruce.

Here was news indeed! All that fuss about me and Mark, with me confiding all, and *not a word* from Emma about her own little affair. I didn't know whether to be annoyed or not. Actually I rather admired Emma. I could *never* have kept so quiet, but then I always have to spout everything. Typical of her, now I thought about it. She is a very *inward* person compared to me, and often amazes me by coming out with things that I would have told her long ago, like having a Lesbian godmother. I mean, good heavens, who wouldn't boast about a thing like *that*?

You can bet I wasted no time getting after her the next morning in break.

"What's all this about you and Adam Scobie?"

"Oh yes," she said, as if it had slipped her mind.

"Why didn't you tell me?"

"You didn't ask."

"You're so *damn* secretive," I accused her. "Fancy letting me find out from Rebecca."

"Is she annoyed about it?"

"Wounded I think's the word. But she's got lots of other irons in the fire, I wouldn't worry. So! Where's he taking you?"

"Oh, I don't know. A disco he said."

"And your parents agree?"

"He's coming to supper with us first. And I have to be in by eleven."

I was silent. A sudden wave of envy had bowled me over. But I'm pleased to say I righted myself and said quite nicely, "You must ring up first thing in the morning and tell me all."

"There won't be much to tell I don't suppose. *He*'s no Mark Collins you know."

"What do you mean by that?"

"Well, only that if you'd been going out with Mark this evening, anything might happen. Adam's a baby in arms by comparison, I'll probably be bored bananas."

That evening we were sitting round the supper-table. I was making a real effort not to throw a damper on the family board by being moody (Mum had had a word with me on the subject). The trouble was, knowing Emma was out with a boy, even miniscule Adam, made it harder not to brood a bit.

Not that there was a shortage of conversation of course. Bruce was full of thrilling football news, having scored two goals that day, and Alastair kept interrupting Bruce's kick-by-kick account of the game with a deeply interesting history of his own struggle with a faulty starting-motor. Daddy was waiting, with increasing impatience, for a chance to tell us a funny story about the producer of the series who had walked off the set. Only Mum and I were not competing.

I think Mum is marvellous, the way she can listen with apparent fascination to all this deadly boring man-talk—she can't *really* care about football and cars, can she? Only sometimes when we're alone together she says, "It's so nice to have a real girl-chat." I honestly don't know why all these idiots keep insisting men and women have, or ought to have, the same interests and talk about the same things and that if they don't it's only a matter of conditioning. Anyone with a family could put them right. It wouldn't have mattered how many trains and soldiers you'd tried to force on me when I was a child, or whether you'd bought miniature dustpans and ironing-boards for the boys. Mark you—I quite enjoy woodwork at school, and Alastair's a super cook, so perhaps it does level out a bit later.

So there was this male voice choir effect going on, without any harmony, when the doorbell rang. Dad said something blasphemous about people who arrive at mealtimes and Bruce said, "It's Neville. We're playing table-tennis at the youth club. I'll go." "Tell him to come back when you've finished eating!" Dad called after him. Then we were all quiet for a minute, expecting to hear Neville Daniels' voice, but instead we heard Mark Collins'.

"I've come to call for Kate," he said.

Dad and Mum both looked at me. I did such a huge shrug it was like Rudy Daniels telling his famous joke about why Jews have short necks. (You ask that, and then when people say "Why do they?" you do this very high Jewish shrug so your neck disappears.) A moment later Bruce, with both eyes crossed and his tongue sticking out of the side of his mouth, came in, followed by Mark in a white shirt and tie looking as if digestives wouldn't melt in his mouth.

Dad stood up and shook hands with him.

"I think there's been a misunderstanding," he said.

"Oh?" said Mark innocently. "I didn't hear anything from Kate so I just thought—"

"You'd better sit down," said Dad. "Have you had supper?"

"No."

Another of those quick looks passed between Mum and Dad. Then Dad said, "Well, you'd better join us. Kate, lay an extra place."

"I'll do it," said Mum. Alastair shifted up, and Mark sat beside him. There was an awkward silence while Mum collected cutlery and stuff. "I didn't hear your bike," she said.

"I left it round the corner," said Mark. "Kate told me you hate them."

"You weren't planning to take Kate out on a motorbike, I hope," said Dad.

"Well—"

"Because I'm afraid that's right out of the question."

"I could take her on the bus. We're only going to the cinema."

Dad looked at me, a "Do you want to?" look. My eyes said, "Yes, *please,*" before I'd had a chance to ask the thinking part of my mind what I felt about it. Dad said, "Well, eat supper first and then we'll see."

Mum had laid the place by now, and went to the Welsh dresser drawer that she keeps the napkins in. She took out a clean linen one and opened the side drawer for a silver napkin-ring. Then she looked up.

"It's gone," she said. "The spare ring." The rings are what we call "the family silver". There are six altogether and one of them isn't used unless we have a visitor.

It was a moment before I realized what this meant. No other losses had been discovered and I'd let myself forget about the pinching—it had been just too awful.

Now I remembered.

There was an awful silence as the significance of the missing ring, in connection with Mark, dawned slowly on everybody. Except Mark.

It was Bruce who spoke out—it would be.

"That's one of your rotten bunch," he said.

"What is?" said Mark.

"Nicking our stuff. They even took a bit of our family silver."

"Bruce!" said Dad.

Mark continued to look quite blank.

"What do you mean, nicking your stuff?"

"There were some small items missing after the party," said Dad reluctantly. "I'm sure Mark had nothing to do with it," he added, without being able to sound in the least sure.

Mark looked round the table. We were all looking at him.

"Let me get this right. Somebody at the party stole some silver from this house?"

"And not only—" began Bruce, but Alastair kicked him and he stopped.

A very odd look now came over Mark's face. A closed, furious look.

"That's a bit past it," he muttered. "That is. That's a bit too bloody much. Sorry," he added, looking quickly at Mum. "Excuse me," he added. "Kate, we'll go out another night. I'm sorry. Excuse me."

Without another word he walked straight out. We heard the door bang.

"Well," said Dad. "What a curious fellow. Where's he gone?"

I said nothing. After supper we watched the programme and then I went up to my room and tranquilly practised different hair-styles. I'm allowed to stay up late on Fridays of course, so at ten o'clock I was still up. I'd done my hair in a weird style that I rather liked and was doing things to my eyes when the doorbell rang again.

I stayed very still. I knew it was him. After a few moments Dad called up the stairs, "Kate! It's for you."

When I got down the hall was empty except for Mark. He stood there very still and calm, and yet tired-looking somehow. His face was rather dirty.

As soon as I got to him he silently began to hand me things out of his jacket-pockets. The alabaster eggs, the silver ring, two ashtrays.

"There may be some more. I'll get it on Monday," he said. Then he turned to go. He hadn't looked at me.

"Well, thanks," I said awkwardly. "Don't go yet."

"You don't want me in this house, I'm sure," he said.

"Why not? You didn't take them."

"No, I bloody well didn't!" he almost shouted.

"Shh! I never thought you did."

"I don't know why not."

"You're not a thief."

He looked at me then, a look that made my heart turn over. It was the first completely *open* look he'd ever given me, a look that laid him wide open to me, letting me see that he could be hurt like anyone else. That he *was* hurt. He stood with his hands spread out a little at his sides, just gazing at me as if he was waiting for me to pass some kind of sentence on him.

"I never thought it might be you," I repeated, and that was true.

"Honest?"

I nodded. He relaxed a little. His arms fell to his sides.

"Well, that's something."

Then his face changed and went back to being two-sided. His mouth twitched. "What *have* you been doing to yourself?"

"Me?"

"Your hair."

Instinctively I turned to look into the hall mirror.

"Don't you like it?"

"Bit far out, isn't it?" We were both looking in the mirror by this time and he suddenly noticed himself. "Crumbs, look at my face! Can I have a wash?"

I showed him the cloakroom, and waited till he came out. Things were back to normal by now. He looked at his watch and said, "What about coming out for a coffee?"

"*Now?*"

" 'I'll have to ask Dad.' I know. Listen, you don't have to ask him —I'll ask him. Where is he?"

I pointed to the living-room door. Mark went up to it, paused for a moment—seemed to straighten himself as if it were an ordeal, which it was—and then knocked and went in. I followed.

Mum and Dad were watching television, but Dad got up right away and turned the set off. Mark said, "I'm very sorry about the stuff, Mr Dunhill. I've got some of it back. If you'll give me a complete list I'll get the rest on Monday."

I had the things he'd brought in my hands and put them on the coffee table. Mum swooped on the napkin ring with a little cry of delight. She looked up at Mark. "They were my mother's," she said. It was her way of thanking him. He nodded as if he understood.

Dad did it differently.

"How did you get them back?"

"That's a long story. Less said the better, really."

"Would you like a glass of something?"

"No, thanks. I wanted to ask if I could take Kate out to that eating place round the corner—the American hamburger joint."

"Do you mean now?"

"I haven't eaten and I could do with something. I thought you might let Kate come with me for a coffee. On foot," he added, looking at Mum. "I'll have her back before eleven."

Dad looked at his watch. He looked at it much longer than it took to see the time. In the end he looked Mark straight in the eye.

"If you're going to have a meal you won't get back by eleven. You can keep her out till quarter past. I'll have the list ready when you come back."

That was his way of saying thank you. It was also his way of letting Mark know he'd be waiting up.

10

"So how *did* he get it back?" Emma asked.

We were gassing on the phone the next morning. We'd been at it half an hour or more already. I'd let her tell me all about her date with Adam (such as it was) before springing my own little surprise. She and Adam had gone to a disco and danced for two hours and drunk so much Coke Emma said she felt fizzy all over, and then he'd taken her home. The only interesting thing really was that he'd missed the last bus home to our district and had had to creep back to Emma's and beg a bed for the night.

"So it was a B and B party!" I teased.

But when I told my story of course it quite put her little outing in the shade. Being Emma she didn't mind, and was full of all the right questions, like how had Mark got our stuff back.

"I made him tell me while we were eating." (I had a baked potato too, in the end, and a milkshake—I found I was quite ready for another supper after all the excitement.) "Well, first he wouldn't say anything, but then when he reached for the salt I suddenly noticed his knuckles were grazed and I positively nagged him till he told me."

"You mean he'd had to *fight*?"

"Only Dave. Vernon gave his up without problems—he only pinched the towel in any case. It was Dave took most of it. He denied it at first, but Mark got tough with him and in the end he coughed up."

"What about Moti? What about Geoffrey?"

"They were both out. Mark says he'll get after them at school."

"What did Dave *say*? What could he say?"

"Not much apparently. Mark was terribly unwilling to talk about it at all. It seems that hooking a few oddments is all part of the fun on these occasions. Mark says nearly all of them help themselves to things like pub glasses and so on, I think he may even have done it himself. It's a question of where you draw the line."

"I think it's absolutely awful even to take from pubs!"

"So do I," I said. I gave a deep sigh.

"What's the sigh for? Because Mark's pinched from pubs?"

"Yes," I confessed.

"You really like him then."

"Yes. Well, sort of. I'm not sure."

"More than Leo?"

"It's terribly different."

"More real."

"Mm. And much more complicated."

"Did he try to kiss you when he brought you home?"

"No. Did Adam you?"

"He never got a chance. Dad was practically under our feet the entire time. But he managed a good squudge while we were dancing. You couldn't help it really, it was so crowded."

"Would you have let him if he had tried?"

"No. Would you?"

"No." I hoped. But he had held my hand on the walk home. That had been quite exciting enough for one evening. I had stupidly thought his hand would be rough (worker's hand—silly stereotyped idea—why should a schoolboy's hand be rough?). Anyway it wasn't, but it did hold mine very strongly, as if he were restraining himself from practically squashing it. It was also very warm.

There was one thing he did which was more—well, *stimulating* than even just holding my hand, though. It had turned very cold out, and Mum had made me take my gloves. I had put them on before we left the eating-house, and when he decided to hold my hand he picked it up and pulled the glove off it so that our hands could touch. It was *that* moment I kept thinking about after I was in bed. Archaeology was nowhere.

After lunch on Sunday Dad came over all fatherly and we had a family outing to the British Museum. There we found it impossible to keep together. Bruce made a beeline for the mummies (there's one little shrivelled-up corpse with the hair and skin still on it that he's devoted to and always visits first). Alastair went to look at the weapons. He's very keen on old blunderbusses, not the swords so much which have no mechanism. Daddy headed for the costume section by way of illuminated manuscripts and Mum and I were left to drift as usual into the jewellery.

We wandered round together, calling each other to look at favourites. I stood for ages looking at a Jacobean pendant. It has a huge baroque pearl in the middle with jewels and bits of enamelling added to make a merman. We played our game ("If you were offered anything you liked from this showcase, which one thing would you pick?"). Mum always went for little, dainty things with very delicate workmanship. I liked the bigger, showier stuff. I think Rebecca's influenced me with all her Beduiney medallions and coin-necklaces with no glitter and lots of dull silver and unprecious polished stones. There wasn't much like that in the British Museum collection. I think if anyone *had* given me one of those wildly valuable pieces I would just have taken it straight out and sold it and bought myself hundreds of records and clothes and shoes and copper-hooded fireplaces and—well, things. Mum said that would be a pity, to exchange an antique masterpiece, an heirloom, for a lot of useless trash. I reminded her that when she and Dad were first married and were both out of work and poor, she'd sold her mother's engagement ring to help with the down payment on their first house. She said a house wasn't to be compared with shoes and records and that even so she often regretted that ring because she would have loved to give it to me when I got married.

I was rather alarmed by the way the words "getting married"—which before had always brought to my mind a large, rosy blank—now quivered nervously in my head as if a name or a face might be about to emerge from the pink mists ... I banished them hastily and started talking about something else. But after a few minutes Mum asked, terribly casually, "Are you planning to see Mark again?"

"Dunno," I said, so shortly that she glanced at me quickly. It annoyed me. She was going to pry. She never pried, but she was going to pry now, I felt it, and got on to the defensive straight away of course.

She sensed this immediately. There are moments when I could wish we *weren't* so damned attuned.

"What's the matter?"

"Nothing," I said, in a silly, tossy sort of voice.

"Well, something is," she said reasonably.

"Only that I know you've taken one of your burning dislikes to him."

"One of my *what*?"

"Oh, you know! Taking just one look and making up your mind. How you can decide the instant you see a person whether you like him or not I'll never know. You don't give people a chance."

I meant to hurt her and I had. No satisfaction in that, naturally; I felt horrible. She didn't say anything, so I had no alternative but to press spitefully on.

"Of course I know *why* you don't like him. Because he's N.O.C."

I said this in a very sarcastic voice. N.O.C., for anyone who doesn't know, means "not our class", and if you think *that* belongs to the era of Nancy Mitford's book you don't know my Auntie Gerry. She's Mum's sister, much older and terribly posh. She lives in Gloucestershire where Dad says she's gone completely native—"your full county-lady, lost without trace in the huntin'-shootin'-and-fishin' set." He's not very nice about her, but then she is the most unashamed snob and that includes thinking Mum married beneath her so you can't wonder. Mum's not like her, of course, but at moments like this it seemed as if a bit of my aunt's prejudice might have rubbed off on her.

But there's nothing that gets Mum madder than being told she's Auntie's kind of a snob. She got mad now.

"I don't think that for a moment!" she retorted, in such a loud voice that the old attendant tutted at her from his stool. She went on more quietly, "You're not fair. I *don't* take instant scunners to people. And I certainly don't judge them by their accents, if that's what you think—I don't see how you can accuse *me* of that." She meant because she'd married Dad's Lancashire one.

"Actors are classless," I said, being clever. "Besides, Cockney's different. Cockney's *common*, isn't that what you think?"

"I don't know what you're talking about, and neither do you."

We were standing in a corner of ancient manuscripts, glaring at each other over an illuminated scroll.

"This is absurd," she said suddenly. "What are we rowing about? I haven't said a word against Mark."

"Not to me. But I bet you've mulled him over with Dad."

"Kate, what do you want from me? I absolutely refuse to go on with this. You're just picking a quarrel."

This was perfectly true, and I didn't even know why. I wished I'd never started it now. It made me feel as if Mark were far more important to me than he was, or than I wanted him to be. Here I was fighting for him as if—and fighting Mum, of all people, who was nearly always on my side. I felt confused and miserable. Mum saw it and tried to put her arm round me but I pulled away because I was ashamed.

Sensibly she let it ride and we walked here and there looking at things till I felt calmer. Suddenly in the porcelain room, right in front of the Portland Vase, I was able to say, "*Do* you like him?"

"I don't know yet, but I don't dislike him, that's certain."

"And you won't make up your mind about him too quickly?"

"No, I promise. And don't you either."

"Okay."

I smiled at her. Funny how you can't make yourself smile sometimes. And then suddenly the stupid babyish anger melts inside and you're yourself again and can love your mother and smile at her and it all passes off.

Arm-in-arm we strolled through to the Greek section where we found Dad gazing up at the Elgin Marbles.

"Thieving swine," he remarked when he saw us. He was referring to Elgin, not to us of course—he's passionately against treasures being removed from their original sites. "Seen anything of the boys? Alastair's got the hold-all, hasn't he? All this culture's making me peckish."

"Anyway," I said to Mum suddenly, "there's nothing at all to worry about yet. After all I've only been out with him once."

Dad looked from one to the other of us and cast his eyes up to heaven. He then called on the son of God to witness that women had no earthly right to claim equality with men when they couldn't keep their minds off sex even when surrounded by the greatest works of civilization.

"And what about those who can't look at a statue for five minutes without starting to whinney for their sandwiches?" asked Mum sweetly. That shut *him* up.

Next day Pamela was back at school.

She'd had a week off to plan strategy, so she didn't give us time for so much as a nudge or a whisper. She marched straight up to me, first thing as I arrived, and handed me a letter addressed to Mr and Mrs Dunhill.

"I'd like you to give this to your parents," she said with all her usual cool. "It's an apology. And I apologize to you too, and so does Geoff. He's signed the letter."

With that she turned smartly about and was gone before I could get my breath back.

"Well!" said Abby. "I hope it's your full grovel, that's all."

"Are you going to let her get away with that?" asked Tina.

I thought of the mess she'd left, the smudges on my pillow, the sick in the basin, and especially about the thefts. But the whole thing seemed old history now. Perhaps she'd been counting on that.

"I'll wait and see if Mark gets the rest of the things back," I said. "If he doesn't, I'll tackle her."

I was half expecting him to be waiting for me at the school gate again, but he wasn't. However, when I got off the bus on our corner, I heard a roar and there he was, racing to catch me up.

"Hi," he said, pushing up his visor-thing.

"Hallo," I said.

We looked at each other. I was glad to see him.

"Jump on," he said.

Mum had made her views on the subject of my "jumping on"

pretty clear but it was only two or three hundred yards. He stopped well short of the house anyway.

He parked his bike and reached into the pannier. Out came the table-lighter and the other bits. There was even a packet of cigarettes.

"Those aren't ours," I said. "Dad's given up smoking."

"Are they his brand?"

"Yes, but—"

"Then maybe he hasn't quite given up. Or maybe they were left over. Anyhow they're yours."

"Who had them?"

"Listen, I've got 'em back for you, now don't ask me to shop my mates no more." Sometimes his accent got stronger.

"I bet it was Geoffrey."

"No takers. Let's forget it."

"Do you want to come in for tea?"

"Okay."

We went in. This time the whole family was at home, even Alastair who'd recently been working later and later. Dad received back his stolen goods with thanks and we made room for Mark at the table.

It was the first meal he'd had with us. At first everyone was a little stiff, but Dad chatted him up and it wasn't long before someone cracked a joke and the atmosphere got easier. It was some time before I remembered Pamela's letter.

"Oh—I've got something for you!" I said, and rushed to get it out of my schoolbag.

Dad opened it and read it, his mouth twitching.

"She's quite a cool customer, the dreaded Pamela," he remarked, tossing it to Mum, who read it and tossed it to me.

"Dear Mr and Mrs Dunhill,

We're frightfully sorry we made a mess of your house on Saturday. I'm afraid the boys got a bit beyond themselves (! ! !) *I* normally don't drink *at all* but I admit I was a little tight too, otherwise I wouldn't have brought so many uninvited guests (! ! !) You have such a lovely little home it is a shame we didn't treat it better. We were all very naughty and we all feel guilty about it. *Do* forgive us.

Yours sincerely,

Pamela Wilton and Geoffrey Gordon."

Everybody read it, and Mum said, "I like the 'lovely little home' touch. Just to make us feel humble."

"That's typical of her," I said.

Bruce said, "D'you think the silly bag knows her boy-friend nicks things from houses she gets him into?"

I looked at Mark. He was reading the letter, his head well down. I tried to imagine how he was feeling. These were his friends we were talking about so scathingly. Yet here he was, "breaking bread with the enemy" as Grandad would say.

"Why *do* they do it, Mark?" I asked.

Perhaps it was unfair of me—treating him like a sort of spy.

"Just for kicks," he muttered.

"They're not hard up or anything?" asked Dad.

Mark drew down the corners of his mouth and half shook his head.

"Do their parents know?" asked Mum.

Mark shrugged. I could see he was getting more and more uncomfortable and suddenly I felt protective towards him. I wanted to get him out of the hot-seat.

"Can Mark stay for half-an-hour and help me with my chemistry?" It was a pure impulse. His head came up at once, and he looked at Dad. Dad looked at Mum. I knew exactly what he was thinking and my face went hot as fire. I always do my homework upstairs in my room and they didn't want to establish a precedent of us being alone up there. "We can work in the glory-hole," I added hurriedly.

"All right then," said Dad, "if Mark can spare the time."

The glory-hole was Mum's little sewing-room and general office. Dad only goes in there to do accounts, which he doesn't do very often. But it has a desk though it's always cluttered with sewing patterns and bills clipped together and in-trays and out-trays. It's not chaos, though it might look it. Mum's the only one of us with any real organization; she doesn't trust any business matters to Dad except just writing the cheques, and then she lays the bills in front of him one by one.

Mark and I went in there and shut the door. I sat down at the desk, cleared a small space in front of me and took out my books. Neither of us spoke.

Finally Mark said, "What help d'you need?"

The fact is, I don't really like people helping me with homework.

"Perhaps you could just check my maths answers as I get them."

"I thought you said chemistry."

"Which are you best at?"

"Whichever you're worst at."

"Do you like science subjects?"

"They're okay when they're well taught."

"Are your teachers good?"

"Not bad."

"You didn't skip school today to go swimming."

"I had to go today, didn't I, to get the stuff back."

"Do you bunk off school often?"

"Now and again."

"Why, if you like it?"

"It gets boring sometimes. There's other things in life, after all."

"Don't you get into trouble?"

"You're dead worried about getting into trouble, aren't you?"

"Now don't start that again!"

"Yeah, I get in trouble sometimes. But when exams come along I generally get down to it. Few weeks beforehand, like. Get good marks. Then Dad and the teachers have nothing to gripe about. I just point to my report-card and bunk off to the pool again, or whatever."

"How many O-levels did you get?"

"Nine or ten—I forget."

"Nine or ten!" I was due to take O-levels next year. I knew I'd be lucky to get six. "You must be very brainy. Bruce said you were."

"It's nothing to do with me. I got brainy parents. Only they didn't have my advantages."

"How do you mean—advantages?"

"Well, my Dad's dad was practically an idiot. Oh, smart enough in his way, I don't mean he was mental, but he was dead narrow. He had no ambitions for Dad like Dad's got for us. All he wanted was for him to take over his little business when he conked out. That was what life was all about, so Grandad thought—the name of the game. You sweat your guts out building up some little shop or works—he made machine-parts in a four-man workshop in Balham—then you hand it over to your son who builds it up a little more, and so on. Well, Dad tried it, but then he started looking ahead a bit. He saw that before he knew where he was, he'd be a middle-class employer, exploiting his labour force with the worst of 'em. So he chucked it and went on to the railways."

"So he's an engine-driver?"

"Yeah. He earns a good screw, stands up for the Union, and keeps his self-respect and his idea of himself as a worker. But still, I think he sometimes feels there's some grey-stuff in his head that's being wasted, and he regrets he didn't learn more. That's why he's keeping me glued to the school bench till he's sure I can't stuff another fact or figure into my head. Or pick up one more diploma or certificate or one of the other 'bits of paper'. Then he'll let me off the hook. He'll turn me loose, when I've learnt all I can, and see what I can make of myself. When I told him last year that I wanted to chuck school and earn some money, he went mad."

"What did he say?" I asked, fascinated of course.

" 'You leave school now, I'm finished with you! You won't come into this house again, I warn you!' Then when he'd calmed down a bit, he says like this. 'Mark, I'm putting the weapons in your hands. I'm putting armour on your back. When you're all set up and they can't get at you no-how, then you can go out and fight the battle!' "

"*His* battle. The one he was never able to fight."

"That's right. Lucky for me I'm not really against it, 'cause he'd push me into it anyway."

"So why did you want to leave school last year?"

"Oh—a lot of me mates were skiving off—saw 'em strutting around, earning good money, getting a start. Cars—birds—good clothes—all that. I saw a programme on the box about it the other night. It's like watching all the others getting a head-start of you in a race. You get panicky, you think there'll be none of the prizes left by the time you're allowed to start running."

"But you're not the only one."

"Course not. But there aren't so many of my sort who stop on. It's the middle-class kids. That's why we hang around together, Geoff and me and the rest of 'em. I don't see eye to eye with 'em about everything but we're outnumbered by all them toffee-nosed twerps from what they dare to call 'good homes'. My Dad hates them—I told you—and there are times I hate them too. And they hate us. They're afraid of us, creeping up on them—we're a threat to them, their privileges and that. They don't like it when we do as well as them in school, or better. I'll tell you something about Willcox. They boast—the Head and the governors and that—that they got a 'cross-section of society' in the school. They imply that if you looked at what all the boys' fathers do, you'd find there was as many workers' sons there as professionals'. Well all I can say is I hope they have to prove it some day, because it's just a bloody lie. They only say it to hang on to the government grant, now Labour's in and talking about enforcing comprehensive schooling across the board. The *fact* is that even at the intake end of the school, before a lot of 'em leave at sixteen, there's not more than ten per cent of working-class kids. If that."

"But Mark, isn't that partly because there aren't so many kids from working-class backgrounds who can pass the entrance exam?"

"Of course it is, of course it is!" he said, getting very worked up by now. "And why? Because those kids *start out* with the dice loaded against 'em from the day they're blooming well born! Everyone knows that. They don't have a chance against middle-class kids with their educated parents, and their ambition and culture in the home and all that lot, that date back generations. It's only one or two generations since the idea come to the surface that working-class kids had any right at all to an equal chance. You can see it clear as daylight in my own family, like I told you. My Dad wasn't *expected* to stay on at school, he wasn't allowed to, even when his teacher went to his house and *begged* his old man to let him stop on!"

"Well whose fault was *that*? It wasn't the middle-classes' fault, it was your grandfather's fault, the workers' own fault. And if there aren't as many workers' kids in good secondary schools even now I don't see how you can blame us for that!"

He stopped, just on the verge of yelling some answer, and stared at me with his mouth open.

"Blame *you*?" he said. "You silly girl, I don't blame *you*."

And he leant forward and kissed me.

He drew back, his face still very close, and looked at me with his kind eye to the fore and said very softly,

"Just the same you're talking right out the back of your neck."

11

He left quite soon after that, and I actually managed to do my homework in a normal way and go to bed. I did this by shutting off part of my mind and sticking a big sign on it saying "LATER LATER". But when I was tucked up in my bunk with the big purple alarm-clock ticking companionably away beside me, the sign came down and I fell into a witless trance.

I had been kissed for the first time.

I had always supposed that my first kiss would be delivered outside our front door, in the dark, after a date. That is when most girls get kissed. It had never occurred to me that it could happen in broad daylight in Mum's glory-hole, in the middle of a political argument, or that it would be from such a boy as Mark, or that it would be that kind of kiss. I thought you kissed standing up with your arms round each other, and that it lasted, oh, perhaps five or ten seconds according to the degree of passion. My first kiss was not at all in this pattern. I was sitting down at the desk; Mark was sort of leaning his behind against a shelf beside me. He had his arms folded across his chest, and mine were in my lap. He simply leant forward and brushed his lips against mine, quite quickly, downward once, then upward again. His mouth was firm, warm, dry. He smelt of school, of cigarettes, mainly of boy. I didn't even have time to close my eyes before he leant back again, his arms still folded. It was the most exciting moment of my life.

But why? Why? It wasn't even a proper kiss! And yet a funny thought came to me as I drifted towards blissful sleep. If it had been a proper kiss—on the porch, dark, arms around, ten seconds even—I would have been planning, at this moment, how I would tell Emma about it the next day at school. But *this* kiss I wasn't going to tell anyone about. And not just because there wasn't much to tell.

Next morning nobody was interested in kissing anyway. All they wanted to know was whether Mark had brought the things back, and who had pinched them.

I reported exactly what he'd said.

"Then it *was* Geoffrey!" said Tina. "He as good as said so. I'm going to *confront* Pamela."

"Oh, leave it," I said. I wasn't in a mood for confrontations. "It wasn't her fault."

"Of course it was her fault!" exclaimed Tina. "She brought them, didn't she? I bet she knew—she must have done. If Tony nicked something at a party, he'd show it to me (and wouldn't I give him what-for!). She can't get away with it."

I begged her not to start anything, but she wouldn't listen. At break she marched up to Pamela.

"I suppose you know your boy-friend's a thief," she said.

Pamela looked at her with complete disdain.

"I don't know what you're talking about."

"Then you ought to. And you ought to be more careful who you go out with. And who you take into other people's houses."

Pamela looked at me. She had on her terrifically haughty look, like royalty being snapped at by horrid little terriers.

"It was Kate's house, not yours. I've apologized to Kate. If she hasn't got anything to say, why should you?"

"Just because Kate's nice enough to let you off—"

"Well, I don't know so much about nice. She only asked me out of spite and curiosity." I blushed. "Anyhow, Kate has a good reason to be grateful to me for bringing Geoff's friends along. Haven't you, Kate?" she asked with a pussy-cat smile.

"Well, at least Mark isn't a thief!" exclaimed Tina hotly.

Pamela was anything but hot. She went on smiling sweetly and remarked, "Well of course, you can't *know* that. Naturally he would say the others took the things. But how can you be sure he didn't take them himself?" She obviously knew all about it. Geoffrey's version.

Tina was speechless with indignation for a moment. Pamela

turned to go. But Tina was not letting her have the last word. She caught her arm and jerked her round again.

"You can just stop putting on airs from now on. We know about you now. We know why you like Geoffrey—it's nothing but sex!"

Pamela flushed darkly for a moment and I saw her swallow. But she recovered. You had to hand it to her—she really was a "cool customer".

"And what's wrong with sex?" she asked. "As if you knew anything at all about it. I don't imagine your weedy little Tony knows what the word means."

And with that she strolled away, leaving Tina in such a state of rage that she couldn't come into the next lesson at all. She just sat in the toilet crying her eyes out.

Half-way through the week I met Rebecca on the way home from school. She said she'd met a heavenly new chap who so far outshone any of her previous ones that she didn't care what happened to any of them.

"I can't think why I ever looked twice at Adam," she said.

She was dying to tell me all, so I was invited in next door for tea. We carried it up on a tray to her bedroom and sat with our backs against the warm mosaic pillar on enormous cushions covered with Moorish patterns and bits of mirror. Rebecca sat cross-legged. Even in her dreary school uniform she managed to look like a houri (or whatever they're called—those Turkish dancing-girls. I don't mean a prostitute of course).

Her new bloke was apparently terribly tall, handsome and exciting, had perfect teeth and played in a student orchestra she'd just joined. Clarinet. He was *eighteen*, nearly nineteen, if you don't mind. I was just starting to feel my usual envy, a sort of conditioned reaction which I'd been having for years during this type of conversation with Rebecca, when suddenly I realized I didn't have to be envious now. Mark, too, was tall and had perfect teeth, and if he wasn't, strictly speaking, handsome, and if he couldn't play the clarinet, and if he was only seventeen, what of it? I didn't want her old Peter, she could have him. It was a wonderful feeling, quite new.

I sat still, my tea warming my hand, looking at beautiful exotic Rebecca and savouring the feeling of no longer dreading her.

"Tell me more about him," I urged her happily.

She did. And when she'd finished, she told me something else.

"Marie-Noelle's leaving."

"Going back to France?"

"I don't think she dares. She's pregnant."

I stared at her.

"Marie-Noelle? Who is it?"

"Goodness knows. Well, *she* knows I expect, but she won't tell. She just keeps crying all the time. It's awful. Mummy's in a terrible state about her."

"Can't she—you know—"

"Oh, no! She's a Catholic."

"Are Jews allowed to do that?" I digressed curiously.

"No. But they do. I think everybody does. Everybody except Marie-Noelle." She sighed. "It's such a pity. She was helping so much with my French. I got quite good marks on my last test."

"Does she have to go? I mean, couldn't your mother keep her on?"

"Well... I have heard them talking about it... Mummy's funny. She's not narrow-minded exactly, but she does like everything to be smooth and organized. I think it's the—well, the sort of *untidiness* of it that upsets her. And the nuisance. On the other hand, she's crazy about babies, and now she's too old to have any more of her own I think she might rather fancy having someone else's in the house. To sort of keep her hand in till she has grandchildren."

"And when will that be?" I asked teasingly.

"Don't look at me! It's Leo's duty first. Did you know he's got a girl-friend at last?"

Anything? Maybe a little lurch of the heart. *Nothing* to what it would have been two weeks ago. But such long-standing loves don't just vanish into thin air.

"Who is she?"

"Fellow-student. Her name's Monique. She's French. Leo always fancied French girls."

"I say! You don't think *he* could be the father of—"

"Oh, you horrible pig," she cried, falling on top of me with a cushion and practically smothering me.

"Is this Monique Jewish?" I asked when I'd finally pushed her off.

"Yes. Daddy's overjoyed. And better still, she's Sephardic."

"What's that?"

"Oh, I can't explain—a sort of Spanish Jew, dark, like us. Not the light-skinned ones from Middle Europe who speak Yiddish. We regard ourselves as a sort of élite." She pranced about being aristocratic.

"I always thought Jews were Jews."

"Oh, goodness me no! We're much posher—we're so rare, you see. The others are sort of common-or-garden Jews, but we all come from ancient families and all that rubbish. Daddy's a frightful snob about it. He can trace his family right back to the seventeenth century or something when Cromwell brought them over from Holland. Terribly aristocratic we are. Bet you didn't know you lived next door to nobility."

She had been draping herself in finery from her old dressing-up box that she still kept. Now she paced the room in a gorgeous floor-length veil-arrangement spattered with sequins.

"Come on! You can be an honorary Sephardi."

I stood up and let her dress me in a long gown. She draped me in bangles and beads, covered as much of my face as possible and smothered the rest of it with jewellery. Finally she drew great black lines round my eyes and stuck on a pair of her mother's old false eye-lashes. Then we stood side by side at the mirror. She looked like Salome. I looked like a dressed-up English girl with two black eyes.

"It's no good," I said. "I don't even look like honorary common-or-garden." I started taking it all off, and added, "One day I'll try dressing you up as a village May-queen and see how silly *you* look."

But I didn't really mind. Mark had seen Rebecca at the same time he'd first seen me, and it was me he had first chosen to dance with. I was very interested in the Sephardics though. There were class-systems where you'd least expect them.

On Friday Mark came and took me to a film.

It was our first proper date. I was careful not to dress up too much for it. I wore my new patchwork jeans and a high-necked silky sweater with a sheepskin jerkin over it. The only thing that wasn't quite me was one of Rebecca's dull-silver medallions which I borrowed from her to hang round my neck.

Daddy saw us off.

"In by eleven-thirty, not a moment later," he said.

"Okay," said Mark.

"And no motorbike!" called Mum from the living-room.

"Okay!" called Mark.

Round the corner was the bike. Mark stopped and looked at me questioningly.

"No," I said.

"Much quicker. Much more fun."

I remembered the ride from school. The rush of wind, the elation ... The temptation was awful.

"No," I said.

He shrugged ruefully and we walked on to the bus-stop.

The film was super. We ate Maltesers and, in the interval, an ice-cream. He didn't hold my hand. I was rather surprised, a bit disappointed, but somehow glad. Anyway his not doing it enabled me to concentrate on the film much better, which was good, because afterwards he wanted to discuss it all the way home, and on rather a high level.

"You seem to know a lot about film-making," I said as we sat on top of the bus. He was smoking. I wished he wouldn't. I hated to think of his lungs getting all that black muck in them.

"One of my hobbies," he said. "I made a film once, at school. That was before the exam-schedule set in and we had time to fool around and really learn things. It was great, that was."

"What sort of film?"

"Horror. Buckets of blood, shrieks and screams. We had a woman teacher then, she nearly fainted when she saw it. I made the maniac come out on top. He couldn't help it really—everyone else was dead."

"I hate horror films."

"So do I, they're all stupid. Hardly anybody really understands what horror is."

"What is it?"

"The secret is to get the audience really fond of the characters you're going to do up. Trouble with most of these directors is, they're so hooked on their monsters and their tricky effects, they forget to make the audience care about the victims. No, that's not quite right either. The truth is you've got to have some different kind of talent to make your characters likeable and real. Writers and directors who can do *that* aren't usually interested in the horror bit. My idea would be to combine the two. Send 'em out of the cinema crying as well as shivering."

I shivered myself.

"Then no one would go."

"Why d'you say that? People pay to be made miserable, they pay to be terrified. To get both, they ought to pay double!" He suddenly gave a shout of laughter. The other passengers looked round at him.

It was still only eleven o'clock by the time we got to our stop.

"What about a coffee?" he suggested.

We went into the American place. It was crowded out with kids. Dominic was in there with some boys and he waved to me.

"Wasn't he at the party?" asked Mark.

"Yes."

"Old lover of yours?"

I was startled by the word "lover". I didn't know how to take it.

"No. He's a sort of boy-friend of Rebecca's."

"The dark siren from next door?"

"Yes." I was so pleased he didn't sound interested.

We sat down at a table with some other people and after quite a long time Mark managed to catch a waiter's eye and order coffee and a baked potato each. It was ages coming and I kept looking at my watch. The noise level was high and in any case since we were sharing a table it was hard to talk, and suddenly I started to get jumpy.

"Mark, it's twenty past."

"Yeah, I know. It'll come in a minute."

But it didn't.

"Mark, I want to go. We'll have to run as it is."

"Oh, come on, surely you don't have to be on the dot."

"Yes, I do. Please come on."

I was standing up. He got up reluctantly. Just at that moment the waiter hove in view with our order.

"Can't we just eat? I'll have to pay anyway."

"We'll go dutch. *Please* let's not be late."

He looked at me. His face had gone stubborn and closed again. He hated rules, I could see that, and besides he was hungry. For a moment I thought he would say, "Go by yourself then." I know he was thinking of saying it—he opened his mouth to say it. Then suddenly he changed his mind.

"Okay then." He turned to the waiter. "You took too long, mate."

"We're awfully busy," said this lad apologetically.

"Do I have to pay for it?"

"No, I've got another order it'll do for."

"Thanks."

Mark gave him a tip, helped me on with my coat, and we went out.

We had to hurry. I was sort of walking ahead, pacing him, all the way home. There was no hand-holding this time and I could sense he was fed up but I couldn't help it. It was for his own good too, if he ever wanted to take me out again. But maybe now he wouldn't. The thought gave me a sinking sensation.

At the gate he stopped.

"Goodnight then," he said. Very short.

I turned back. "Want to come in? I'll make you some coffee."

He hesitated.

"No. I'll be getting home. Thanks," he added grudgingly.

We turned away from each other. I got as far as the door, then I *had* to look round. He'd got about twenty steps along the road towards his bike. He'd stopped too.

We looked at each other through the lamplight. Then, slowly, we both turned and walked back to the gate.

It was closed between us. He put his arms round me and kissed me over the top of it. Gently and quietly. Everything reeled and spun. He lowered his arms.

"Thanks for a lovely evening," I said.

"It's been great."

"Sorry about the end."

"Not to worry." He let his eyes wander over my face for a few seconds. "It's a damned bind you being so hooked on the rules, but I'll have to learn to put up with it."

Then he walked away. I stood there leaning a little over the gate. At the corner he turned and lifted his hand for a moment. Then he was gone.

Mum and Dad looked up as one man the moment I opened the living-room door. The last thing I wanted was to be looked at or asked questions—I wanted to be *alone, alone, alone*—but if I hadn't gone in they'd certainly have smelt a rat.

"Hallo, darling! Have a good time?" asked Mum.

"Super, thanks. Sorry I'm a few minutes late."

Dad grunted. "Four, to be precise."

I didn't argue.

"I'm going up now. 'Night."

I closed the door. Then I did an awful thing. I put my ear against it to hear what they'd say. I can't excuse it, but that's what I did.

"Well?" asked Dad. "Did he?"

"Oh, yes," said Mum.

"*Oh?*" said Dad. "How do you know?"

"I just know," said Mum complacently.

12

Several weeks went by. The weather was still fine, though it was officially winter. I kept wishing it would rain so that I wouldn't go on wanting so desperately to have another ride on the forbidden motor-bike. Apart from that, Mark and I were happy.

We saw each other most Friday nights, and occasionally after school, and once in a while on a Sunday. Saturdays were no good because he worked nearly all that day in a shop. He hated it but it put a bit of money in his pocket which he needed, not only to take me out (he'd never let me pay my share) but to pay for his driving lessons. His Dad and older brothers had clubbed together to give him a course for his birthday, but, to his shame, it hadn't been enough.

I think it was the first exam he'd ever failed. He swore the tester had failed him on the length of his hair.

"Rotten little ponce with his short-back-and-sides!"

The ponce had told him snootily to "polish up his gear-shifts". Mark said he'd have liked to polish *him* up. But he had no choice but to pay for more lessons, though his brother took him out for a practice in his car once in a while.

One sunny Sunday a couple of weeks before Christmas we'd just finished lunch when there was a honk outside. I rushed to the front window and saw a clapped-out old car juddering to a halt at the gate. Mark was leaning out of the driver's window.

I ran out. The car had L-plates up, and sitting beside Mark was a thicker, older version of him.

"This is my brother Walter," said Mark. "This is Kate."

Walter and I shook hands across Mark's chest.

"Pleased to meet you," he said. He was red-faced and cheerful, tending to fat though he wasn't more than twenty-three.

"I'm having a free lesson," explained Mark. "We thought we'd drive over and see you."

"I'm glad you did. Would you like a cup of coffee?"

"Personally I'm only here for the beer," said Walter.

"You'll have to forgive my brother, he's a boozy type," said Mark, looking a bit put out.

"She don't mind, do you, love?" said Walter cheerfully.

"Not if we've got some," I said.

I took them through into the kitchen. Dad was washing up the lunch dishes with Alastair drying. They usually do this on Sundays to give Mum a rest. They both had aprons on and were a very pretty sight.

I thought they might be embarrassed, and felt quite proud of them for not being. Dad merely wiped his hands before offering one to Walter, and Alastair did the same. Then they went back to their task and we sat down round the kitchen table, or rather, Mark and Walter did, while I combed the back of the fridge for a stray can of beer. To my surprise I found a set of four.

"Who's taken up beer-drinking in this house?" I asked.

"I have," said Alastair.

"*Oh?*" said Dad.

"Do you want one now?"

"I don't mind."

So I poured out three and somehow after that I found it was Alastair who was seated at the table and me who was drying the dishes. It took my brother no time at all to find out that Walter was in the garage trade. He started pumping him for professional tips without a stop till Dad (who I'd noticed always got tetchy when Alastair went on too long about the innards of cars) finally suggested they take their beers out into our garage and practise their skills, if any, on his defective clutch. This they cheerfully did.

Dad finished the dishes, took off his apron, folded it neatly, bowed to us in a pleasantly actorish fashion and took himself off to join Bruce in front of the Sunday afternoon old movie.

Mark and I had the kitchen to ourselves. We hadn't seen each other for a week because that Friday he'd had to go out with the family. It was extra nice to see him after such a long gap, and when I hadn't expected to. We had lots of news to catch up on. We were telling each other all sorts of things by this time, gossipy things about our families and friends. He knew all about the cast in Dad's series, about Tina's ups and downs with Tony (there was a lengthy down going on at the moment) and Rebecca's (all ups so far) with Peter. I, for my part, had heard a good deal about his family, though this was the first time I'd met any of them. I'd begun to suspect he hadn't been joking when he had said his Dad wouldn't approve of me.

I heard very little, however, about any of the "gang" at Willcox. I had the welcome impression he wasn't seeing much of them out of school hours especially since the day Bruce limped home with a bloody knee, come by in mysterious circumstances following a game of squash in which he'd accidentally clouted the dreaded Geoffrey with his racquet. Mark had been around at the time and had interrogated Bruce pretty closely. Next time I'd seen Mark, *he'd* obviously been in a fight. No amount of nagging could make him reveal the details, but I remembered his words about Geoffrey being dangerous when "cheeked" by the younger boys, and I concluded that Mark had taken it on himself to exact revenge on Bruce's behalf.

The first person he asked about now was, of all people, poor old Marie-Noelle.

"Oh, she's still around. Every time I go in there, there's Marie-Noelle at the table, dripping tears into the matzo-meal. I never know what to say. Once I said something futile like, 'Don't cry any more, Marie-Noelle, it's not as bad as all that,' but she just dropped what she was doing and ran upstairs simply howling. So perhaps it is."

"What?"

"As bad as all that."

"I should think nothing could be much worse."

"Oh, I don't know," I said carelessly.

"What d'you mean?"

I wasn't really thinking very deeply about it. "It might have been the end of the world once upon a time to have a baby like that, but it's not any more, surely."

He looked at me strangely. "You are a funny girl," he said slowly.

"What's funny about me now?"

"So prim and proper, won't be a minute later than Daddy says, won't sneak in to X-films, won't go into pubs even, and as to having a little blow on the bike—cor! The jaws of hell fair gape for you every time you let yourself think of it! But an illegitimate baby, now—a little thing that's going to grow up without a Dad to tell it when to come in nights, let alone buy it its cornflakes, that's quite okay."

"I didn't say it was quite okay!" I exclaimed indignantly.

"Well, you don't give me the idea you think there's much wrong with it."

"I wouldn't do it myself."

Mark was given to suddenly raising his voice. He raised it now.

"I should bloody well hope not!"

I blushed.

And well I might. Those wonderful, exciting goodnight kisses had extended themselves in length and conviction in the past weeks. I would like to say that I felt they were quite exciting enough for me without going any further, but to be perfectly honest I had experienced, once or twice, a feeling that I could very easily be carried away. *Right* away. I was quite alarmed about it, to tell the truth. The physical feelings were glorious, of course, but I didn't care for this odd business of losing control of the situation. Once when we were kissing I was overcome by an absolute *need* to get closer and closer to him and suddenly he kind of put me away from him. Not *pushed*, just *put* me away, holding my shoulders. I felt a bit wild, and he looked sort of sick. I didn't like it, I felt it was all getting too much. Especially having to come in afterwards and face Mum.

Apart from my own feelings of uneasiness, Mum's beadiness about me had a very restraining effect. It had given me quite a turn to discover that she knew by instinct, or by looking at me, or something, when I'd been kissed. We'd always been very close but this was a bit much. One does like *some* secrets. She never pried, mark you; but then she didn't have to. She'd just give me this beady look when I'd come in from a date and she seemed to *know*. It's as good as a chastity belt any day to have your Mum guess everything you've been up to without even having to interrogate you.

Anyway I ignored Mark's sudden outburst and got the conversation back on to Marie-Noelle.

"I don't believe in coming over all Mary Whitehouse about other people's weaknesses," I said (rather priggishly I fear). "I'm very, very sorry for Marie-Noelle, of course it's awful for her, with strict Catholic parents, and not even around to help if they wanted to. I'm just not prepared to tut-tut about it, that's all."

Mark was playing with some breadcrumbs left on the table and not looking at me. He didn't seem to be listening particularly either.

"I thought I'd knocked a girl up last year," he said suddenly.

I sat very still, waiting for the familiar objects round me to settle down into their normal positions. After some moments, when I didn't seem to have breathed for some time, I sighed deeply and felt better. A bit, anyway. I still couldn't say anything, though, and at last he looked up at me from under his dark eyebrows.

"I'd have married her," he said loudly, as if I'd accused him.

Still I didn't speak. He *did* this sort of thing. He'd spring something on you without warning, something shattering, like saying, "My Dad was in the nick once." Then, having shocked you, he'd add that it was for lying down in Trafalgar Square in an anti-H-bomb demo and resisting arrest. Another time he told me he'd been thrown out of his first secondary school when he was thirteen for smoking pot. Of course he'd stopped all that now (the whole drug scene was practically a thing of the past, he told me casually) and he looked back on it as a childish lark. But of *course* he knew I'd be shocked. I think he liked shocking me.

But this time was different. He was looking, not slyly sideways to see my reaction, but straight at me as if determined to get something off his chest even at the cost of hurting me. And he had hurt me. I *hated* to think of him with other girls. Of course I knew he had been. I knew it by instinct, just as surely as I knew that Alastair, Ian, William and Tony hadn't. I'd thought about it, right at the beginning, and discovered that I didn't mind *in general* so long as I didn't have to hear about any one girl *in particular*. Now I found my voice and said rather shakily, "Thanks, I don't want to know about it."

"But I wanted you to know," he said, so tensely that I knew it had been weighing on him. "So you'd understand why—"

"Why what?"

"Why I won't take the slightest risk *with you. I* know what it can all lead to even if you don't, I've seen it. Just the terror of thinking it *might* be going to happen was enough for me. 'A baby's for life,' my Mum said to me. She made me see that—I didn't want to—I wanted to run—but she made me see it. I'll never forget what she made me see about kids like that and their mothers, specially when they're too young for the job. You don't have to worry. And neither do your parents. If you was on your knees *begging* for it, I wouldn't."

He stopped, gazing at me. Then he sank back into his chair. He reached for his empty beer glass, tried to drink out of it, and put it back on the table. His hand was shaking.

"What is it, Mark?" I asked gently.

He put his head in his hands and shook it.

"Do, please, tell me."

"Well, I do want you. It's not so easy." He put his hands down and looked at me again, more calmly this time; he was even smiling in his lopsided, cynical way. "I'm not grousing. There's plenty of Denises around if I'd wanted 'em, or Pamelas come to that. I chose you. And I'll stick to your rules. Come to that, your rules and mine aren't so very different in some things."

I felt a strange jolting sensation inside, like something exploding. It was physical and a heart-thing at the same time. I thought, "I love him." And then quickly I thought, "No I don't! That's stupid." I didn't want to be in love yet—it was too serious. But just the same I went round the table and stood close to him and he put his arms round me and rested his head against me. I kissed his hair and stroked it. After a few moments we heard Alastair and Walter coming back from the garage. We separated quickly and I took the dirty glasses to the sink to give me something to do.

In they came, all hearty and self-satisfied the way men get when they've been to a football match or mended some bit of machinery or done something terribly masculine and brilliant like that. They'd fixed Dad's clutch and were practically blood-brothers as a result, banging each other on the back pretty nearly and crying out for more beer. There was only one can left so they shared it. I watched Alastair sort of hurling it back into his throat as if he'd been lost in the desert for a week. His voice had got loud to match Walter's. They were both bawling away about their triumph so much that Dad left the film and came in to see what was up.

"I'm pleased to tell you, Mr Dunhill," said Walter, "that this boy of yours has hands of gold. Hands of gold," he repeated enthusiastically.

Alastair grinned as if he'd had a medal hung on him. He was all flushed and had far more oil about him than seemed necessary for one little clutch.

Dad didn't look as pleased as he might have done.

"Oh, you've fixed it?"

"Not me—Al, here, fixed it. Single-handed. Give him a year or two and he'll be fit to run his own workshop. Take my word for it, he's got the knack. That's what he's got. The knack."

"That's nice," said Dad, rather sourly I thought.

There was a brief pause, and Walter glanced at Alastair, who lost his pleased look and muttered, "I don't think Dad's too keen on me making it a life's work."

"Wha-a-t?" roared Walter. "Finest trade in the world! Inflation—recessions—why worry? A good mechanic need never go hungry. Want to travel—up stakes—pick up your tool-bag and off you go. Take you anywhere. And if you want to settle—no sweat. Bit o' capital—buy a little garage somewhere—build it up—"

"Belt up, Walt, you sound like Grandad," said Mark. He was obviously rather embarrassed at the tactless way his brother was going on.

"And what's wrong with that? The old man had the right ideas if you ask me. What's wrong with having a few blokes working under you? Better than working under some other bugger."

Mark, who doesn't know how Daddy talks when nobody but the family's listening, stood up sharply and said, "I think we'd better be off."

Walter didn't want to leave. He gave Alastair another whack on the back and insisted on scribbling his own name and phone number on a cigarette-box.

"Here, you keep this. You ever want to change jobs, give me a buzz. I'll put in a word with my guv'nor. He's always on the lookout for likely beginners, and I could show you the ropes."

I saw them to the gate. Mark turned back to say, "Sorry about that. Walt never did know how to put his feelers out, did you, big-mouth?" He aimed a punch at his brother's meaty shoulder.

"Here! Watch it, big-head!" said Walter, pretending he was going to wallop him. Then he winked at me and went round to the other side of the car.

"Mark," I said suddenly. "When am I going to meet the others?"

He hesitated.

"I thought you'd better get Walt over, so at least they're not *all* strangers. Four of us together, plus Mum and Dad, are a bit much in a lump."

"Fine. But when will you invite me home?"

I had a strong impression that he felt he was in a trap. But at last he said reluctantly, "What about Friday?"

"I can't this Friday. It's Hannuka."

"It's what?"

"Hannuka. What the Jews have instead of Christmas. Rebecca always asks us to their party. It's a sort of tradition."

"Oh." He looked relieved. "Well, then, we'll have to put it off." And he got into the car.

On complete impulse I called after him, "What's wrong with right now?"

Mark, who had just put the car in gear, stopped. "What do you mean, right now?"

"I mean why don't you drive me back now?"

Mark opened his mouth, but Walter got in first.

"Now there's a girl after me own heart. A creature of impulse! Who needs an invitation? Go on then, get your coat. Mark, move over. I'll drive. We're taking no chances with this one in the back."

I don't know what got hold of me. Mark's face showed quite clearly that he thought the whole idea was lousy, and actually it *was* fraught with horrible possibilities, so horrible that I rushed indoors without giving myself time to think another thought about it. I grabbed my coat, gabbled a word of explanation to Dad (Mum was off somewhere) and shot out and into the back of the car. Walter, who'd come round to take over the driver's seat, held the door open for me with a flourish worthy of Dad at his most actorish.

We were half-way there, with Walter telling jokes all the way before I let myself notice Mark's silence and my own ever-more wildly beating heart.

I leant forward with my arms along the back of Walter's seat.

"Walter—"

"What, love?"

"Maybe this isn't such a bright idea? What'll your mother say?"

"*Now* she asks," said Mark.

"Belt up, you," said Walter, adding kindly over his shoulder, "Don't you worry, love, she'll be tickled to death. She loves surprises, Mum does."

Mark muttered something that sounded like "Like holes in the head" which hardly calmed my heartbeats at all.

13

We were driving through a shopping area north of the river. At last we turned off into a maze of small roads behind the high street. Some of them had trees, but they were so narrow that where cars were parked on both sides there was only room for one other car to squeeze through. The houses were terraced, and had no real front gardens, just a yard of yard. We pulled up outside one that had Mark's motorbike standing in this little area under a canvas cover.

Walter let us in with his latchkey. We went straight down a narrow passage, past the foot of the stairs and through into the kitchen at the back.

It seemed to be jammed with people. Mark had said "the four of us plus Mum and Dad" but he'd been understating the case. There were the four of them—one could recognize the brothers easily—and Mum and Dad, plus the eldest brother's wife and baby daughter, plus the youngest brother's friend, plus an old lady, plus a neighbour. How they all fitted into such a small space was the mystery.

When I appeared a dead silence fell, but luckily it didn't last. The baby started yelling for her tea almost at once, and the general uproar engulfed me. But I had my eye fixed on Mark's mother, and she (you can bet) had hers fixed on me.

In appearance, Mrs Collins was to my mother what my mother is to Rebecca's. Mum has her hair done for parties; the rest of the time she pins it up herself (when she gets around to it). She wears mainly Marks and Spencer clothes, slacks, skirts, sweaters and so on, or summer dresses. And for make-up she normally just wears lipstick and a bit of powder. In other words she's comfortable rather than smart, whereas Mrs Daniels is smart all the time—I bet she even goes to bed looking smart.

Mrs Collins was just a mother. I don't know how else to describe her. She was too plump ever to be very smart even if she'd tried, her hair was quite grey (I often wondered why Mum didn't get grey and I finally found out) and she didn't wear even lipstick. She wore an overall and flat shoes, and her face was Mark's face, the very same lopsided look which couldn't ever have been pretty. The French word for her, which I'd picked up from Marie-Noelle, was *formidable*.

Now she was watching me as I threaded my way across the room to her. She was laying tea for all those people on a big formica-topped table, and had stopped with a tray of cups in her hands. As Walter brought me up to her she put it down and automatically wiped her hand on her overall.

"Here, Mum—I brought you a surprise," said Walter heartily.

"So I see." She shook hands with me. Her hand was slightly cold and damp as if she'd just been washing up. She held mine for a minute and looked at me. "So this is Kate." I couldn't tell what she thought of me, just as I couldn't often tell what Mark was thinking.

"I'm sorry to come without warning," I said.

"Well. You'll have to take us as you find us." She looked at me straight for another moment, and then turned to her husband, who was already sitting at the table, reading the *Sunday Mirror*. I don't think he'd noticed me. "George, look who's here. Mark's girl-friend."

His father started up. He was a huge man, with stiff short dark hair just greying at the sides, a tough bristly face (being Sunday I suppose he hadn't shaved, like Dad when he doesn't have to rehearse) and a pot-belly. Mr Daniels is fat, but not like Mr Collins. Mr Daniels is sort of fat all over, but Mark's Dad hadn't an ounce of extra flesh anywhere about him—his shoulder and neck muscles were like smooth rocks—except just this big round stomach that stuck out over the top of his belt and meant that when he sat down he had to spread his knees.

He shook hands with me, and here was the worker's hand I'd expected Mark to have—hard as wood with callouses like little pebbles under the skin. He also fixed me with this piercing look under beetling black eyebrows.

"I'll say one thing for my sons," he said, "they know how to pick the lookers."

"Thank you," I said.

"Mark, Kate don't know the family. You do the honours."

Mark introduced me. There was his eldest brother Brendan, and his wife Linda and the baby, Mark's niece, Sharon. Linda was a very pretty red-head. I'd heard about her from Mark of course. I knew about all of them really. I knew Brendan had been named after a crazy Irish playwright that Mr Collins had admired, before he (the playwright) drank himself to death. I knew about Linda's fiery temper and the rows she and Brendan had (they lived just across the road, and Mark said that when the wind was right you could hear them yelling). I'd also heard a lot about Gran, the old lady, who now gave me her still-strong old hand to shake and the same beady look I had had from her daughter and son-in-law. She lived in one of the ground-floor rooms.

"So you're Mark's bit o' stuff," she said. "Very nice too. I'm not sitting up to table, love, I like me own chair here by the storage heater. Why don't you go and get us both a cup and come and keep me company."

"Gran always tries to grab off the visitors," said Mark. "Hands off, you old poacher!" He shook his fist at her and she cackled with laughter.

The youngest brother, Derek, was sniggering in a corner with his pal. He was about Bruce's age or a bit less and just the same pestiferous type of little monster so I felt quite at home with him. The neighbour, having looked me over, had let herself out of the back door, so that just left the eleven of us. Lucky it was a fair-sized table.

Gran wasn't to be left out of the conversation for long, even though she was outside the tight circle of us sitting elbow-to-elbow round the table.

"We see your Dad on the telly," she called from her corner. "Always watch him nowadays." I waited for her to say something nice about him, but all she added was, "He tells 'em off proper, that's what I like."

Derek had unexpectedly insisted on sitting next to me.

"Could you get me his autograph?" he asked.

"Oh, let her alone, Derek," said his mother. "Always asking for things." She passed me a plate of bread and butter and some sliced ham, an unthinkable luxury in our house where tea consists of a marmite or peanut butter sandwich. Here there were all sorts of delicacies including those delicious little individual apple pies you can buy in station buffets. Mum scorns them at home, preferring to make her own, which would be fine only she hardly ever does. But nervousness had had its usual effect on my appetite.

"Go on, have another," said Walter, who was tucking in. "Don't take no for an answer, Mum. She needs building up."

"Not everyone eats like you do," said his mother shortly. "I hope Kate knows she needn't stand on ceremony."

She hadn't once called me "love" or "dear" yet, as most of the others had. I sensed she *was* a bit put out at my arriving unexpectedly. I noticed she kept touching her hair and glancing round the room, which was filled with a homely clutter, as if wishing she'd had a chance to tidy up. I knew how Mum would have felt if Alastair had brought a girl home for the first time and caught us in our usual muddle.

Still, I must say none of the others seemed bothered. They all chatted away to me as friendly as you please, except Linda who was completely taken up with Sharon and who in any case seemed to be in a bit of a mood. She wasn't speaking to her husband at all, I noticed, and he was being very noisy and jolly to everyone else to show her he didn't care.

"You going to follow in your Dad's footsteps?" he asked me.

"No fear," I said. "I wouldn't go into acting for anything. Too uncertain."

"I want to be an actor," said Derek with his mouth full.

"Forget it," growled Mr Collins. "You'll learn an honest trade. That's no job for a man."

There was an awful silence. He glanced round the table, then he clapped both hands over his mouth. "Gawd. Me and my big mouth. Sorry, love," he said to me.

"That's all right," I said.

The silence persisted. Linda looked up in surprise.

"What did he say?" she asked.

"Never mind," said Brendan.

"No, I want to know."

"I just put me great big boot in it as usual, that's all," said Mr Collins cheerfully. "I really am sorry, love, I wasn't thinking. We all got our prejudices. I've often told 'em. I'd rather see a boy of mine in his coffin than poncing around on the telly—"

"Why don't you just shut up, Dad," muttered Walter. "You're only making it worse."

"I'm trying to explain!" shouted Mr Collins. "Nothing personal, I like watching your Dad do his stuff. Very entertaining and that. But it's not what you'd call productive, now is it? It don't do nothing to increase the resources of the country. And don't you tell me to shut up!" he added with sudden fierceness to Walter, as if he'd only just realized what he'd said.

I decided to be bold.

"Well, you know, it does in a way. I mean, the series my Dad is in has been sold in America for thousands of dollars. It brings wealth to the country, just like any other successful export."

Mr Collins put down his knife and fork and stared at me.

"Is that right," he said.

"Oh, yes. Our television's the best in the world, and that's partly because our actors are the best."

"And where do all them dollars go to?" Mr Collins asked, recovering from his surprise. "Straight into the pockets of them ponces at the BBC or whatever. Just goes to make the rich richer."

"Most of it goes into the pockets of a lot of poor hard-working technicians and prop-men and make-up girls and all the craftsmen who make the dozens of different things they need. Cameras and furniture and lights and—"

"All right, all right, don't kick me when I'm down!" said Mr Collins, pretending to protect his head with his arms. Everybody laughed, and the old lady called out, "You've met your match now, George! She knows more about it than what you do!"

"Oh, she does, does she?" shouted Mr Collins, well roused by now. He leant across the table to me, nearly knocking over a bottle of ketchup which his wife rescued just in time from under his chest. "Listen here then, Mrs Thatcher! If you want to get the better of me on politics, you'll have to come and spend a whole evening—"

"A week, more like," said Walter.

"A month," said Mark.

"Why don't she just come and live with us?" cackled Gran.

"Belt up, the lot of you! This is between me and young Kate. You think you know a lot. Right. Maybe you know about television but I can knock spots off you about where the money comes from and where it blooming well goes. You get Mark to trot you round here one Sunday when I got plenty of time and when I'm not so lumbered with big-headed sons and we'll have it out, you and me. Met my match, have I? What d'you say?"

"Okay," I said.

He reached across and gave my ear a gentle box. Then he looked over at Mark.

"She's all right is this one," he said. "Got a head on her."

Mark said nothing. I wondered if everyone was thinking about the other girl, the one he thought he'd got pregnant. There was another of those brief family silences and then everyone started talking. I glanced quickly under my eyelashes, not at Mark but at his mother. She was looking at me. Suddenly she gave me a tight little smile.

"Have another pie," she said.

It was dark long before we left. There was a crispness of real winter in the air and the narrow little street had a frosty glitter.

"Let's go home on the bike," said Mark.

"Right," I said instantly.

He stared at me in astonishment. I was astonished at myself. Every time we'd gone out together he'd said something about going on the bike and every time I'd refused. Now, suddenly, without even thinking about it, I'd changed my mind. I don't know why. It had something to do with that afternoon I'd spent with Mark's family. I'd been afraid, but I'd managed to overcome my fear and come through with all flags flying. A real barrier between us had been knocked down. I felt elated, almost as if I were drunk. Only a ride on the bike would be a fitting end to the day—to go home tamely on a bus would be a let-down.

I put the thought of Mum out of my head.

Mark put the helmet on me, wrapped his own scarf tightly round my neck and over my mouth, and then from the pannier produced an eye-screen arrangement like he had and fitted it to my helmet.

"I bought this ages ago in case you ever changed your mind," he said.

We got on the bike. Mark revved up and in a moment we were flying through the frosty streets.

Being Sunday evening there wasn't too much traffic. We were able to go really fast, faster than last time. It was glorious. I felt the world was ours. I understood why men want fast cars, why they spend far too much money on things like Concorde, and even more going to the moon. It's part of our nature to want to go faster and faster. But one couldn't have this thrill in a plane or a rocket. Only skiing perhaps, or flashing down those mountainous waves in the Pacific on a surf-board, could equal this.

I could have cried when it ended.

"Do you like it?" he asked.

"It's better than anything!" I said breathlessly.

He gave me a hug and whispered, "Not than *any*thing." I blushed and hid my face against his coat. He turned it up with both hands and kissed me. It had begun, very lightly, to snow.

He tucked my hand in his jacket-pocket and walked slowly off towards our house. (As always he'd parked the bike round the corner.)

"I liked your family," I said.

"They liked you." But something was bothering him. "What do you think of the house?" he asked at last.

"I didn't see much of it. It seems very nice and homely."

"It's a slum," he said harshly.

I looked up at him, frowning.

"A *slum*? Of course it isn't!"

"It is compared to your house."

I laughed. "Like ours is compared to Rebecca's, and like Rebecca's is compared to Kath's. But you can't call it a slum."

"I do."

"But in what way?"

"It's so small. Do you know I have to share a bedroom with Walter? Even now Brendan's moved out we're crammed in like sardines. When we're all in the sitting-room together you can't move about. We've got a garden the size of a table-top. If Derek kicks his ball out there it lands three plots along. When I look at your garden I could—"

He stopped. His head was down. "I hate our house," he said furiously.

I didn't know what to say. I had let myself think that here was a typical working-class family, three generations living under one roof, all warm and cosy and communal, helping each other, the way it ought to be. But Mark was muttering about what problems Gran made, forever nagging and interfering and making extra work for his mother, and how they could never really invite friends back because there was no room and Mum was always so short-tempered and overworked . . .

"I've been putting it off and putting it off," he said, "asking you back. If you hadn't pushed it today, I might never have really done it. I'm ashamed of the place, that's the real truth. It's so different from yours. I thought it'd put you off."

"Silly," I said. But he'd upset me. I didn't like him saying he hated his own home.

"Dad's so bloody stubborn!" he burst out.

"What do you mean?"

"Well I mean to say, he could have moved us all years ago if he'd liked. He makes good money, Brendan was earning well and living at home till he got married, Walt brings in a good screw as well from the garage. We could have got a decent house in a nicer district. But Dad never would. Do you know what he used to say, when Mum'd ask him? (She's given up now, poor old Mum, she's resigned herself to living in that little rabbit-hole the rest of her life.) He used to say,

'No bleeding bourgeois semi for me! This is where we belong, and this is where we'll stop. They know me in the pub, they know you in the shops, all our neighbours are our mates. Am I to cut meself off from me roots?' But what he really meant was that he wanted to stop in a working-class area. Said he'd lose touch with himself if we tried to move on. But he never thought how Mum felt and how we felt. He just didn't care. So the house gets shabbier and shabbier and Mum gets older and we get bigger and we all hate it more and more—except him. *He's* quite happy, is Dad, master of all he surveys, king-frog in his own little mud puddle . . ."

We'd reached home and were standing by the gate. I was listening to him with all my attention, with all my sympathy, until I noticed Mum watching for me at the front window. Suddenly the most awful wave of guilt swamped me and drove Mark and everything else out of my mind.

"I should never have come back on the bike!" I whispered.

"What?" said Mark, brought up short.

We looked at each other. Obviously he thought I hadn't been listening to him. His face closed up again. It was the first time he'd really opened up to me about his life at home, and here I'd cut him short. He looked as if I'd thrown a pail of cold water over him.

"I'm so sorry—" I said. "It's just that I won't be able to tell her—"

But he couldn't be expected to understand.

"I'm glad I haven't got your conscience," he said shortly. "Too delicate by half. You got to start making your own decisions sometime, and if it'd hurt her to know you came home on the bike tonight then keep it to yourself and no harm's done." He kissed my cheek briefly. "'Night."

He strode off without looking back.

I went in feeling flat and unsettled and moody. Mum asked how it had gone.

"It was interesting," I said.

"How did you get home?"

"On the bus," I said after the briefest pause. I felt faintly sick. It was my first lie to her for ages.

"Was it so cold on the bus he had to lend you his scarf?" she asked. I looked up quickly. She was busy getting supper and didn't look at me. I felt a sudden anger. Everybody lies to their parents sometimes. Why did I have to feel so *awful* about it? I ran upstairs to my room without answering.

14

Rebecca had said that our party was horrid. But it wasn't half as horrid as her Hannuka one turned out to be that year. I have to say that, even though it wasn't her fault and it didn't go wrong in the same way ours did. It was worse.

I had begun to realize, about a year before, why the Danielses always included us—Alastair, Bruce and me—in their family celebration. There weren't many Jewish families living in our district. If we had known that the Danielses had special religious-type celebrations from which we were kept out, or if their children hadn't been allowed to come to our Christmas do's and so on, we might have felt there was something strange about them. As it was, we accepted Hannuka and Passover and all their festivals as perfectly normal because we knew all about them. We even looked forward to them.

Hannuka is really lovely. It goes on for eight days, with more candles being lit in their special nine-branch candlestick each night. On the final night, when all the candles have to be lit, they have this party to which we're invited. We always eat special traditional food and sing Hannuka songs and play a game with a top and mountains of nuts, figs and dates. Actually we consider ourselves too old for it now, but that night we played a couple of go's of it with Neville, Rudy and Bruce, just to be friendly. Then I went to see if I could help lay the table.

The Danielses have this huge dining-table that opens out, which they need for occasions like this. There were six of them, three of us and Marie-Noelle.

Marie-Noelle had stopped crying for the moment. Mrs Daniels had showed no signs of getting rid of her and she seemed on the surface to have calmed down. But she wasn't the same girl. She used to be happy in her lumpish way, quite chatty and good-natured, but now she was all shut-in and sullen. Mum had told us she was getting dreadfully on Mrs Daniels' nerves, and watching her now as she finished laying the table, not looking at anyone or even answering when you spoke to her, I could well understand it.

I tried to talk to her, but it was rather hard to think of things to say. After all, how could she put her mind to anything except that one thing she must be thinking of all the time? Still, she didn't have to snatch the napkins out of my hand when I tried to help her with them. I wandered off to find Rebecca.

She was sitting in the living-room with Alastair and Leo. She looked heavenly as usual in this terribly feminine velvet skirt and a see-through blouse with ruffly sleeves hanging down to her finger-tips. She never wears jeans at all and whenever I see her I wish I liked elegance more than comfort. I wonder if Mum feels that when she's with Mrs Daniels.

Alastair and Leo were bridging the rather wide gap between their job-interests. Leo was still studying at London University and spending all his free time in museums, while Alastair was getting more and more stuck in at the garage. While Alastair was talking, trying to make Leo understand something of his difficulties with Dad, I was glad to see Rebecca watching him sympathetically. (I couldn't help thinking it was a bit of a pity about this Peter, who isn't Jewish either.) Suddenly she drawled,

"What Ah say is, a man's gotta chew—what a man's gotta chew."

We all looked at her. It was a TV slogan that the twins and Bruce were always using. It had come, in both our families, to mean roughly that you have to do your own thing. Alastair said, "That's all very well, but Dad's got his heart set on me going back to school somehow."

"Well, why don't you go to night-school, and study engineering?" suggested Leo. "That way everyone's happy."

"I thought of that," said Alastair. "I just wonder whether I could cope. I'm pretty tired in the evenings. Besides . . ." He didn't go on—he didn't need to. We all knew each other well by now and Leo certainly realized that Alastair, rightly or wrongly, had no confidence in his ability to study.

From the twins' room upstairs came a roar as somebody won a big "pool" of nuts and figs.

"Those kids won't want any dinner," said Leo.

He seemed restless and kept getting up and moving around. When he was down at the far end of the big room, I whispered to Rebecca, "I wish Monique was coming!" I hadn't seen her yet.

"So does Leo. But she has her own party at home," said Rebecca. "How's Mark?"

"Fine," I said quickly. I hadn't heard from him since the previous Sunday so I didn't want too many questions. "How's Peter?"

"Fine," she said—in such a similar way that I gave her a sharp look.

"Has something happened?"

"No. Not really. It's just—" She lowered her voice. "Daddy says I'm seeing too much of him. He keeps coming round. Daddy wasn't very nice to him last time and I got annoyed. I'm not really talking to Daddy at the moment," she said, tossing her head a bit.

Pretty soon Mrs Daniels called us all to the table. She is the most motherly woman I know, despite her elegance. She just can't keep her hands off children, and if you don't want to be hugged and kissed and plied with things to eat, you had better keep out of her reach. She's never happier than on occasions like this one, when she can pull out her dining-table to its full length, surround it with kids and stuff them full of food. Now she bustled round like a mother hen, showing us where to sit and fitting all the boys with little satin skull-caps. Even Bruce and Alastair had to wear them for the occasion.

I was to sit between Rudy and Mr Daniels, with Marie-Noelle opposite on Mr Daniels' other side. My heart sank a bit. Mr Daniels is a businessman and it's hard to think of things to say to him, since I don't know much about business. Besides, there is this *foreignness* about him. He's plump and smooth with olive skin and grey curly hair and these dark, dark eyes like plums behind his thick glasses. He's always very kind to me but I never really feel at home with him.

Now he lit a white candle and handed it to Neville, who's the youngest in the family by twenty minutes, and all the Danielses said a Hebrew prayer while Neville lit the other eight candles from the white one and stuck it into the topmost branch of the big silver candlestick. Then we all sang a traditional Hebrew song that I like very much and almost know the words of by now, though I don't know what they mean.

After that Mrs Daniels went into the kitchen and returned with a platter heaped with dozens of crisp golden potato-pancakes called "latkes", a traditional Hannuka dish. There were all sorts of olives and things to go with them, and chopped liver and hardboiled eggs. We were all tucking in, feeling very cheerful, while Mrs Daniels sat at the head of the table beaming from ear to ear, when I suddenly noticed one person who wasn't eating. Marie-Noelle.

The poor girl was sitting there with her head down and her hair falling in a gingery curtain towards her untouched plate. I saw a tear fall into the latke. Her head was going lower and lower. Mr Daniels saw me looking, and looked too. He put down his fork and leant towards her, putting one arm round her in a fatherly way and saying something to her. Nobody else had noticed what was going on.

Suddenly she jumped up. Her chair crashed over on its back. Everyone stopped talking of course, and looked at her. She stood there, her fists clenched, staring wildly round at us.

"You are all so 'appy!" she said. "Why can you be 'appy when I am so in despair?"

The smile fell off Mrs Daniels' face.

"Marie-Noelle—my dear—"

"You don't call me your dear!" cried Marie-Noelle. "You sink I am a bad girl and a big trouble! Well, is not only my trouble, is also your trouble, madame." She opened her mouth to say more, but then seemed to catch herself. She looked at Rudy and Neville, and at Rebecca. "You come," she said to Mrs Daniels. "Come out in ze kitchen, madame. I 'ave decide to tell you something."

She stalked out with her head thrown back and her arms stiff. Mrs Daniels looked at her husband and they both shrugged. She put down her napkin, said "Excuse me a moment," and followed Marie-Noelle into the kitchen.

There was not much conversation till she came back a few minutes later. She had gone absolutely grey in the face.

"Maurice," she said.

Mr Daniels stood up, threw his napkin on to the table, and strode out into the kitchen.

We all gazed at each other. Nobody said anything. Then Leo stood up and followed his father out.

"What can it be?" I whispered to Rebecca. She shook her head. She looked frightened. "I don't know," she breathed.

We just sat there for what seemed an age. We could hear angry voices coming from the kitchen. The boys grew restless and began to nibble their latkes, furtively as if we were in church or somewhere where you mustn't eat.

After a long time, Mr Daniels returned. He also looked awful, but he tried to cover it up.

"Oh come, children, your food is getting cold! Eat up."

"What's going on, Daddy?" asked Neville.

"Nothing to concern you. Now eat."

He sat down in his wife's place and served more latkes. The boys ate them, but Rebecca, Alastair and I refused. An appalling thought had occurred to me. I couldn't have swallowed another mouthful. Rebecca just sat there looking at her hands in her lap. Suddenly she broke away from the table and ran out, not into the kitchen but into the hall. We heard her rushing upstairs.

I looked at Mr Daniels.

"I've finished, Mr Daniels. May I go and see her?"

I knew the meal, under ordinary circumstances, was nothing like over, but he just nodded. I hurried up to Rebecca's bedroom, and found her, as I'd expected, crying her eyes out on the bed.

"It's not true! It can't be, it can't!" she sobbed.

"Of course it's not!" I said.

She stopped crying and rolled over to look up at me.

"You guessed what she's saying?"

"It's only a guess. Maybe we're both wrong."

"We're not. She's saying Leo did it. But he didn't! She's only saying it because she wants Mummy and Daddy to feel responsible for her and help her!"

"But they were going to anyway."

"I suppose she wants to make sure. The rotten little liar! Oh, I'd like to strangle her!"

I didn't know what to say. I just sat there with her for a long time. We didn't talk much. After a bit Alastair knocked on the door and peeped in.

"We're going," he said to me.

I got up from the bed. On an impulse I bent down and kissed Rebecca, who was still lying on her face.

"If I can do anything—"

She shook her head without turning.

On the way down, Alastair whispered, "It's awful. She claims Leo's the father of her baby. She's making a terrible to-do, throwing herself about . . . Poor Leo's right up the creek. He denies it but I'm not so sure his father believes him."

"I believe him," I said.

"Oh, so do I! He's always been nice to the girl but I know for sure he's never thought of her like that. Anyway, he wouldn't."

"Surely Mrs Daniels believes him?"

"She says she does, but she's terrifically upset. We'd better just creep out the front way without saying goodbye."

We hiked Bruce out of the living-room, where he was messing about with the twins, and went home. Bruce pestered and pestered and pestered to know what the mystery was. Finally Alastair gave in and told him.

"Cor!" said Bruce. "Poor old Leo. Ah well, a man's gotta chew what a man's gotta chew."

"Never mind chewing. You just keep your trap shut about it," said Alastair, quite threateningly for him. "Don't say anything to the twins. Their mother may not want them to know."

Mum and Dad had taken the opportunity to go out for the evening to a theatre, so they didn't find out what had happened till the next morning.

Mum was in a state. She didn't know whether to go next door and talk to "poor Zilla" (Mrs Daniels) or not. Eventually Mrs Daniels came to her and we were all shooed out of the way while they had a long session over endless cups of coffee in the kitchen. Poor Mrs Daniels must have cried a lot, because when I caught a glimpse of her leaving her eyes were all swollen and she looked as un-smart as I'd ever seen her.

15

The Leo–Marie-Noelle scandal kept us lively all over Christmas. I know that sounds an awful way to put it, but looking back on it it's a fair description. We hardly seemed to have time for Christmas actually, because nearly every day of the holidays brought some new development next door and it came to seem positively selfish for any of us to get on with things like shopping, decorating or cooking because of the piling-up agony going on at Number Eight. (We're Number Ten.)

Rebecca, with no Christmas to distract her, was round at our place most of the time. So were the twins, though not from choice. Their mother now had no help, because Marie-Noelle was on strike until she was convinced that her word was believed by the whole family. Mrs Daniels simply couldn't be doing with the twins, and foisted them on us during almost all daylight hours and quite often at night as well. Luckily Bruce took them off to the rec. or the swimming pool quite a bit, otherwise Mum would have gone bananas with them hanging around all the time.

Alastair and Dad kept out of the way as much as possible. They crept about with a furtive air as if trespassing and not wanting to be noticed. Dad had taken to pub-crawling with Alastair, most unlike both of them, but it showed how desperately they both needed to get out of the house and away from the drama.

As for me, there wasn't much I could do except keep Rebecca company as much as possible. My private thoughts were unsharable even with her. She had never known about my thing about Leo, and wasn't I thankful now that I'd never told her! I kept wondering how on earth I should have been feeling about this whole business if it hadn't been for having Mark. All my love was for him now and so I could be almost objective about Leo's dilemma, but that didn't stop me feeling desperately sorry for him and wishing I could help him somehow.

I must say Marie-Noelle turned out to be a proper little monster. Well, not so little. She spotted right away that Mr Daniels half believed her lying tale, and she played on his doubts for all she was worth. It wasn't Mrs Daniels she cried in front of now—she knew she'd get no sympathy from her any more. But whenever Mr Daniels hove in view on would go the taps, and she'd trail about the place sniffing and gulping until they were all ready to scream. In fact Mrs Daniels did scream at her one day, so loudly we all heard it. Soon afterwards she rushed in to Mum looking perfectly distracted and stayed closeted in her bedroom with her for so long that I had to make the lunch.

The ironic thing was that if only Marie-Noelle had left things alone, I mean if she hadn't accused Leo, I'm positive the family would have kept her on, looked after her when the baby was born and generally treated her like their own daughter. It would never have surprised me if Mrs Daniels had adopted the baby! As it was, the stupid girl had just played the wrong card. Mrs Daniels was now itching to get rid of her. Leo had solemnly declared his innocence and she believed him and that was that so far as she was concerned, but the trouble was, Marie-Noelle wouldn't go. She stuck to her story and threw herself on Mr Daniels' mercy. Mr Daniels didn't say in so many words that he believed her but he certainly wasn't prepared to throw her out into the snow, so to speak. In the meantime he was dreadfully short-tempered with everyone, including Rebecca, who was banned from even seeing Peter for no better reason than because Mr Daniels had enough troubles without "hairy musicians" (let alone non-Sephardic ones) hanging about the house. You may imagine that Rebecca, who was already genuinely upset about Leo, threw herself into quite a fit about *that*.

While all this was going on, Mark and I kept seeing each other. During the holidays he got a job in a restaurant as well as his Saturday job. He told me he was saving up for something special, which I supposed was a second-hand car when he'd passed his test.

But there was a lovely feeling of no-homework in the evenings and he came round three or four times a week. Sometimes we'd just mess around together at home, sometimes we'd go shopping or to a flick. Once he took me over to visit Emma. (Yes, on the bike. I'd decided, in for a penny in for a pound, I'd disobeyed Mum's ban and I'd be caught eventually so I might as well enjoy my vice in the meantime.) Emma was fed up with Adam and was feeling a bit pallid, so we took her out with us to a pub-theatre and then had a Chinese meal afterwards which we all enjoyed.

Christmas itself produced its own trials, not connected with our unhappy neighbours. The Danielses kind of cried off for those few days out of respect and we were left in peace—or it would have been peaceful, if it hadn't been for Uncle Steve, who, as usual, brought his family down from Lancashire to visit us.

I think I've mentioned before that I like Uncle Steve, Auntie Alice and our cousins Jenny and Reggie, but I'm afraid if we saw them more than once a year the strain might prove too much. It's Uncle Steve mostly. He kind of bears you to the ground, with his great booming Lancashire voice echoing all over the house and all that back-slapping. And jokes. The jokes are the worst. The best way with him is not to let him know you're sensitive about *anything*, from the colour of your eyelashes to the state of your love-life. If he senses any weakness in you he'll simply tease you to death.

For this reason I would have hidden Mark's existence from him altogether if I could, and I did try. I warned Mark not to come while Steve was about, and he didn't, being busy with his own family. But need I say that my revolting little brother lost no time in betraying me utterly? Steve wasn't in the house five minutes before he was roaring and bellowing about "Kate's intended" to all and sundry. Of course I nearly throttled Bruce but it was too late. He should have been throttled at birth, if you ask me.

Still, there was Jenny. Jenny's my friend though she's only thirteen. She's very quiet and mousy but she has hidden depths. When you can get her on her own and she's not being drowned by her family, she blossoms out and tells you all sorts of fascinating things. There are advantages in being mousy. Nobody guesses you've got any devil in you, but Jenny has plenty, and in the course of a year she accumulates a good collection to tell me when we're tucked into my bedroom at night.

In exchange for Jenny's latest stories of daring and secret rebellion, I told her about Leo and Marie-Noelle. She amazed and rather shocked me by saying she betted it was really *Mr Daniels*, whom she'd met the previous Christmas. She said he was definitely the sensual type who went after young girls, she knew it because she had a piano-teacher who looked a lot like him and he was always pinching her knee under the keyboard. When I digressed to ask why she didn't complain to her mother, she asked in surprise what there was to complain about? She liked it very much and often left her foot on the bass pedal too long so that her knee would be more available, and furthermore never changed out of her uniform into jeans before her lesson. Stupidly I asked why, and she said, in her rather flat, matter-of-fact voice, that there were two reasons, one, because being pinched through jeans wasn't so nice as being pinched through even rather thick black tights and two, because she suspected that school uniforms turned him on. I was riveted, and asked what she'd do if he tried to go further than a pinch, and she said she would cross that bridge when he came to it and gave me the impression she hoped he wouldn't be too long about it.

I didn't feel like telling her too much about Mark because it seemed in quite a different category from her and her music-teacher, but she already knew about him so I told her a little about how nice he was without going into details which might sound like competing with her and her pinches.

Having four extra to every meal made so much work that I didn't really have much free time until the evening of Boxing Day, when they all went home and we were left lying about in heaps of exhaustion. But I was not too exhausted to crawl to the phone and ring Mark, as I'd promised to do when they'd gone.

I could tell at once he was in a bad mood.

I asked if he'd had a nice Christmas and he said "Horrible". I said why, and he said he couldn't go into it now, but basically it had been noisy and crowded and boozy and he'd missed me. "When can

I see you?" I said he could come over now if he liked, and he said "Good" and hung up.

I met him at the gate twenty minutes later. It was a damp, cool evening and I said, "Let's not go in, they're all very pallid and don't want anybody. Let's go for a walk."

He took my hand and we walked. We didn't talk much at first, just walked slowly through the streets, looking at Christmas trees through the windows and saying a few odd things that came into our heads, like, "Sharon kept being sick", and "My cousin Reggie failed nearly all his O-levels". Neither of us was very interested in the grisly details of the other one's family but it was necessary to sort of get us together again. Finally I said, "My Auntie Alice thinks she'll have to have a hip operation," and that was just one too many for him. "I don't give a *shit* about your Auntie Alice," he said, and turned round and kissed me rather violently between lamp-posts.

It was so absolutely lovely to be in his arms again after five days of not even seeing him that I simply abandoned myself, and we kissed about ten times before we moved on. This time he had his arm around my shoulders and I felt entirely different. All the subtle strains of Christmas eased away and were gone—for him too, I hoped. I wanted his bad mood to melt away.

Suddenly he said, "I feel like a *proper* Christmas drink—with you. Come on." He'd spotted our local pub, The Roebuck, all lit up still with its string of fairy-lights outside, looking very inviting I must say. "I don't feel I've celebrated at all really. Let's have a drink together."

I hesitated, but only for a moment. This was no time to be prim and priggish.

I'd never been in a pub before properly, apart from one in the country which let children in to a special section where you could eat. Dad was always saying what nonsense the licensing laws were, that pubs on the whole were the most harmless places and that half the trouble with the British was that their children grew up with the idea that drinking was deliciously wicked and forbidden, so that as soon as they got the chance they started swigging like maniacs instead of learning to drink sensibly like the French. Anyway some of this feeling of a taboo must have infected me, because I did feel a proper devil going into a pub like that and breaking the law. I think I was expecting the bartender or whoever to spot that I was under age and chuck me out. But to my surprise he took no notice of me. I hovered in the background while Mark ordered the drinks at the bar and then we sat down in a dark corner.

As soon as I saw I wasn't going to be pounced on, I had a look round. There were a lot of men around the bar, and a few more playing darts near us, and one or two women who didn't seem to belong to anyone—I mean, the men didn't seem to be their husbands. There was one of those fruit-machines which two young lads were playing with. When they left, Mark asked me if I wanted a go.

"No thanks," I said.

"Oh, come on."

"Those things are silly, you never win anything on them."

"Watch me."

He went and played and I watched him, sitting there. I don't know why, but I was feeling suddenly rather miserable. I didn't seem to fit in that place. The men playing darts kept looking at me as if I were in their way. I became aware that I was bored, that I had been bored almost from the moment I came in. I'd never been bored with Mark before.

I finished my wine and went over to the fruit-machine. Mark was wrestling with it, and just as I arrived three plums lined up and ten p. clinked into the metal cup. Mark showed it to me in triumph.

"You see? You can win."

I'd seen him put in at least thirty p. to get ten out, but I didn't say anything. He had another go with his winnings, lost it, and said, "Would you like another drink?"

"No thanks, Mark. Let's go."

"Why?"

I shrugged.

"Don't you like it here?"

"What's there to like? It's dreary and it smells awful."

His face closed. "Maybe you'd be more comfortable in the saloon bar."

"Where's that?"

He looked at me. "Through the other side. Didn't you know there were two bars?"

"No. What's the difference?"

"I'll show you."

He led me through into another room on the far side of the bar. The atmosphere here was quite different. It was quieter for one thing, and the people were better dressed. There were more women, and they seemed to be in couples with the men. Also I noticed there were more short drinks and fewer beers being drunk. There was no dart-board and no fruit-machine. Nobody looked at me here. Straight away I relaxed and said, "Maybe I will have another drink, after all—just a shandy—"

I looked at Mark. His face was strange. He was watching me very closely with his eyes narrowed.

"I thought you'd feel better on the snob side," he said oddly.

"What do you mean?"

But he'd left me to go to the bar. He came back with my shandy and a short drink for himself—a whisky by the look of it. I blinked at it. I guessed he was waiting for me to say something, but it wasn't the drink that was worrying me, it was his sudden change of mood.

"What's the matter?" I asked. "What did you mean about the snob-side?"

"That's what we call the saloon bar, in our family."

"But I don't get it. Why are there two bars in the first place?"

"In the *first* place? That's easy. In the first place everyone knew there were three social classes in this country. You probably call them upper, middle and lower, or working. I call them nobs, snobs and yobs. And in the first place, everyone knew which they were, and liked being with their own sort. So innkeepers—who always aim to please—naturally had two or three separate compartments for boozing in, so the nobs didn't have to mix with the yobs or the snobs with either of them."

He paused to drink half his whisky and then went on.

"Now look around you, and what do you see? An anachronism. That means—"

"I know what it means. Something left over from another time."

"Exactly. Aren't they always telling us the class war's over? We're the great classless society now. No more 'us' and 'them'. It's true the politicians haven't quite ironed out all the little inequalities that make life so interesting. But those are culture differences, money differences, not class differences, oh dear no. Only, what? Right down here where we all meet, in the good old British pub where we show ourselves as we really are, what do we find? Built-in class distinction, that's what."

I looked round again. I began to understand what he was getting at.

"And," Mark went on, "it's not just a hangover from a less civilized past either. If they build a new pub today, don't you think they make sure there's a snobs' side and a yobs' side? And here's another interesting thing. Once you could have written 'Bosses' and 'Workers' or even 'Rich types' and 'Poor types' on those doors instead of the code-names 'saloon' and 'public'. But now some of these blokes are poorer than some of the ones next door, and some of *them* are less ignorant than the ones in here. But the funny thing is that every man in Britain turns automatically into one bar or the other, whatever pub he goes in to. Why do you think I feel happier over there while you couldn't wait to come here?"

I was listening with all my ears. "I don't know," I said. "Why?"

He leant towards me. His eyes were hard.

"Because you can't get rid of it," he said. "You can't, Kate, no matter what you do. Laws can't do it, politics can't do it, even education can't do it. And that's something the Labour government had better look into before they go much further. We're not a classless society and we never will be, *because we don't want to be.*"

I'd stopped listening, and was looking over Mark's shoulder at a man who was watching us. Now he was coming towards the little round table we were sitting at. I tried to warn Mark, but he was still drinking up his drink when the man put a hand on his shoulder.

Mark jumped.

"Excuse me, son," said the man, quite politely, "would you mind telling me your age?"

"Eighteen," said Mark instantly. "What's it to do with you?"

"Mark—"

"And your young lady?" asked the man, looking at me.

"She's eighteen too." The corner of the man's mouth curled up, and I saw Mark begin to bristle. "Look, who—"

"I'm the landlord here. Do you realize you two could lose me my licence?"

Mark stood up slowly. I was suddenly thrown into a panic. What had panicked me was that I saw in Mark's face, in his whole body as he got up, that the smouldering anger I had felt in him ever since I'd spoken to him on the phone was about to break out.

"Listen," said Mark, and I'd never heard that tone in his voice before. "I'm not eighteen—you're right. I'm seventeen. I'm old enough to hold down a job, to drive a car—"

"To join the army and get killed in Belfast, and to get married and have a baby," interrupted the man sarcastically. "I know, son. I've heard it all before. Now if you don't mind—"

"I'm also old enough to knock your thick head right off," Mark went on in a louder voice. "And if I can do all that, I'm old enough to drink in public, and anyone who says I'm not had better watch it."

With that he started towards the bar as if to order another drink.

The landlord was a burly man a few years older than Dad. He grabbed Mark by the shoulder and spun him round.

The next bit was awful—really awful, so that I hate to remember it. Mark hit him. Not hard luckily, because the landlord ducked, but Mark was absolutely beside himself with rage, I could see it. His face was dark red and snarling and I felt I hardly knew him. But I did know him, I even loved him, though not at that moment. So I jumped up and grabbed his arm and tried to hold him.

All the people in the saloon bar had drawn back in horror, except for two men who leapt forward eagerly to help the landlord. They laid hold of Mark very roughly, and in another second were rushing him out of the door.

It seemed so unfair, three of them against him, he hadn't a chance. I ran after them calling, "Let him alone, I'll take him out—" But no one listened to me. When I got through the door—which had swung back behind them right in my face—I saw Mark actually sitting on the pavement outside the pub. The smart men from the saloon bar were dusting off their hands as if they'd got rid of some old rubbish, and grinning in a satisfied way at each other.

They'd *enjoyed* it. And when I saw that, I felt so angry—partly with Mark, but for that moment mostly with those men—that I shouted at them,

"You didn't have to do that! He hadn't done anything to you!"

One of them, a tall youngish man in a smart blazer and a club tie, turned to me with such a superior smile I could have hit him myself.

"I think your boy-friend came into the wrong bar," he said.

"He came into the wrong pub," said the landlord. "And so did you. Go home and dry behind your ears. Be thankful I don't call the police."

They went back inside, their hands chummily on each other's backs. I crouched beside Mark and said, "Are you all right?"

He didn't say a word. He wasn't hurt, but he didn't move for quite a while. He just sat with his head between his knees. Several people went past and looked down at us. I knew they thought he was drunk. I tried very hard not to be ashamed of him, and I think I succeeded.

"Do come, Mark," I said at last.

I took his arm, but he jerked it away. Then, without looking at me, he stood up and walked quickly away towards where he'd left his motorbike.

I wanted to run after him, but I didn't. I knew he'd heard what the man had said about him being in the wrong bar. And I knew he didn't want to be with me at that moment—me of all people. He'd talked about "us and them". And for the moment I was "them", maybe only because I was more at ease among the "snobs". The snobs who'd humiliated him . . . I didn't know how to heal the wound they'd made in his pride.

And yet I knew in a way he'd brought it on himself. The landlord was right about losing his licence. We should never have gone in there.

I walked home alone, too stunned even to cry. That night I wrote my first letter to Mark. I was so miserable, I had to do *something*.

"Dear Mark,

I hope I did right tonight in not coming after you. I felt you wanted to be alone for a while.

I hated those rotten men as much as you did, and you were right, you should be allowed to drink in a pub if you want to.

I wish none of it had happened but I wanted you to know that I'm basically on your side, and now I'd like to forget all about it. Only let's not go into pubs any more. I don't think I feel much at home in either sorts of bar yet.

Please ring me up soon.

Love,

Kate."

I hesitated about the "love". I'd never told him I loved him. But in a letter it didn't seem too committing.

I put a first-class stamp on the letter so it would get there sooner. Then I waited for the phone to ring.

Tina once told me how ghastly it is to sit waiting for a boy you've had a row (or something) with, to phone you. Rebecca too. And Mum says there'll never be real equality of the sexes until women feel free to phone men after a quarrel. Not that Mark and I had quarrelled. It was something worse in a way. If we'd rowed, I could, at a pinch, have apologized. But you can't apologize to a man for seeing him put down.

Something else was worrying me. Did it matter that Mark felt more comfortable in the public and I in the saloon? Despite my row with Mum in the museum, *I'd* never really thought there was a class barrier between us, but he'd made me feel that perhaps there was and I just wouldn't admit it. He'd made it seem like something so fundamental—sort of inescapable. Those men playing darts in the public bar seemed to know I was an intruder. They made me feel it before I knew I didn't belong there. And Mark obviously hated the "snobs" next door even before they attacked him. I wondered if they'd *sensed* he was working-class? Did they resent him, as the dart-players resented me? Did it mean anything to us if they did?

I thought and thought about it. I had plenty of time as the long lonely days went by. If his class resented me and my class resented him, what about our families? Maybe his family was just being polite about me, and vice versa. Maybe they only weren't making a fuss because they were hoping it would all peter out. I hated to think that, but I supposed even if it were true, we couldn't do anything about it.

In the meantime, why didn't he phone?

Never had I felt more mixed up and miserable. And I couldn't tell anyone. Not even Emma. A brawl in a pub!—No, I couldn't explain that without making Mark sound like a hooligan.

It was while I was in this depressed state, getting worse every day, that I ran into Leo in the village.

It isn't a real village, just a suburb that was a village once. We call it that to give us the feeling that we haven't been completely swallowed up by London. I was out shopping for Mum in the local bakery, where there's a little counter for coffee and sandwiches, and there was Leo having a snack-lunch. This seemed odd, only a few steps from home, until I remembered his situation. I'm afraid I'd completely forgotten about it.

After buying my bread, I hesitated a minute, and then sat on one of the stools beside him.

"Hallo, Leo," I said.

He started, and looked at me as if he'd never seen me before. His eyes had changed. They looked sharp and strained; the soft, liquid look was gone. Funny, I thought, how I never see him without remembering he's Jewish. I don't feel anything special about it, I just am always aware of it. Yet when I look at Mark I never think, "He's different from me." Or I never had thought it. I wondered how I would feel if I saw him now. With a queer, sick sinking of the heart, I suddenly and for the first time wondered if I would ever see him again.

Now Leo was doing his best to smile at me.

"Oh—hallo, Kate. How are you?"

I felt like saying "Awful", and after a moment I did say it, not so he would pity me but so that he would feel free to talk to me if he felt awful too. (Well, obviously he did feel awful. One only had to look at him to see that. He looked as if he hadn't slept for days.)

"What's *your* trouble?"

"It's not as bad as yours."

"I hope not." He stared at me. "I hate to think of you knowing. There's no getting away from it."

I stood up, but he put his hand out and held my arm.

"No, I'm sorry, I didn't mean it quite as it sounded. Don't go. Do you want a coffee?"

"Thank you."

We drank our coffee together, not saying much. Being so close to him physically I could almost feel his misery. It piled itself on top of mine and smothered mine right out of existence for the moment. I longed to say the right thing, to comfort him, but, like the other night outside the pub, I was just not old enough or wise enough to have anything to offer so I kept quiet. After a while he said, "Tell me about you."

"Oh no. Mine's just baby stuff."

I could have bitten my tongue out! But after an awful moment, he suddenly gave a laugh.

"And what, pray, is mine?"

He put his head in his hands for a second, then rubbed them through his curly hair and stood up sharply.

"Come on, I'll carry your stuff home."

He carried my shopping in one hand. The other held my arm lightly at the elbow to guide me across the main road. Then he left it there. After a short time it just slipped down and took mine. It was such a strange feeling. Not at all like holding hands with Mark. There was none of the strength and tension. Leo's hand was soft and cool and held mine so gently I wanted to squeeze it to make sure it was really touching me. I don't think he was much aware that he was holding my hand. It was as if he just needed contact with someone in his trouble. Although I thought I'd completely got over my thing about him, I found myself feeling such a strong sympathy for him that I forgot Mark, and our linked hands became important, as if some current passed between us. I felt it tingling up my arm.

We reached our house and without anything being said he came in with me. Everyone was out. I'd left Mum cooking and wondered where she'd gone. Next door, perhaps.

Leo put the shopping-bags on the kitchen table and stood there, as if unwilling to leave.

"Don't you want to go home?" I asked. He shook his head. "Stay a bit then."

He sat down at the table. I put the shopping away. Suddenly he said,

"Do you know what my father said to me?"

"What?"

"That it was a forgivable fault in a young man. But why couldn't I have been more careful? And why couldn't I now be more honest?"

His voice had a queer, almost childish shake in it. I had a moment of absolute panic, thinking he was going to cry, but I believe it was only a sort of furious desperation because his father wouldn't believe him.

"I never touched the wretched girl!" he almost shouted. "I never wanted to! If I had, I wouldn't lie about it. If it were my child, wouldn't I take responsibility for it? Even if that lying, stupid, mean-spirited little cow was its mother?"

I swallowed. I suddenly felt like crying myself. It was so absolutely obvious to me that he was telling the truth—not that I'd ever thought anything else. "Have you said all this to your father?"

"No. If he doesn't trust me, I won't plead with him. Mother believes me. So does Beccy." He gave me an odd look. "So do you. That'll have to satisfy me."

"I suppose," I said hesitantly, "the question is, if it'll satisfy Marie-Noelle."

He laughed again, that same short, hard laugh. "Marie-Noelle won't be satisfied with anything less than a pension for life."

"She doesn't expect you to marry her then?"

"That," said Leo grimly, "thank heaven, has not been mentioned."

"So what'll happen?"

"I don't know. I don't much care any more."

"Your mother won't keep her on, will she? She's making you all so unhappy. Why can't she go home to her parents?"

"The short answer is she's much more comfortable here."

"But she must be as miserable as you are!"

"Miserable? She's loving every minute of it! She loves the tears and the drama and all the fuss. Look at her, silly fat lump that she is. Who could ever have made such a to-do about her in her life before? It's meat and drink to her, the whole rotten hornets' nest she's stirred up."

"She's not worth all the trouble she's causing then."

"Not for a moment. But what about the baby? If there wasn't a baby involved I'd throw her out on the street myself."

He said it so bitterly that I was startled. I'd never known Leo could be so un-gentle—vicious almost. I said awkwardly, "I wish I could help you."

"No one can," he said shortly. He just sat for a few more minutes. "Seems awful of me just to sit here, not wanting to go home . . ."

There was another short silence. I sat opposite him. He wasn't looking at me, but I was looking at him, at his dark skin and full lips and sad, angry eyes, remembering how I had dreamed about him and tried to catch glimpses of him ever since I was twelve . . . Infatuation . . . yes, but still, you don't just shed that sort of feeling, or even outgrow it all at once just because you meet someone nearer your own age. I thought how I would once have treasured a situation like this. Now it was real; he had held my hand, confided in me; I had him to myself. The whole dream no longer seemed a complete impossibility. And yet—there was Mark. Like a wall between me and my old crush on Leo. A real wall, hard and solid, even though at this moment it seemed so cold.

Leo sighed, and glanced at me with a half-smile.

"You haven't told me yet what's the matter with you."

"Oh . . . It's just . . . this boy-friend I have, he's bombed off, and he doesn't ring. It's just nonsense compared to yours."

"No it's not. My girl-friend's also—bombed off, as you call it."

"Monique?"

"Mm. It was all getting too complicated for her, she said."

"You told her—about all this business?"

"I was foolish enough to think one did tell one's troubles to one's girl-friend."

"Leo, that's terrible. So that creepy Marie-Noelle has even spoiled *that*."

He got up. "This won't do, I can't take up residence here. Your mother's coming back." And I heard her too, saying a last few words to Leo's mother across the fence. "I'll go out the front way, I don't want to meet her."

I went through into the hall with him. He turned at the door and, taking my hand, gave it a quick kiss. Perhaps his fondness for French girls had taught him that! I couldn't possibly imagine Mark kissing my hand. The contrast shook me somehow. And the touch of his lips on my fingers shook me too.

"Thanks," he said softly. "You have helped. You're very sweet."

And off he went, leaving me in a fine old state.

"Who's been here?" asked Mum as soon as I walked back into the kitchen.

"Leo."

"Oh."

She didn't seem to want to talk about him. I wondered for the first time whether *she* thought it "a forgivable fault in a young man", and whose side she was on.

16

Two days before school was due to start, I decided that the age of equality had arrived, after all.

"I'm going to phone Mark," I announced to Mum as we did the breakfast things.

"I wouldn't," she said.

I suddenly felt furious.

"Oh, I know *you* wouldn't!" I retorted rudely.

Mum didn't answer, which made me still more unreasonably angry because I knew just what she was thinking. She was thinking that it was for Mark to phone me and that I mustn't make myself cheap by running after him. Perhaps she was even thinking it would be a good thing if we broke up—that's if I was right in my idea about what Mark's parents and mine secretly thought about it.

The main trouble with really loving your parents is that you want them to be sort of *with* you on all the important issues of your life, and when they're not you almost hate them for not being. Sometimes when I was younger I used to shout, "I hate you! I hate you!" at Mum when she disagreed with me about vital things like friends and opinions and behaviour. Of course now I know that what I should have been shouting was, "I love you, I love you, I want you to be on my side in everything!" I also knew by now that this was impossible if only because of the generation gap. But it didn't help me to feel calm and philosophical when I suspected that she didn't really approve of Mark and might even be trying to wean me away from him in her subtle way.

"I know you don't like him," I said. "You *and* Dad."

Mum stopped washing the dishes and looked at me. I dreaded that look. It was the look that said, "I don't like you when you talk like that." It made me feel quite wild inside. She said, "Kate, we've been over this, you know it's not true. Mark's a very interesting and attractive boy."

"*But*. But, but, but!" I heard my voice getting shrill but I couldn't control it. "Interesting and attractive! But 'common' and not good enough for me. Isn't that true?"

She continued to give me that quiet look for a moment and then went back to the dishes.

"Isn't it?" I persisted idiotically.

"You said it, I didn't," she answered.

Oh, I did hate her then for a bit—I really did. I threw down the dish-towel and rushed upstairs to the phone in her bedroom and dialled Mark's number before stopping to think about anything, even the fact that he wouldn't be there.

His mother answered the phone. I nearly panicked and put it down, but the rebelliousness I felt against Mum stopped me.

"Mrs Collins? This is Kate."

"Oh. Hallo Kate," she said in a flat, non-committal voice.

"May I speak to Mark?"

"He's at work."

"Oh—of course. How silly of me." I didn't know what to say next and she wasn't going to help me either, so we just breathed down the line into each other's ears for an eternity and then I said, "Will you ask him to phone me when he gets in?"

"Very well. He's got your number."

"Yes. How—how are you all?"

"We're fine," she said shortly. I began to feel sweat prickling my armpits and wished with all my heart I hadn't phoned, or that *any* other member of the family had answered. Mrs Collins had never really come round to me, and I saw in her shortness to me a reflection of Mum's feeling about Mark.

"Well!" I said brightly. "I'm sorry to have troubled you"—like the operator when she rings you by mistake. Mrs Collins said, in the same flat tone, "That's all right." She hung up without saying goodbye.

I couldn't stay in the house. I took my bike and went for a ride. I rode and rode till I was a long way from home and after a while it dawned on me that by the weirdest coincidence I was riding down the street where Mark's restaurant was.

I looked at my watch. It was eleven o'clock. The lunch-hour wouldn't have started and perhaps he wouldn't be too busy. Perhaps he would be glad to see me. Perhaps . . . I pulled up at the kerb near the restaurant and tried to think, to foresee the scene if I decided to go in. It was two weeks since the incident in the Roebuck. I'd been miserable, but what about him? Maybe he'd found another girl, maybe he never wanted to see me again . . . If he had wanted to, wouldn't my letter have given him an opening? Wouldn't it in any case be better to give him one more chance to make the contact, when he got my message? If that didn't make him phone, I would know the worst.

But knowing he was so close to me made it impossible just to turn and ride home without seeing him. I longed to see him, so much that even the utter dread of a cold look couldn't put me off. I parked the bike against the front of the restaurant and went in.

It was more of a "caff" than a restaurant really. Its menu was written up on the wall over the counter, on which were perspex containers for ready-made sandwiches and doughnuts and chocolate snacks. There were rows of cans of Pepsi and bottles of Tizer and Fanta against the mirror at the back, and big tea- and coffee-urns. The cooking was done in a kitchen at the back. That was where Mark worked, I knew.

The man behind the counter was the owner. I'd heard about him and recognized him from Mark's description—a fat, jolly type with an eye for the girls. He rolled it at me as I came in.

"What can I do for you, my love?"

It was my last chance. I could still order a cup of coffee and a Mars bar and take them to a table and think about it a bit more, and then go out and ride home if I liked. But something pushed me to say, "May I see Mark?"

The man rolled his eyes even more and said roguishly, "Oh-ho! Goin's-on at work, eh? I dunno if I can allow that!" Then he called into the kitchen, "Mark! There's a smashin' bit o' goods out 'ere askin' for you!"

Mark came to the door immediately and stood there looking at me.

"Well don't just stand there gawpin' at her! Ask her in," said the owner. He opened the counter-flap and bowed to me. "Step into my parlour, said the spider to the fly. Go on, love, 'e won't bite—I won't let 'im."

I went through and into the kitchen. I hadn't thought that Mark might not be alone in there, and was dismayed to see a rather straggly sort of girl sitting on a high stool in a corner peeling potatoes. Mark closed the door of the kitchen behind me and said, "Kate, this is Dawn."

Dawn looked at me out of pale, pink-rimmed eyes, said "'Ullo," faintly, and went on with her work as if I weren't there. But I couldn't pretend she wasn't. I looked round despairingly. What madness! It was even more sordid here than in the café-part, about as suitable for a romantic reunion as a—well, I can't think of anywhere less suitable. Everything was old and chipped and grey and there was a smell of stale cooking and washing-up water. Mark was wearing a long shiny apron and looking as if he'd like to go through the floor.

"I wanted to see you," I said hopelessly.

"You certainly picked your time and place," he said.

We looked at each other. Dawn peeled away in her corner and every now and then gave a great sniff.

"Well why didn't you pick a better one?" I said finally.

He didn't say anything, just took up a huge knife and started chopping onions with savage movements as if he were killing them.

"I'm going," I said abruptly. The smell of the onions had hit me and reminded me forcefully that I was on the edge of crying anyway. I turned round and was just opening the door when he dropped the knife and grabbed my wrist.

"Can you come back at three? I get off then."

"No, I can't! I biked all the way here. If you want to see me you know where I live."

"Kate." He stood up close to me, holding my wrist so tight it hurt.

Dawn pushed her lank fair hair off her face with a wet hand and looked at us with her mouth open. "I'm sorry," Mark said very softly with his back to her. "I'm sorry. Thanks for coming. I'll be round this afternoon."

My heart, which a moment ago had been like a boulder in my chest, suddenly became so light it was hardly there. I squeezed his hand and said, "Don't get up to anything in the meantime." I flicked my eyes in Dawn's direction. Mark made a funny face—crossing his eyes and letting the corners of his mouth droop. It was such a Bruce-face I stifled a hoot of laughter. I suppose it wasn't very nice of us to make fun of her but she was so ghastly and so *in the way* we couldn't help it.

I rode home singing madly and tinkling my bell at every corner.

Of course I'd forgotten my row with Mum, but I was soon reminded of it because of how quiet she was over lunch. Nobody else noticed it because Alastair was so full of the fact that the boss of the garage had suggested he should have driving lessons for which the boss would pay—he said Alastair would be more useful to him if he could drive, and in the meantime he was putting him on to much more difficult jobs.

"You remember Walter saying I had good hands?" Alastair said, quite excitedly for him. "Well, our guv'nor said the same this morning. He was watching me working on this carburettor—I've just about learnt how to strip one down and put it back together—and he said, 'You've got good hands, Al'. Maybe I really have, Dad. What do you think?" He held them out, black-rimmed nails and all.

"I think you're going to have to decide pretty soon what you're going to do with your life," said Dad, "never mind your hands so much."

Alastair looked at Mum, then at me. Then back at Dad.

"The thing is, Dad," he said, "I really think it comes to the same thing."

"What do you mean?"

"What I do with my hands and what I do with my life. I want to go on doing what I'm doing now."

Dad put down his knife and fork. It can't have been unexpected, but he wasn't going to give in without a fight, so he tried to appear incredulous.

"You mean you want to be a mechanic? As a *career*?"

"Yes."

"Work with car engines all your life?"

"What's wrong with that?"

"Nothing really. I'd have liked to see you aim a bit higher, that's all."

"Higher how? If it's the money that's worrying you, let me tell you that in a year or so's time I can be earning—"

"That's only part of it. When I say 'higher' I mean literally higher than lying on your back in a puddle of grease. You talk about hands—look at yours! And that's the way they'll be all your life—like a sign pinned to your chest saying 'Manual Worker—Social Category D'. Have you thought a bit about what that'll mean in terms of how you live, who you meet, how people react to you? A man isn't judged by his accent nowadays, or the school he went to, or what his father did. He's judged by his job. And whether it's fair or not, whether it's right or not, a mechanic is judged to be a whole lot lower down the scale than a man with some education who can wash the day's dirt off his hands easily after he's finished work."

Alastair had listened to all this carefully. Now he just said, "Well, Dad, I must say you disappoint me." And went back to eating his lunch.

Dad threw his napkin on the table and stamped out. The rest of us ate on in silence. Alastair was the least upset. After a while he said, "What's your view, Mum?"

"My view," she said, "is that you're old enough to decide for yourself."

"And if I do decide to be a grease-monkey, will you be ashamed of me?"

"No," she said, but with reservations in her voice.

"Oh dear," said Alastair, and he winked at me.

That was when I knew that he had grown up. It wasn't that he didn't *care* what Mum and Dad thought. It was that he didn't have that awful feeling of hating them when they opposed him. He was himself. He'd made up his mind; Dad could roar the place down and Mum could go as quiet as she liked, and Alastair wouldn't change. He knew he wouldn't, and he accepted the cost and didn't fight against it, even inside. I envied him suddenly with all my heart—and I think it was the first time I ever had envied Alastair (at least since we were very small and he got things first just by being the eldest). I had always been cleverer than he was. Perhaps I had even looked down on him because of it—I had certainly called him "dumb" and "dopey" about a million times, up until just the last year or so. And all of a sudden I remembered Dad, in the car that day, telling me not to run him down, and only now I knew what he'd meant. I felt absolutely certain I would never run him down again, even in my mind. He was streets ahead of me as a person, and brains had nothing to do with it.

I'd hoped Mum would do dishes with me again so that I could say something nice to make up with her, but after lunch she stacked them and left them, without even checking to make sure I would do them. I did do them, and dried and put them away too, which I don't always, and tidied up rather more carefully than usual. I hoped she'd recognize it as a kind of signal of goodwill. Then I went up to my room and crammed in some late holiday reading. I need hardly say that at the end of half an hour I couldn't remember a word I'd read even though it was *Far From the Madding Crowd* which I love. I was waiting for the hands on my purple clock to point to three-fifteen, and at long last they did, and right on time I heard the bike, roaring to a stop just round the corner.

I forgot all modesty and restraint and rushed out. We met about four doors down. We stopped dead and stared at each other. Then he said,

"Well, say something."

"You're a rotten swine," I said.

"Very nice. Charming."

"What do you expect?"

"What did *you* expect?"

"I expected you to get over it and ring me, or come."

"Then you don't know me."

"Apparently I don't. I thought you were more sensible."

"Well I'm not sensible," he said loudly. "I'm not sensible or stable or even quite sane, I often think. If what you want is somebody *sensible*, you picked the wrong guy."

"What *is* eating you?" I asked.

"Don't you know?"

"No."

He smiled his crooked smile.

"Well, there do seem to be different opinions. My class teacher says I've got a superiority complex. My headmaster says I've got an *in*feriority complex. Gran's view is I'm getting a bad case of family-gap—she blames Dad for educating me above our station. *Dad* on the other hand says the thing he did wrong was not belting my aggressions out of me when I was a kid. Mum says it's all your fault for making me want what I can't have. And my brother Walter simply says I'm losing my marbles." He looked at me for a moment and then said, "What do you think?"

"Oh, I agree with Walter."

Then we fell into each other's arms, and our first bad row was over.

17

I say the first. We had others, of course. Some major, some minor. And while they were on, I was unbearable, to myself and everyone around me, even though I tried to take it out only on anyway-enemies like Jammy and Pamela (not that I had much to do with her any more) and not too much on the family. But the important thing was that each row we had seemed to bring us closer together in the long run, even though they each seemed like the final, ultimate end at the time.

One thing we agreed on. Whatever problems we had, we mustn't give weapons into our families' hands. In other words, we each faced up to the fact that, no matter how well Mr Collins and I got on together *on the surface*, and no matter how polite and charming Dad was to Mark *on the surface*, they didn't really approve.

So when we were rowing, we never ran to our parents to grizzle about each other. This rule was harder on me than on Mark, who hadn't been as used to running to his parents all his life with every little moan as I had. But I had begun to realize how restricting it is, to be tied too much to your parents and their prejudices and opinions.

I used Alastair as my model. He behaved beautifully to Mum and Dad—he was loving and very thoughtful; helped round the house, phoned if he was late, etc.—but any unpleasantness from their side, Dad sulking and so on, he just ignored. I once asked him how he managed it. "Don't you care that Dad's furious with you?"

"Of course I care. I love him. I don't want to go against him. But it's my life. If I let myself think too much about how disappointed he is, I might do what he wants just to please him, and that'd be fatal. He'd regret it more than me in the end."

It goes without saying that Alastair didn't disapprove of Mark. They got on very well, and sometimes we were invited to the Collinses together, usually for Sunday tea. Mr Collins and I had loads of fierce political arguments. Gran usually cheered for me, Brendan for his Dad, while Walt and Mark, and Mrs Collins, stayed neutral. (Derek, having got Dad's autograph out of me, took no more notice of me.)

Meanwhile at Number Eight the drama reached its climax just before my birthday in March.

Marie-Noelle had been keeping what the papers call "a low profile" for a couple of months. She'd stopped ranting and sniffing, had called off her strike, and was going on as if nothing had happened. This was rather a good tactic since Mrs Daniels desperately needed help in the house and wasn't very good at managing without. She always, according to Rebecca, tended to take the line of least resistance; as long as Marie-Noelle wasn't bawling out accusations, it was easier just to keep her on than kick her out and find someone to replace her. It seemed a very odd situation to me, considering how Rebecca and Leo hated her and wouldn't speak to her, but it had become obvious that Marie-Noelle had a hide like a hippo and couldn't have cared less as long as she was still comfortably ensconced in her little *au pair*'s suite (complete with own bathroom) and didn't have to go home. No doubt she was counting on Mrs Daniel's passion for babies to take over as soon as she'd produced hers.

And then one day Leo blew his top.

I think he'd been building up to it for a long time. Every time I'd seen him for ages he'd given me a feeling of passing close to a volcano which was just smoking a little before it erupts.

One evening we were sitting down to supper in the kitchen when the most frightful row broke out in the kitchen next door. You could hear crashes and bangs and shrieks and roars—we all just sat there paralysed, looking at each other. When the first outbreak subsided a bit, Dad said to Mum, "Do you think you'd better go over there?"

"What's wrong with you going?" said Mum.

"*Me*?" said Dad. "Not if my life depended on it. That's woman's work if ever I heard it."

Just then we heard the gate that links our two gardens squeak open and crash shut, and then a long knocking on the glass in our kitchen door. Mum got up and opened it. I think the very last person we expected to see was Marie-Noelle, but there she was, streaked with tears, bosom heaving, hair on end. Dad and Alastair took one look at her, grabbed up their plates as one man and fled the kitchen.

"Madame, madame!" she cried wildly and dramatically. "You must 'elp me! You must save me from zose 'orrible people!"

"All right, Marie-Noelle, calm down, nobody's going to harm you," said Mum. Marie-Noelle flung herself into the room and into Dad's chair, still warm no doubt. She put her head down on the table and began to wail. "You don't know, you don't know what zey 'ave say to me—such terrible sings! Zat Leo—I 'ate 'im, I 'ate 'im, 'e say he srow me out of the 'ouse, 'e call me names, 'e—"

"You called him something first," I reminded her brutally.

She stopped wailing instantly and looked up at me. Her mouth was a straight, hard line and her little eyes were aimed at me like daggers through the jungle of her red hair.

"You," she said. "I know why you defend 'im. You are not my friend."

"No I'm not," I said. "Why should I be?"

"Now, Kate—" said Mum.

"I am not stupid," said Marie-Noelle. "I know you are jealous of me."

Mum, who was getting her a drink of something at the dresser, turned sharply.

"That will do, Marie-Noelle. Bruce, haven't you got any homework?"

"I want to stay here," said Bruce, naturally riveted.

"Go upstairs. This minute."

Bruce heaved a sigh and went slowly. As soon as the door closed behind him Mum came quickly to the table. She plonked a glass of brandy or something in front of Marie-Noelle and said, in a voice that thank goodness I don't often hear, "Drink that up and pull yourself together. You're not going to turn *this* household upside-down."

Marie-Noelle looked up at her, opened her moth, shut it again and picked up the glass. She drank it down in one swig.

"Now," said Mum. "What was all the noise?"

"For no reason 'e suddenly shout at me. Leo. 'E say 'e won't stand it no more. 'E say I spoil 'is life, with 'is family, with 'is girl-friend—'e say 'e can't work or do nothing because of me. What 'e sink, *I* can work and be 'appy? 'E sink *I* 'ave no feelings? 'Ow can 'e speak so when 'e 'as cause all my bad troubles . . ."

She began to blub again and suddenly I lost my temper. I thought of Leo's misery, which I had seen so clearly and felt in my chest like a weight. I don't get really angry often, but when I do I've got a temper just as fierce as Dad's and I don't stop to think. I didn't now. I pulled both her hands down from her face as she sat opposite me and held them down on the table and said,

"Shut up! Stop that silly crying! Don't you know *not one person* believes a word of your lies? Why don't you tell the truth?"

"I 'ave tell ze truth! I 'ave! Meester Daniels believes—"

"When are you going to have your baby?" I asked suddenly.

She hesitated. Too long. "In May—"

"Rubbish! You only arrived in England at the beginning of September. Are you telling us Leo jumped into bed with you practically the moment you got into the house? If he had, more fool you for letting him. If you ask me, you got pregnant before you ever left France!"

She stared at me. Her mouth hung open. All the redness drained out of her face. I knew suddenly that quite by accident, I'd hit on the truth.

"You say your baby's going to be born in May. Well I'll make a bet. I bet it'll be born sooner. And you'll say it's come early. Well, no go, Marie-Noelle. So you'd just better write to the real father of your baby and get him to do something about it. Or better still, get on the first plane and go back home and find him."

There was a silence. She panted at me through her hair like a wild thing, as if she'd like to pounce on me and tear me to bits. Then she flung herself up and over to the door, where she turned.

"You sink you are so clever, Mees Kate Dunheel!" she shouted shrilly.

"I must say I think she's absolutely brilliant," said Mum in a surprised tone.

Marie-Noelle gave a strangled noise and dashed out, leaving the door wide open. Mum went to close it. Then she turned to me.

"I meant that," she said.

I felt a sudden rush of elation. I could have jumped up and down with sheer excitement.

"What'll happen, do you think?"

"I think she'll take herself off. And the Danielses will have you to thank if she does."

And so she did, and so *they* did. Not that I told them I'd had anything to do with it, but Mum couldn't resist telling Mrs Daniels when she came skating in to announce Marie-Noelle's sudden departure—virtually a midnight flit, she was packed and gone by the next morning. Mrs Daniels left a message for me that I was to come in to see her after school, and when I did she was absolutely all over me. She hugged and kissed me and cried over me and it was only with the greatest difficulty that I stopped her rushing out to buy me some enormous present—she kept asking what I wanted most in the world and so on and so forth, but I managed to persuade her that I was glad to have helped and didn't want a reward.

I got one anyway, of course—a vast bunch of spring flowers all done up in cellophane and ribbons, plus a fabulous five-pound box of chocolates. I'm not very keen on sweets, so I handed them over to Bruce and Dad (who was in the throes of yet another attempt to give up cigarettes).

My real reward, though, was Leo's and Rebecca's gratitude. Rebecca did more kissing and hugging. (They really are a very kissy family. I've even seen Leo kissing his father and the twins kiss him every time they meet or leave him. Dad never kisses Bruce any more, Bruce wouldn't stand for it. It's probably a Jewish thing. Rather nice, I think.)

As for Leo, he wasn't exuberant about Marie-Noelle's defeat, like the others. It went much deeper with him. He came to the front door two days later and asked for me, and when I went he said, "Kate, I've got rather a lot to say to you. I wonder if your parents would agree to my taking you out to dinner on Saturday?"

I wasn't worried about them, I was worried about Mark. And Leo seemed to sense what I was thinking, because he added, "I realize your boy-friend might not like it. If you like I'll ring him up and ask his permission." He said this quite seriously.

"No, don't. I'll explain," I said.

Mark was a bit grumpy about it but he did know the background so in the end he said okay. "But no funny business, mind," he added.

"Of course not!" I retorted.

Leo was coming to pick me up at seven o'clock sharp on that Saturday. I wore a new Laura Ashley dress that Mum had bought me. It was an advance birthday-present (my birthday was three days off). She said she realized this was probably the only time she'd ever see me in it, since I hardly ever wear dresses. I'd often thought, from her silent looks up and down as I left on a date with Mark, that his liking me best in jeans was one of the minor points she had against him. Tonight she actually came in to my room to watch me dress. I could see what she was longing to do, and for once I submitted myself. After all, going out with Leo was hardly part of my normal life. It was a sort of extra, so I was prepared to let Mum have her fun dressing me up and playing dolls with me a bit, as she used to when I was little. It was actually rather nice to feel her hands tinkering with my hair, to let her choose my shoes, and lend me an evening bag. I even made a complete martyr of myself and let her touch up my make-up.

"There!" she said at last, standing back from me. "Now you look like a girl."

"'A young lady', you mean," I said.

"No," she said, "I don't want a young lady. I want a girl. I always wanted a girl. Every now and then I have to take steps to remind myself I did get one."

I looked at myself in the long mirror in her bedroom. I did look rather nice. It's not that I despise femininity. It's just out of fashion. Seeing how nicely feminine I could look, I couldn't help hoping that jeans and hulking shoes and unisex tops and so on for everyday wear would go out some time.

The doorbell rang. I jumped, and blushed stupidly and suddenly Mum grabbed my hand.

"Don't you go falling back in love with him now," she said.

I looked into her eyes.

"Wouldn't you rather Jewish Leo than working-class Mark?" I asked, not joking though I tried to sound as if I was.

"I'd rather happy you."

"Which means neither of them."

"Which means plenty of time ahead to meet and fall in and out of love with some of the other ten million assorted young men in Britain."

"Gosh!" I said. "Ten million? Are there really? What a gorgeous thought!" I hugged her. She held me close for a minute and then I ran downstairs to open the door.

The evening out with Leo was not like anything I'd ever done before. He made me feel something I had never felt with Mark, or with anyone—not grown-up exactly, but as if being grown-up and mixing with adult men was going to be an experience quite apart from the thrills of teen age. Funny how you seldom project yourself forward into a different time of your life. You do wonder, of course, how it will feel to be eighteen or twenty or whatever it is, but that's just a matter of a few extra years. What Leo gave me a taste of that evening was a different *era* up ahead, when I would be a full-grown woman. I must say it gave me a new perspective, even on the present.

He almost seemed to have planned it that way. For instance, he didn't ask me a single question about school. It was as if I'd left school ages ago. He didn't once talk down to me or patronize me the way men usually do young girls. He treated me exactly the way he would have if I'd been his own age. I'd expected he'd take me to a Schooner Inn or something like that, with fishing nets and fake beams and a ship's figurehead and all sorts of novelty touches to amuse me. Instead he took me to a lovely place, a very expensive

Italian restaurant in Chelsea with beautiful décor and what they call "discreet" lighting.

I was so *flattered* at his thinking I would appreciate quiet elegance! Another thing was that he kept sort of deferring to me. In an old-fashioned way. I can't explain exactly, but it went with my dress. When I went out with Mark we were equals and partners (at least in everything except that he wouldn't let me pay). He didn't stand aside to let me go first, or pull out chairs for me, or hold my coat or anything like that. I think I would have felt silly if he had. He helped me in a sensible, practical way if I had things to carry or couldn't manage something, but the *formal* "good manners" things he didn't bother with. Leo was like someone from a different generation. He did all the polite, male things Daddy did—and I liked them. From him. It didn't make me feel disloyal to Mark to like them, not at first anyway. It was just different—but super.

He didn't mention anything about Marie-Noelle until we were in the middle of dinner.

I kept expecting him to because, after all, that was why he had asked me out, I didn't kid myself it was anything but gratitude. But we ate our way Marie-Noelle-lessly through a delicious first course (I had something called quenelles—little soft fish-balls; I'd decided privately not to order anything that I had ever had before, or even knew what to expect from its name). The second course was osso buco, which he recommended—veal baked round its bone—with a choice of lovely vegetables like something out of the paradise gardens, all drenched in butter. We had a dry white wine with this. Leo evidently knew a lot about wine, and when I asked him he told me a bit about what one should drink with what, not in a snobby way but just to help the food taste better. Frankly I haven't really learnt to like very dry wines yet, but I was determined to have the proper things that evening so I was glad when he ordered the right wine to go with the veal. It was part of his not patronizing me, and I gladly put up with its rather mouth-shrivelling taste.

He toasted me.

"To the girl next door."

"To the boy next door," I replied. Then, as I drank, I nearly snorted into my glass. I had suddenly thought how funny it was, having Leo as the boy next door. *William* was the boy-next-door type—plain, ordinary, nice, irritating sometimes. Leo was the boy you hope to meet abroad, the face glimpsed on a cruise-ship, the gorgeous, unattainable film star. He was far too—well, glamorous, to be living next door to anyone.

"What's the joke?"

"I was just thinking how lucky I am to live next door to you," I said without thinking how soppy it might sound.

"Why?"

I must have been a bit drunk, because I said straight out, "Well, you're sort of exotic."

He roared with laughter. "Idiot! I'm not exotic in the least. I'm just Jewish."

"Maybe that's what it is."

He leant over to me and said very sincerely, "I'm the lucky one."

It was my turn to fish for a compliment now. "Why?"

"Because if I hadn't lived next door to you, everything would be as ghastly as it was last week. You got me off the hook, and I don't think anyone else could have done it."

"Oh, that's rubbish. I just happened to say the right thing at a moment when she was in a vulnerable mood. You blowing up just beforehand softened her up for me."

He leant back, frowning.

"Does that sound too callous?" I asked quickly.

"N-no . . . Not really . . . She was a dreadful creature, tough as old boots and calculating and ruthless . . . But there was a baby. Somebody's. One hates to think what's waiting for it. If she'd only been a decent girl—I mean nice, not moral—we could have looked after her, and it."

"You don't regret her going?" I asked in horror.

"No! God, no, Kate. I'm not a saint. She was making my life a perfect misery."

That reminded me of Monique. I wondered if I dared ask about her. But as if he'd read my mind he said, "I rang Monique yesterday."

"And?"

"Told her Marie-Noelle had gone. What had happened. She sounded so—relieved—" he said with an effort. "I suddenly knew she'd half-believed I was lying to her, that I *was* responsible... Straight away I didn't want anything more to do with her. Beautiful and—'suitable'—and all as she is. She didn't trust me, so what's the use of it?"

"Well, your own father didn't quite believe you either."

"Yes, well I'm stuck with *him*," he said grimly.

"You won't hold it against him?"

"I'm not sure."

"I wish you wouldn't. It'll mean that Marie-Noelle keeps on spoiling things even after she's gone."

He gazed at me. His eyes looked black in the candlelight.

"Hm. True. But you know, it does make me wonder a bit what he got up to when he was young."

"I expect all our Dads got up to things. It's none of our business."

"It is if they claim the right to tell us how to live and behave."

"It's like Daddy says about smoking—'Do as I say and not as I do'."

We both laughed, and he suddenly reached over and took my hand, which was just about to lift a forkful of osso buco to my lips. The osso buco fell off.

"You really are a super girl, Kate. If only you were a bit older—"

I gawped at him. It was hard to read his expression in the half-darkness but his face looked serious.

"I won't even be sixteen until Wednesday," I said stupidly. "Besides—"

I stopped, mainly from shock that the "besides"—namely Mark—had been an afterthought. Only about five seconds after, but wasn't that very late if I was really in love with him?

Leo let go of my hand, which automatically started groping around on the plate for the dropped bit of meat. I was going to cry. I wished with all my heart Leo hadn't said that. I'd been so entirely happy before. Now I felt unbalanced. Had he meant it? Had *I* meant it when, for just a moment or two, I'd actually hoped he did?

Would I—oh, most horrible thought!—have ditched Mark if he *had* meant it and if—

"Oh Katie, I'm a fool," said Leo's soft voice through the misted-up candlelight. "Forgive me. You looked so sweet and so much of a woman, and you made me laugh, that was the fatal thing—I haven't laughed for weeks, not properly. I didn't mean to spoil anything, or interfere in your life, that wasn't the idea at all."

I made myself look up at him. Beautiful, sweet, gentle Leo! I could love him again easily. But I mustn't. For a bundle of reasons, I mustn't. But he didn't make it any easier by reacting with horror to my tears and looking as if he'd like to kick himself for causing them.

"Darling! Don't cry!" he said with a sharp little gasp. I knew he had felt my sadness, the way I had felt his.

"It's nothing, Leo! Excuse me a moment."

I went to the Ladies and tried to mop up. But the stupid, awful thing was that suddenly it turned into a real cry and I couldn't stop. I felt so bad about Mark! Not for anything I'd done of course, but for what I'd felt when Leo had called me darling. A great pain had gone through me, the sort of pain I felt when Mark kissed me. I knew well enough what it was in both cases. What the old-fashioned books call desire. How could I feel it for Leo when I was Mark's girl?

It made me feel split in two. It was a hateful feeling—as if I didn't know who I was any more.

Well, I managed to stem the flood at last and put on some fresh eyestuff. (I'd rather scoffed at Mum for making me take a bag—usually I just carried what I needed for repairs in my coat-pocket. Wasn't I glad I had it now!) When I got back to our table, Leo jumped up and looked at me quite wildly.

"I thought you'd gone! Kate, what did I say? What did I do to make that happen? I could cut my throat—"

"Sh-sh! It's all right, Leo, honestly."

I sat down and got on with my meal, which was cold but still good, and oddly enough I was starving. I often am after crying.

"But tell me! You must. I couldn't forgive myself if—"

"Leo, I can't explain. You know how silly girls are at my age," I added in the very same patronizing voice he hadn't used to me ever.

"The least thing sets them off. *Us* off. It's all over and it was really nothing to begin with. Please let's eat, I'm famished."

So we went on with our dinner, but he watched me all the time with an anxious, tender look that went through me like little attacks of pins and needles, especially along my arms. I made a terrific effort to talk normally, which was very good for self-control and social sense and all those things girls, or rather women, are supposed to develop to get them over awkward situations. I pinned my battered old "LATER LATER" sign up in my mind against the horror of thinking I might be in love with two men at once and just made chat and tried not to meet Leo's eyes too often across the candles and flowers. I must confess that the indescribably delicious things called profiteroles that we had for dessert took my mind off the sign completely while I was eating them.

He took me home in his little car. It was nothing like as exciting as the bike, but it was undoubtedly more comfortable and ladylike and romantic. All the way home I was trying not to look ahead to the moment when we'd arrive and he either would or wouldn't get out to see me to the door. Of course I knew he would. And he did.

I had had two or three charming appreciative remarks ready for the doorstep but when we stood there together none of them came. We just stood there and I thought, quite frantically, "Don't let him try to kiss me because if he does I shall let him because I want him to and then I shall never be able to face Mark again." That sounds like quite a long thought or prayer or whatever it was, when I write it down, but it actually only took a second to think it several times, each time more desperately, and by the last time I thought or prayed it I saw it was useless because he *was* going to kiss me.

I need hardly say that I thought about it over and over again afterwards, always asking myself whether I could have helped it or rather helped myself if I'd really tried hard. I have come to the conclusion I couldn't. That doesn't let me off, of course. It taught me a very valuable lesson. Even the things you do that you couldn't help doing, you have to accept responsibility for.

The kiss was the most—oh dear, what word is left that hasn't been ruined? Divine, blissful—no good. I was totally swept away. I felt as if, in the most beautiful way, I might be going to faint. It was just too much. Everything disappeared, drew back into the darkness, and the kiss was left in the middle like a glowing white light.

Then it slowly stopped and everything drifted back and I was left with real life and the knowledge that I'd been unfaithful.

I lay awake nearly all night. Mum sat with me. She'd never seen me like that. I told her what had happened. I thought I might as well, she knew anyway that it was something tremendous. There wasn't much she could do or say, but I was glad to have her with me.

But after a while she did start talking. She said everyone has to learn sooner or later that nothing is easy or straightforward, love less so than anything. She told me something else, something terribly private. That she'd fallen in love with another man *after she was married* and without ever stopping loving Daddy. If I felt bad, she said, how did I think she'd felt? She'd thought she was quite immune to that sort of double-feeling but she found out she wasn't. And what had she done about it? Nothing. Just struggled with it, all by herself, without telling anyone. She said she looked back on it as a period of madness. She said being in love was always like that, that was why you had to be so careful—as careful as you could anyway—while you were in that state, not to do anything final. I said, did that mean you shouldn't get married while you were in love, and after a long, long silence she said she thought she did mean something like that. At least, she said, you shouldn't have children until the first madness was over and your love had settled down to being something more solid. She said it was better to live together first, until you were sure. Then I asked her if she'd lived with Daddy before they married and she said yes, for two and a half years on and off, and I was absolutely staggered, but not shocked after what we'd been talking about.

So then of course I asked the obvious question. Would she object if I wanted to live with someone? And she said—again I was staggered—no she wouldn't, provided I was old enough to know what I was doing, and of course sixteen wasn't old enough, nor seventeen either in her opinion. Personally she hoped I wouldn't get really involved with anyone for years yet because I could get so hurt.

I saw what she meant. Look how affected I was about just a kiss!

"What shall I do about Mark?" I cried out to Mum in the darkness. Why were we bothering to talk about *anything* else, when there was this awful dilemma to be faced?

"You'll have to just play it by ear," said Mum.

"I'm supposed to be seeing him tomorrow! He'll sense something—"

"Put him off. Give yourself a chance to get the thing in perspective."

It was about four o'clock in the morning—must've been. I was at long last dropping off to sleep. I sensed dear faithful Mum getting quietly to her feet. I reached out and clutched her hand.

"Do you think I'm awful?"

"*No*, darling. Of course not." She kissed me. "Go to sleep now and don't worry. It'll seem better in the morning."

18

Well, it did and it didn't. I certainly felt—after sleeping till well past eleven o'clock—that the whole thing wasn't quite so much on top of me as it had seemed the night before. But I still felt desperately guilty.

I'd read in a novel once about a girl, madly in love with her husband, who kissed (or was kissed by) another man, and it made her feel very sexy but all that feeling turned round somehow and flowed straight back to her husband. Kissing the other chap made her more in love with *him*. I kept remembering this all that Sunday. Why, if I was properly in love with Mark as I'd thought, did kissing Leo make me feel I might be in love with *Leo*?

I got up courage to ring Mark at lunchtime, hoping (coward that I was) that he'd be out and I could just leave a message that I couldn't see him that day. But he answered the phone himself. Naturally.

I said as casually as I could that I was busy at home and couldn't see him. This had happened occasionally before to both of us and I saw no reason for him to suspect anything, but there was a very odd silence at the other end of the line. And then he said, "What's happened?"

My heart leapt. He could tell! I didn't know whether to be glad or sorry.

"Nothing! I've just got a lot to do for tomorrow."

Another pause. Then he said slowly, "All right. I'll see you on Wednesday." Wednesday was my birthday. We weren't celebrating it properly until the following Saturday, but of course we'd planned to see each other that day.

I thought that would give me three days to calm down and "get things into perspective". But how could I, with Leo right next door? In the old days of my "crush", when I was dying to catch a glimpse of him, *weeks* could go by and somehow I always seemed to miss him coming and going from the house. Now, when I most particularly didn't want to see him, needless to say I bumped into him every time I put my nose outside my door.

"Hallo, Kate!" he would exclaim, looking terribly glad to see me. "How's my saviour today? Why don't you come in after supper and listen to some music? Dad's just bought a new hi-fi, and look—I got this to go on it—" And he'd show me some classical record. "Do you know this quartet? They're glorious, you must hear them. Come in about eight-thirty."

"I can't, Leo, I've got a mountain of homework."

His face would fall. It was horribly upsetting.

On Tuesday night I eavesdropped again. It seems to be my vice. I excused it to myself by thinking that Mum can practically read my mind, and since I can't read hers it really isn't fair. I knew Mum had talked to Dad about what was going on. Several times since Saturday I'd walked into a room and they'd gone suddenly quiet in a significant way. It's awful to know that people are talking about you and not know what they're saying. I do realize it's dreadfully sneaky, but I was feeling so guilty anyway it hardly seemed to make things any worse.

So after I'd done my homework I came downstairs to get myself a snack, and as I passed the living-room door I stopped to put my ear to it.

". . . really very cross with him," Mum was saying. "Upsetting her like that. He can't be serious, at his age what can he see in her?"

"What can he see in her?" echoed Dad indignantly. "She's an extremely attractive, not to say beautiful girl."

"She's not beautiful at all," said Mum. (Humph! I thought, though she was right of course.)

"Well not in a classic way perhaps, but anyone can see she's going to pull the boys round her like so many wasps round a honey-pot. Not just the boys, evidently, but the men."

"I think you should stop sounding so smug about it and start being a little concerned. She's barely sixteen. Getting her all steamed up with sex at that age is a great mistake. She ought to be getting on with her schoolwork. That's why we sent her to an all-girls school if you remember."

Oh? I thought. I never knew that came into it.

"Nonsense," said Dad, surprisingly. "She's just at the right age for getting steamed up. Best years of her life. There's nothing in the world so beautiful or important as a boy–girl relationship at that age. I wouldn't want her to miss it for anything. You can do what you like—douse the glow of their pretty little bodies with hideous uniforms—incarcerate them in all-female institutions—it'll break out somehow. Good God, what are you worrying about? Have you looked at her these last few days? She's absolutely lit up like a Christmas candle! And why not? Two handsome fellows running after her, both heartily disapproved of by us which makes it all the more exciting, her lips a-tingle with forbidden kisses, her soul in a turmoil of lovely guilt and the thrill of not knowing what's coming next—what the hell more does she need to bring her up to the peak of her adolescent form? If she were plain and fat and nobody wanted her, if her sexual instincts were lying around unstimulated and unaroused, would you be happy then?"

There was a long silence and then Mum said, "You *are* the weirdest fellow I ever knew. Most fathers are worried sick that their daughters are going to get into jams with young men. Here ours is in one, with *two*, and you're bursting with satisfaction."

"Of course I am. It's part of her natural role in life."

"Well," said Mum with energy, "it's part of *your* natural role to worry about her."

"If you mean I should be worried about her 'losing her virtue', she won't. She's too sensible. Also we keep her too well supervised, and that's how it should be. All that tension and conflict between the demands of the flesh and the restrictions of the home are part of the thrill. They sharpen up the instincts to a fine point. No permissiveness around here—not because I disapprove of sex for the young, but because I want her to put it off till she's mature enough *really* to relish it properly, and also because she'll relish it better if all the doors aren't flung open."

"I see," said Mum drily. "Meanwhile, what are we to do about Leo?"

"Nothing. Just see she doesn't stay out too late. If you like you can brief Zilla to see that they're not left alone too much if she's with him next door."

"I can think of no instructions she would obey more willingly. She can't be exactly overjoyed at recent developments herself."

"Why not? Aren't we good enough?"

"We're not Jewish enough."

Dad said a rude word meaning rubbish. "They're not going to get married, you know. It's only an interlude."

There was another silence, and I was just going to tiptoe away (with much food for thought) when Mum said, "And what about Mark?"

"Ah! Mark. We were bound to get back to him. I must say it's been quite a relief to talk about something else for a change." I pricked my ears even further at that—so they talked about him a lot! I'm ashamed to say I felt a pang of regret for all the times I *hadn't* listened.

But I was not to hear any more, because just then the phone rang and I leapt two feet into the air and flew upstairs like the wind before Mum could come out into the hall to answer it.

Next day was my birthday.

Birthdays are great events in our house, and are often spread over several days. They start with breakfast in bed (for those who like it —I do) with two trays, one for the food and one for cards and presents. The younger you are, the more of these you open immediately, but I had recently come to see the fun of saving a few till after school. But of course I had to open Bruce's straight away because he couldn't stand the suspense.

It was a box he'd made in woodwork class, absolutely lovely with proper hinges and a carving of a sun on the lid.

"It's for all your bits of tat," he explained, jumping about. "Make-up or jewellery or just any of your old rubbish."

"Or love-letters," put in Alastair.

Alastair's present was a record of a group I was absolutely insane about called the Winds of Change. They were quite new on the scene, and entirely different from any other group *ever*—I can't describe them if you haven't heard them—just a totally new sound, but the best thing is their lyrics, which are like great poetry only better because it honestly seems as if each one is a message meant for me. They really speak to me, I mean they're just my thing, and in the ordinary way their latest disc would have given me unmixed delight. The *only* thing was that this passion was something I shared completely with Mark, and the sight of the shiny sleeve with its abstract design forced me to realize that I would be seeing Mark today and that I didn't know what I would feel when I did.

Still, I was very pleased, and managed to hide my dark thoughts from Alastair as I hugged him, leaning down from my bunk. (A bunk is rather inconvenient on these occasions.)

Then I opened my cards. There was one of those long narrow cards from Jenny. It had a mad musician type on it saying, "Play, Maestro, Play! It's Kate's birthday today!" I knew why she'd chosen that one—because of the secret we shared about her sexy piano-teacher—but no one else knew why I laughed so much. There were lots of others from my relatives (I must say they're all very good about remembering), and one huge landscape one from the whole Daniels family. I noticed Leo alone hadn't signed it, so presumably he was going to send me a separate one, but it wasn't in the pile. There was one from Mark, though. It too was a funny one, and he'd written "See you tonight" on it. No "love" or anything. I felt strange, almost sick. How women can carry on intrigues as a regular thing I don't know.

I left Mum's and Dad's presents (separate ones) to open later. They were both too big to go on the tray, and were sitting in their bright paper on my desk in front of the window. I had a good idea what Dad's was—an old-fashioned pub mirror with a design on it. I was dying for one. I hoped it would be an Aubrey Beardsley type. I'd dropped a couple of heavy hints to that effect, but Dad really doesn't have a lot of spare time to shop around so I was determined not to be disappointed if it should be another kind, even a tobacco advertisement. Though come to think of it, I doubt if he'd have bought me *that*, considering his own struggles with "the weed" as he called it.

I took the shattered remains of the Daniels' box of chocolates to school and shared them around, and in a fit of perversity wrapped up five or six in a paper napkin from lunch and left them on Jammy's desk with a note saying, "*Chère Mademoiselle, c'est aujourd'hui mon anniversaire. Ces bonbons-ci signale ma promesse d'essayer plus fort en français cette année.*" We had our French lesson in the morning and it had gone worse than usual so why I did this odd thing I don't know—it was part of the strange mixed-up mood I was in. I wouldn't have been surprised if she'd simply hurled them furiously into the waste-paper basket, but I was surprised when she sought me out just as I was leaving at four. She was actually smiling—a very strange phenomenon.

"How very sweet of you to leave me those chocolates, Kate," she said. "My favourite kind. But your promise means much more to me of course. Here's a little present for you." And she pressed something into my hand and scuttled away.

"Whatever is it?" asked Emma.

I opened it. It was a little book of easy French poems, not new.

"It must be her own book," said Emma wonderingly. "Fancy her giving it to you when she hates you so much! Look, it was hers, it's got her name in it." Sure enough, there it was, and the date, *1939* if you don't mind. It had been awarded to her as a prize when she was at school! But she'd crossed all that out and written over the top, "To Kate Dunhill on her 16th birthday. First Prize for Future Effort. Emily Jamieson." I looked at Emma and we both burst out laughing.

"The old thing's got a sense of humour after all!" Emma said. "It just needed your chocs to bring it out. Wonders will never cease!"

I lingered in the cloakroom to stagger through the first couple of poems in the book. Partly, of course, I was lingering because I knew Mark was either waiting outside or would meet me at the bus-stop near home, and I was grabbing at any excuse to put off our meeting.

But also I had this funny feeling that I owed it to Jammy not to just stick her book in my pocket without looking. The first poem was some old nonsense, but the second one was nice. It was about a field of wheat and poppies and two young lovers saying that the wheat was life and the poppies were love and that they were so mixed up you couldn't sort them out, even though it looked so easy to tell the difference from afar. And there was something sad at the end about how the poppies which were so beautiful could sometimes poison the crop when it was harvested . . . I think it was that . . . Anyway it read very touchingly in French, even though I didn't quite understand it, and suddenly tears came to my eyes. I slammed the book shut, stuffed it in my schoolbag, and ran outside.

Everyone else had gone, but there was Mark at the school gate.

As I ran across to him he straightened up sharply and threw his cigarette away. As soon as I was through the gate I felt his big hands take hold of my arms, and his eyes were looking down at me in such a piercing way that I knew that the craven hope I'd had—of just passing it all off as if nothing had changed—was simply stupid, and insulting to him as well, because he was very sensitive, for all his rough ways sometimes.

"What happened, then? Did he kiss you?"

I didn't answer. He gave me a hard little shake and let me go. We began to walk along to where he'd parked the bike. I longed for him to take my hand and be like always. I just wanted to get back to things being more or less simple, as they had been before Saturday, but they weren't going to. We got on the bike together in silence and roared away. After a few minutes though I saw we weren't heading for my house.

"Where are we going?" I shouted in his ear.

"Down to the river," he shouted back.

We went to Richmond, to that place where the town ends up on a hill and the rest of the hill drops down to a sort of little park, which is partly fields. We left the bike and walked by the river, climbing on to the wall every now and then when the tow-path was too muddy. We didn't talk. Only once Mark pointed to a police-launch careering down the river and said, "Wonder who they're after."

After a while we were clear of the town and walking by ourselves through the mud. We'd given up worrying about our shoes by then. On our left was almost country, though there were some houses. It was getting on for twilight. Once in a while we'd pass someone walking a dog, and once some kids on bikes swished past. I wondered if we oughtn't to be getting back, but Mark just walked on and on, his hands in his pockets, looking to his right at the river with me splodging along a little way behind. I knew something would have to happen, and finally it did.

He stopped, and I stopped beside him, and we looked out at the river together, just watching the slow grey water slide by with an occasional lump of wood caught in it.

At long last he said, "Happy birthday, by the way."

"Well it's not just now," I said.

He turned to me.

"*Did* he kiss you?"

"Yes."

"And you—it turned you on."

"Yes."

"I knew it. I think I knew it when it was happening. I was pissed off all that evening. Hardly slept. And then the next day—the Sunday—I was waiting for you to phone. I expected it. I knew just how you'd sound, what you'd say, and I knew why."

"I've been pretty miserable too, if that helps."

"I know you have, and it doesn't." Then he said a few perfectly unprintable things about what he'd like to do to Leo, which I took no notice of—a good thing because almost immediately afterwards he took them all back. "I suppose the poor idiot couldn't help himself any more than I could," he said. That would have made me feel like some sort of *femme fatale* except that I was feeling so rotten.

He turned to me again.

"Look. I can't ask you to choose between us or anything of that sort. You're only a kid. You wouldn't be human if some part of you weren't enjoying this." I remembered what Dad had said and blushed, though God knows I wasn't enjoying it as far as I knew. "I don't blame *you* at all, Kate. I just know how much I personally can take, and it isn't much, not of this. I'll compete for you, if that's the name of the game, but not for too long. One of these days very soon if I see you like him best I'll bunk off. Just because I won't be able to stick it. The thought of you kissing some other bloke makes me want to do murder. I've been wanting to do murder for four days and it's churned me up till I feel as if I'm getting an ulcer or something." He stopped, looking at me, and swallowed. I shut my eyes. I felt his pain on top of mine like a real weight, the way I had with Leo, only worse because I'd caused this. I didn't want to cry, but all of a sudden that damn poem about the poisonous poppies came into my head—it sounds ridiculous in English, but the French words just ate at me somehow—and I felt the tears starting. Then I felt him take me in his arms. He didn't kiss me, just held me tightly against him, and I cried and cried and detested myself, as if I were asking him to be sorry for me, or playing some kind of corny woman's trick to win him back—but honestly, how can you bear it when a boy is so nice and generous, instead of hitting you for hurting him and being unfaithful? That's what got me, that and the strain of the last few days, and its being my birthday, and knowing that when I saw Leo again I *still* wouldn't be sure who I loved best. But that I did love Mark was absolutely definite, and I put my arms round his waist and hugged him suddenly with all my strength to tell him so.

19

There's no doubt that Mark had behaved as beautifully as any man could over the business, and I was almost awed about it, but there was one thing I wished he hadn't said and that was about competing. It was especially unfortunate that, being my birthday, there was a special opportunity for him and Leo to "compete" in the matter of presents. And since Mark had used the word, it was almost impossible for me to avoid thinking of their two presents to me as being—I don't know—bids for my favour or something like that.

Mark gave me his when he took me home. He didn't come in, just walked me to the gate and then took this little package out of his pocket and gave it to me with another "Happy birthday" and started to walk away. But he turned round and said, "Is Saturday still on?"

On Saturday we were going to hear "our" group, Winds of Change, playing live. We'd looked forward to it for weeks.

"Of course!"

"I'll pick you up at six, okay?"

"Okay."

He was very quiet and didn't walk tall the way he usually did. The "worst" was over—our meeting, him knowing, having it out about Leo—but watching him slouching along I felt the worst wasn't over at all.

I went into the house. Mum was bustling about getting dinner ready. It was to be dinner and not supper tonight because of my birthday. The table was laid in the dining-room—a rarity when it's just us—as if for a party, best tablemats and napkins and silver and even the best glasses, and a lovely bunch of freesias in the middle scenting the whole room. And candles. My unopened presents were beside my place—Mum's and Dad's, some things which had arrived by post from Lancashire and Gloucestershire (where Auntie Gerry lives), another great sheaf of flowers from next door—and beside my plate a little packet, much the same size and shape as the one Mark had given me. I knew as soon as I looked at it that it was from Leo.

Funny what *little* things bother you in a situation like that. I almost had a trauma about which of the boxes to open first. I felt that whichever I did open first would be "winning". At last I did a most childishly silly thing, to get over what seemed like a huge problem. I put both the boxes in my school hat, closed my eyes, and reached in and grabbed one. It was Mark's. I was so glad that I wondered why I hadn't just opened Mark's in the first place.

The box inside the wrapper had held soap. For a moment I thought it was soap. But then I realized it was too light. I took the top off and then a layer of cotton-wool. Underneath was a pair of silver ear-rings. Real silver, and absolutely beautiful. But they were the kind for which you have to have pierced ears.

I stared at them. Several times Mark had surprised me by asking me why I didn't have my ears pierced. He seemed very insistent. Frankly I didn't want to. Auntie Gerry once mentioned to me that pierced ears were "common". Of course I never take any real notice of anything Auntie Gerry says on this subject but just the same it wasn't a thing I wanted to do And now here were these gorgeous objects—the first real jewellery I'd ever had, I mean apart from junky, fun-things—real grown-up ear-rings, in my favourite metal, and if I wanted to wear them I would have to do what Mark wanted.

I didn't know whether to be terribly pleased, or annoyed. I ended up being quite a bit of both. It was so like Mark. Wildly generous on his own terms. And now, longing as I did to wear his present, compelled to anyway so as not to hurt him, I would have to give in to him.

Slowly I picked Leo's box out of the hat. I knew it was also jewellery and I thought, "If it's some glittery thing, even if it's a real jewel, I shall put him right out of my mind because it'll prove he doesn't know me." I opened it, half-praying it *would* be some gaudy expensive thing so that my life would be simple again. But it wasn't. Damn it all, it was a *genuine*, *Beduin* old silver medallion on a chain of hand-wrought links, interspersed with dark amber beads and an engraving on it, every bit as beautiful as Rebecca's.

I took it up in my hands. I could have cried. Of course he'd cheated—he must have. He'd asked Rebecca what I wanted. Irresistibly I hung it round my neck, looking at myself in the oval dining-room mirror. Then, quickly, I took it off again, ran upstairs, tore off my school clothes and put on my new dress. It had a high neck and was in dark-coloured cotton with a tiny flower design. All it needed was the medallion, which gleamed against it with the lovely dull shimmer of an antique, something from another time and place, a piece of history.

I held Mark's ear-rings to my ears. Let the new shine go off them and they would match. But I couldn't wear them tonight. I put them back in their box.

Dad's present *was* an Aubrey Beardsley mirror. The figure on it was a long, long woman in a flowing gown with her slim graceful arms raised to her snake-like hair. She was gorgeous. I rushed to kiss Dad as he came in tired from his rehearsal and he instantly spotted the medallion and said, "And where did madam get *that* little bauble?"

"From Leo," I said, blushing.

"Oho! And from her other swain?"

I showed him.

"And which does madam prefer? Or shouldn't I ask?"

"No, you shouldn't. I like them both the same."

He examined the ear-rings. "I see these will necessitate a major operation."

"Yes. I'm going to have it done tomorrow after school," I said, much to my own surprise.

"Indeed," said Dad, not looking too pleased. He took my ear-lobes gently into his fingers. "Poor little ears. Well, well. Girls will be girls, I suppose. Just have to be grateful it's not the fashion to wear nose-rings or discs in your lower lip." But I knew another black mark had gone down on the score-card against poor Mark, and that perversely made me quite determined to have my ears pierced the very next day.

After our festive dinner, Rebecca came in to give me her present—a silk Indian scarf, much more her than me but as I'm always wanting to be more exotic and foreign I was delighted with it. She insisted that I come over. As I was dying to hear my new record on a stereo I succumbed. I had a strange reluctance to see Leo, especially now that I had to thank him for this dangerously-perfect present. I didn't want to be too gushy about it, but the trouble was I felt gushy.

Mum sensed my dilemma. She wrapped round my shoulders the lovely crocheted stole she'd given me to go with my dress and said, "Now take it easy. Don't overdo the thank-you's. I know it's a lovely present but it's no more than he owes you for getting him off the hook, and besides—" She stopped. I knew she had been going to add, "—he can well afford it," but she had decided not to bring money into it. Just as well. I'd have been cross if she had. I *hate* this grown-up obsession with how much money people earn and what things cost. I must say the relative *prices* of Leo's and Mark's presents never even occurred to me.

I was welcomed like royalty at Number Eight. Even the twins had presents for me, both things that Bruce would be delighted with—a box of metal puzzles from Neville and a jigsaw puzzle from Rudy. "They were all set to give you a whoopy-cushion, "said Rebecca, "but I drew the line at that."

Mr and Mrs Daniels made a terrific fuss of me and toasted me in sweet sherry, of which I had a small glass too. Leo was nowhere to be seen. I was really relieved. Pretty soon the grown-ups went off, leaving Rebecca and me to the hi-fi, though not without Mr Daniels giving Rebecca a list of do's and don't's a mile long. Obviously it was *his* toy.

We put the Winds of Change record on. Rebecca doesn't quite share my devotion to them, but she does like them and was suitably envious when I told her I was going to their concert on Saturday. Then we settled down on two great brocaded sofas, shoes off and feet up, to listen.

From the first track I was off—drifting away into a dream-world. The gentle, mysterious sounds carried me away, and the magic words went right into my brain, curled up there and made pictures—strange and exciting and new. I thought being drugged must be something like this and half-understood why people smoke pot or even take LSD, though the mystery to me always is why they need to when you can get the same effect from music or kissing or even just thinking, sometimes. Euphoria. That's the word for it. I was so glad I could have euphoria without any artificial help. You need it sometimes. I only wished Mark had been here with me instead of Rebecca. To be kissed while that music was going on must be just like heaven on earth . . .

While the second side was still keeping me on Cloud Nine, the door opened and in walked Leo.

He stood in the doorway, looking at me. He hardly noticed Rebecca. I looked back at him. He was beautifully dressed as always—I don't think I've mentioned how well he dresses, but he's got that kind of slim tall build that any clothes look good on. He'd been out somewhere and hadn't even taken his overcoat off before coming to the living-room door. It hung open rather like a cloak. It sounds so silly to say he looked like some kind of beautiful sheikh standing there in the shadows. My heart stopped for a moment and then raced on. I sat up and put my bare feet on the floor quickly. It felt so *sensuous* to be lying down while he looked at me.

"Thank you for my beautiful present, Leo," I said.

"It suits you," he said. "You look really lovely tonight."

He took off his coat slowly, and then came across the room to the patch of light I was sitting in. He bent over and kissed my cheek with his dark, warm lips. "Happy birthday, *dear* Kate," he said.

Then he seemed to remember that Rebecca was there too, because he straightened up and said, "Hallo, you," to her. "Is this nice record yours?" he asked me in quite a casual tone, not at all like his happy-birthday one which had been terribly intimate and had sent shivers all over me.

We chatted for a few minutes and then he went off to have his supper. The second he was gone Rebecca fairly fell on me.

"*What's* going on between you and Leo?"

"Nothing," I said, my face on fire.

She sat beside me on the sofa and looked from one of my eyes to the other in a very beady way and then said slowly, "I don't believe you."

"Look, don't go getting ideas! He thinks I got rid of Marie-Noelle and he's grateful."

"Well, I know *that*, but that doesn't account for him talking to you in *that* sort of voice, as if you were grown-up and he were in love with you."

"I'm not and he's not, and don't be so silly or I shall go home," I said with an edge to my voice. I did *not* want Rebecca questioning me or suspecting how I felt.

But she wouldn't leave it alone.

"So he gave you that," she said, pointing to the medallion. "*Of course* I thought Mark had."

"Didn't Leo ask you what I wanted?"

"No. And if he had I wouldn't have dreamt of suggesting anything like that. That's a sort of love-present, not a friendly or a thank-you one." She went on looking at me, almost accusingly. "Did he kiss you goodnight when he took you out on Saturday?"

"That's none of your business!"

"So he did!"

"Rebecca, shut up. You're spoiling the music and you'll spoil the end of my birthday too. You're cooking something up that doesn't exist. Leo's far too old to be interested in me."

"But you're not too young to be interested in him. Or you wouldn't be absolutely scarlet in the face."

"I'm scarlet in the face with fury at you. Now stop it or I'm going, right this minute."

"Okay, but I'm just warning you. Mum's not going to be much keener on you than she was on Marie-Noelle."

Suddenly I really was angry. "Don't be so disgusting! Comparing me to that horrible creature. And even if Leo and I—" I stopped sharply. "I'm going," I said, instead of whatever I'd been about to say.

I started towards the turntable to get my record which had just ended, but Rebecca rushed after me. "Please don't touch it, Dad'll go spare." She took the record off as if the whole thing were made of fine glass and handed it to me. But when I tried to take it from her she held on to it. "Kate, listen," she said, "I'm sorry I pounced on you. It just came as a shock. Hearing him talk to you like that, and then I thought of a few other things I've noticed lately . . . Maybe he really does like you, *that* way I mean. No, don't say anything. I want to say something so you'll understand why I jumped on you about it. *I'd* like it if you were Leo's girl-friend, of course I would, in a way, but Kate, it would be bound to make trouble at home. We've only just got over the other trouble which made Mum and Dad impossible to live with and I couldn't stand any more of it—all those hushed conversations and Mum crying in her room and Dad being awful about Peter—"

Now *she* stopped, but of course I understood at once what was at the bottom of it. She was almost in tears.

"Parents are such a nuisance with their fixed ideas!" she burst out. "Don't tell me you haven't had trouble about Mark not being posh enough—well I have all *that*, which mine call being 'not in our circle', but on top of it I have this Jewish business which makes it almost impossible to find any boy they approve of. Maybe you think they're very free, letting me go out with boys a lot, but they're not. I'm *never* allowed to stay out after ten even at weekends. Dad takes me everywhere and brings me home. When I've got a boy here either Mum or Dad is in the room the entire time. No boy'll stand that for long. Oh, I know I've had plenty of boy-friends, so-called, but you may have noticed none of them last. And I never really fancied any of them till Peter. He was the first one who wouldn't be put off by all Dad's madnesses. Do you know during all these horrible weeks when I haven't been allowed to see him, except at orchestra practice, he's kept ringing up and writing to me—it's like Romeo and Juliet—I think he'd come and carry me off tomorrow if I asked him to! And being separated from him has made me like him more and more, I keep thinking and dreaming about him all the time. Yesterday I asked Dad, very casually when he was in an awfully good mood, if I could see Peter again, and he said yes if I 'behaved myself', which means sticking to the rules. And now you come along and if Leo's going to get fond of you in any way that gets Mum and Dad worried, awful things are going to happen! They won't affect you, but they'll affect all of us and especially me because I'm a girl. I'm treated just about like that hi-fi, as if the least jar might break me. That's how it is in families like ours. The boys can do what they like more or less, while the girls are treated like hot-house flowers. I'd give *anything*," she added passionately, "to be you, with your nice sensible English parents who haven't any religious hang-ups!"

"They have other hang-ups," I said. But Rebecca didn't really want to talk about my parents. Her mind was on Peter.

"I'm simply longing and longing to be with him again," she said. "It's been sheer torture, seeing him across the room at orchestra practice and hardly being able to talk to him because Dad always sits there watching me like a hawk . . . Kate, please, don't spoil it! If you're my friend, you won't."

"It's not fair to put it like that."

"I can't help it. Give me a chance to get started with him again, *please*, before you go out with Leo any more. They accepted that once, thinking it was just a gesture of gratitude, but even one more date and they'll start getting jumpy."

"Just because I'm not Jewish, all this is?" She nodded. "Then why won't they get jumpy about you and Peter?"

"Because I'm not ready to get married and Leo is. They want him to get married, they expect it, they look at every girl *he* looks at from that point of view. Wait till I'm twenty-two and see how they chain me up if I so much as look at a goy!"

"At a boy?"

"At a goy. That's a gentile. Oh, it all makes me sick! As if there's any real difference! A man's a man, isn't he? Sticking them in categories and saying 'You can only choose from this box'—it's *stupid*! Don't you think so?"

"Yes," I said feelingly. "Oh yes, I do."

"So you'll hold off, if he asks you out? Just for a few weeks?"

I thought quickly. It would be just as well. I really couldn't see *how* I could square it with my conscience if I were going out with both of them at once. It would only make me unhappy. It might end in complete disaster. Hearing that Leo was "ready to get married" scared me. It made the age-difference between us look like a huge gulf again, because *I* wasn't ready to get married or anything like ready, and wouldn't be for years and years, I was sure. I wanted a career first, and travel, and I wanted to feel I could run a home and cope with children and so on before I even dreamt of calling myself "ready to get married".

And the way I felt about Leo was an oddly un-teen-age feeling and always had been, no matter how I'd tried to disguise it as a "crush" so as not to be frightened by it. If he was going to get at all serious about me, I sensed that it couldn't be just what Dad had called a boy–girl relationship. It had to be a man–woman relationship. And I didn't want to be a woman, not really, not like that. Not seriously, with some kind of—well, final goal in view. With Mark it was different. We were on the same level. We might or might not be in love, but neither of us thought a step further than just what we felt about each other today. No plans, no heavy thoughts—the future didn't come into it. And that was better.

"All right," I said.

"Oh Kate!" said Rebecca, her eyes shining. "You are sweet! Thank you! I'll do something for you one day." And she hugged me and kissed me, and then I took my record and went home.

20

When I thought over this promise I'd made to Rebecca I felt like laughing. How noble of me to say I wouldn't go out with Leo when he hadn't even asked me! And probably never would.

But he did. He rang me up on Friday and asked me to go to a concert at the Wigmore Hall next day. Luckily there was absolutely no question of my going because I already had this longed-for date with Mark. I put down the phone after explaining this with a huge, pent-up sigh of relief. Perhaps that would be the end of it. Leo knew about Mark. He'd *said* he didn't want to interfere. If he really didn't, he would take that "no" for a final answer. But if he really didn't, why had he kissed me? Why had he given me the medallion? Weren't those the acts of a man who's decided to—well, to compete? My anxiety about the whole thing flared up but died down again. I'd decided, hadn't I? And I meant to stick to it.

Mark called for me at six sharp the next evening.

I'd decided to try my new dress out on him. Without the medallion—I didn't want to ask for trouble. But the very first thing he did when he arrived was to push my hair back and look at my ears. A great complacent grin broke out on his face.

"You did it!"

"All right, don't crow. I hadn't much choice."

"Did it hurt much?"

"Hardly at all—to my surprise."

"That's good. And when can you—you know, wear my—"

"When the holes have healed. Meantime I have to wear these little sleeper-things."

He beamed at me, glanced round the hall, and pulled me to him. He kissed my ears, first one and then the other. Wow—who *ever* would imagine ears could be so (pause while I look that word up, I always forget it) ah, yes: *erogenous*? "You're smashing," he whispered to me. He only ever said things like that in a whisper.

"I'm a fool," I retorted, trying not to let him see how erogenous my ears were still feeling, "to let myself be pushed into a thing like that."

"Are you ready?"

"Don't I look ready?"

Then for the first time he looked over the rest. "Cor, aren't we ponced up," he remarked, broadening his accent.

"You don't like it."

"Too got-up for my taste. But maybe it'll grow on me. Push your hair back, then when all the rest of it gets too much I can get comfort from looking at your lug-holes."

"I suppose you'll regard my ears as your own bit of private property from now on, just because I've mutilated them for you," I said, making a pony-tail in the mirror.

"They're my foothold on the rest of the premises."

"*Pardon?*"

"The thin edge of the wedge."

"Talk about mixed metaphors," I said, showing off a bit. But you can't get the better of Mark in schoolish things. He immediately answered, "They're not only mixed, they've got demotic overtones which is even cleverer."

I wasn't going to challenge him on "demotic" because I've never been sure of it and I was pretty confident he was, so I just gave him a look.

Dad came into the hall to see us off.

"What time will you be bringing her back?" he asked as always.

"The concert ends at ten o'clock, so we'll be back by ten-thirty at the latest," said Mark smartly.

"Take care of her," said Dad, also as always, and kissed me. "Have a good time, darling."

It wasn't till we got round the corner that I remembered the bike.

"How will you ride in that dress?" Mark asked.

I had a quick think. I'd much rather have gone by bus and

arrived unblown-about, but I didn't want to make problems so I said, "Hitch it up."

"You'll be cold."

"Well that's my fault."

Whoever's fault it was, I was pretty nearly frozen from the hips down by the time we reached the cinema in South London where the group was playing. We parked in a street behind the place. There were hundreds of kids all trooping along, chatting excitedly. As I stiffly dismounted from the bike and stood rubbing my icy legs while Mark locked up, I noticed something.

"Aren't they all terribly *young*?"

Mark looked up. A group of little girls was just going by, all giggling and shrieking. They looked about twelve.

"A mature appreciation of good music seems to be starting earlier these days," he remarked. But he was frowning. Winds of Change is definitely not for the teeny-bopper, and these kids we were walking with towards the cinema were the teeniest and boppiest you ever saw. We were like grown-ups beside them, a good head taller than most of them.

"Why have they got 'Chuck' and 'Dukie' on their sweat-shirts?" I asked uneasily.

"I don't know," said Mark. "Who *are* Chuck and Dukie, anyhow?"

"They're members of the Bo Janglies," I said.

Mark gave me a look of horror. I knew the dreaded Bo Janglies only too well because Bruce had recently woken up to the pop scene and started watching them whenever they appeared on TV. They have about as much in common with the Winds of Change as the Bay City Rollers have with Simon and Garfunkle.

As we came to the final corner, the tide of infants we were moving in swelled to a torrent.

"God! You don't think—" began Mark.

Then we saw the marquee. There it was in big letters. "The Bo Janglies Live Tonight."

Mark let fly with the worst swear word he could think of. "Wait here," he said. "Don't *move*. I'll be right back."

I stood against the wall while the crowd flowed past me. After what seemed like ages, Mark, swimming upstream, fought his way back to me. His face was like thunder, and my heart sank.

"It's not my fault, Kate, you must believe me! They changed it last week. Well—maybe it is my fault—maybe I should've checked—they say they advertised it all over the place, on the radio and everything, and in *What's On*—"

"*I* didn't see it either—I don't blame you—" But oh, I was disappointed! I felt almost as furious and miserable as he did.

"They offered to give me my money back. They're packed out with this lot, they could sell our tickets ten times over. What do you think? You don't want to see this other group, do you?"

Well of course I didn't. On the other hand, what would we do instead?

"Maybe there's a good flick on near here?"

Mark looked despairingly round. It was a wilderness-area. "I doubt it."

"Or we could go for a meal . . ."

Neither suggestion really appealed. We'd come to hear a live pop concert. Mark looked so depressed I only wanted to cheer him up.

"Listen," I said, "let's go to this. Even if it's ghastly it might be good for a giggle. I can always drive Bruce wild by telling him about them." I didn't really fancy it but I didn't want Mark to feel bad.

"Derek's gone on them too. Pity we can't go and get them and send them in instead of us."

So, feeling terribly let down but trying to make the best of it, we joined the crowd and were swept in.

We really were almost the oldest people there. Well, no, there were a few middle-aged women, Mums possibly, though they looked just daft enough to have come on their own account. Sorry if I sound snobby, but the Bo Janglies really were the dregs of the pop scene. Their sound was really crude. That was why the very young kids went for it. It was all noise and beat and glitter. Their gimmick was to drape themselves in as much junk-jewellery as their bodies would possibly hold. They wore bangles right up their arms, Morris-dancer-type bells round their knees, ankles and waists, jingly ear-rings (they were all men of course), necklaces of metal whistles, believe it or not, and even little cymbals attached to their fingers that they clashed as they moved. Underneath all this they wore tight-fitting lamé suits smothered in sequins and loads of make-up so that when the full lights hit them it hurt your eyes to look. They hurt your ears worse, and I didn't discover until that evening just how painful really loud noise can be.

I'd never liked the very noisy groups, even when I was younger, but with a record or telly you can always turn it down. There was no turning it down here. There were loud-speakers in every part of the cinema, so the sound blasted at you from all directions. And as if that weren't enough, the kids in the audience went totally mad right from the moment the group came on.

I'd seen them do it on telly but I'd never realized what it would be like to sit in the middle of it and see and hear it going on all round me. It wasn't only agonizing to listen to, so that I put my hands over my ears, it was really frightening. The kids—girls mainly, but quite a few little boys too—simply stood up in their places, opened their mouths and shrieked and shrieked and shrieked. I never realized what a shriek really is—I mean, how it's different from, say, a scream or a yell—until then. A shriek tears your ears. It's high, shrill, piercing. And these shrieks went on and on. How they could do it continuously like that without damaging their throats I don't know.

And meanwhile the Bo Janglies were doing their stuff up there on the stage. They weren't far away from us, because darling Mark had thought only the best was good enough for my birthday and had bought seats only about four rows back. They seemed almost on top of us with their frenzied movements and dazzling costumes and deafening, monotonous beat. At the risk of repeating myself I must say again that I've never heard such a noise in my life. I don't believe a battle could be louder, and as the concert went on I began to be almost as scared as if we *had* been caught up in a battle.

Those kids went really wild. The group kept gyrating down to the very edge of the stage and reaching out their bejewelled hands to the crowd, who would strain forward to try and touch them. Then the group would dance tantalizingly away again and the shrieks would change to a high-pitched wail of frustration. One girl next to me, a little kid of about eleven, started actually clambering over the back of the seat in front after they'd done this manoeuvre a few times. "Chuckie! Chuckie!" she kept screaming. "Let me touch you! Just touch you!" One of the boys on stage seemed to reach directly towards her. She stretched both hands towards him and I swear he beckoned to her to come closer. His face—which I thought quite horrible with its slimy green and silver eye-shadow and bright red cheeks—leered at her like some tempting demon. She got one leg over the seat-back, scrambling almost on to the shoulders of the girl in front, clawing and struggling to get nearer to the hand reaching towards her as if it were a magnet pulling at her.

On my other side I saw Mark suddenly jump up and catch hold of the little girl beside him who was almost falling on her face over the back of the next row. He pulled her back and I heard him shout at her, "Sit down, you'll hurt yourself!" She gave him a glassy look, her mouth hanging open. Her face, turned towards me, was quite wild and streaked with tears. Her hair was all over the place as if she'd been rubbing her hands over it. Suddenly her face twisted furiously. "Lemme alone! Lemme go!" she screamed at him, wrenching away. He doubled over and I saw she'd kicked his leg.

He turned to me, and put his mouth to my right ear.

"They're all mad," he shouted. "Let's get out!"

But you could forget *that*. We couldn't have got out without a bulldozer to clear the way. The kids in the row behind ours now started to clamber forward, pulling and clutching at our clothes to help them climb over the seat-backs. When I looked back, there seemed to be a movement forward all the way into the depths of the cinema. The faces straining towards the stage looked absolutely demented, hardly like children's faces at all any more. We have a book at home of paintings by Hieronymous Bosch, and those kids reminded me of some of them—especially the mouths—wide open and letting out these terrible mindless sounds.

Now we were being shoved and trodden on as the kids scrambled almost *over* us to get closer to the stage. And suddenly I saw that some huge men had appeared from nowhere and had ranged themselves between the edge of the stage and the front row. It was easy to see what their job was. They had to keep that crazy mob of hysterical girls from actually reaching the group and tearing them to pieces. They weren't fussy about how they did it, either—they couldn't afford to be by this time, the state those kids were in. Nothing but sheer brute force could have held them back. The audience pushed forward in waves, the ones behind driving on to the ones in front. Now the screams all round us began to sound different. Frightened and even panicky. Very near me I suddenly heard a scream that was different again—it was a scream of pain as someone got trampled, and I saw the little girl who had been next to me go down on the floor under the seats while a wave of others seemed to hurl themselves right over her.

"Mark! Mark—help her—" I shouted, but it was a wonder he heard though he was right beside me with both arms round me to protect me from the crush.

He saw where I was pointing and yelled something like "Don't crouch down!" Keeping between me and the forward surge, he managed to reach down, hiking the little fallen girl up by getting one hand into her armpit while forcing the other kids off her with the other. All the time we were struggling to get her upright the beat of that horrible music was going on and on as if the group up there was quite oblivious of the uproar and danger we were in, which they'd deliberately caused. Looking at that poor kid's scared dirty face, and seeing those big bruisers in front of the stage hurling themselves at the heaving masses of bodies like policemen dealing with a street-riot, I just felt *so angry* and sick I wanted to scream myself.

Suddenly in the very midst of the nightmare, everything seemed to go slack. The glaring lights which had been like part of the madness went out, the throbbing beat stopped, the screaming died down. I looked round. The curtain had fallen, the men had gone; the house-lights came up. The audience was still in chaos, but the terrible compulsion which had seemed to drive them mad a moment ago had been turned off. The kids who had been pushing and straining forward now sank back into their seats. They looked battered and exhausted; many of them were sobbing on to each other's shoulders, or just sitting there blankly with tears running down their faces.

The girl Mark had rescued flopped into her seat. She pushed her hair back with hands that trembled and after a moment gave a little giggle.

"Cor, I wet myself!" she said brightly to the girl next to her.

"In't they smashin' ?" the other one replied.

Mark and I looked at each other. His face was grey.

"Let's go," he said grimly.

We tottered out.

"No re-admission!" the doorman called as we pushed through the swing doors.

"Who needs it ?" Mark shot back. Then we were out in the fresh night air, leaning against each other in stunned silence.

Finally Mark straightened up. "That", he said, "was one of the most horrible experiences of my life."

"Mine too!"

"Kate, I feel lousy. You might have been hurt!"

"I think I was," I said, peering over my shoulder. Mark turned me round.

"Good God! Look at your dress! It's all ripped. And your shoulder's been scratched—"

"Oh well, if that's the worst. If you ask me we were lucky to get out alive."

We walked back to where we'd left the bike, our arms tightly round each other. I was trying to stop shaking.

"Those kids—" I began.

"Don't," he said. "Just to think, if we'd had our kid brothers here we'd have sent 'em into that hell-hole without thinking about it."

"I wonder how many parents know—"

"I should think seeing your kid come back from a session like that just once'd be enough for any parent with a grain of sense."

"Wait till I tell Bruce!"

He turned to me. "Look, maybe you'd better not say too much at home. I'll get the blame."

"It was my idea to go in."

"Try telling them that. I'm responsible for you. When I think what could've happened—"

"Maybe you're right. I'll say we went to another concert instead of our one, but I won't go into details."

"What about your dress ? Won't your Mum ask ?"

"I'll keep my coat on and mend it myself."

"So long as they don't think I did it in a moment of passion!"

When we reached the bike Mark turned me to face him.

"You're still shaky. And you'll get cold again. Maybe I'd better take you home on the tube."

"Oh, nonsense. That'd take hours, and you'd have to leave the bike here and come back for it."

He looked doubtful, but in the end I persuaded him. He gave me a quick kiss and said ruefully, "You know what ? We've just had our second adventure together. We'll have to try to have some *good* adventures sometime." Then he fitted on my crash-helmet and we climbed on the bike and took off.

21

All might yet have ended well except that half-way home we both realized we were starving.

Mark pulled up at the kerb.

"Listen, this was supposed to be your birthday treat. I'm not going to let it go at that. Let's at least have a good nosh-up somewhere."

I'd have been quite satisfied with a Wimpy or some fish and chips, but Mark was having none of that. He was determined to make it up to me. So in the end we turned into the West End and he took me to a very nice place. Far, far too expensive, but he'd got that stubborn look so I didn't protest though the food nearly choked me when I thought of what it was costing.

Try as I might I couldn't avoid comparing Leo with Mark in this sort of place. Leo had been completely at ease, and had made me feel at ease too. Well, of course—he'd had dinner in swish restaurants hundreds of times before. Mark was different. It wasn't that he didn't know how to behave, it was more as if he resented having to "act posh" for the benefit of waiters and other diners. There was a sort of aggressiveness buried in the perfectly polite but rather tense way he gave our orders. This made me nervous. I felt as if I—or maybe Mark—might be going to spill something or cause some sort of disturbance. Perhaps the ghost of that awful incident in the pub haunted the very back of my mind, too. I found myself chatting brightly and not-quite-naturally to keep Mark's mind off our surroundings. The fact that I'd had to keep my coat over my shoulders to prevent my torn dress from showing didn't help me to feel comfortable.

And yet although being with him at times like this was so—well, strained, I understood so well how he felt that in a way it made me love him more. He was doing this for me, trying to fit into what he thought of as my sort of place. Actually it wasn't, or only on special occasions, but he thought it was, or perhaps he thought it was the sort of place I deserved. Anyway I knew his bringing me here was every sort of compliment and even though I did wish we were having a hamburger and Coke in the American place round the corner from home, I kept that to myself.

I couldn't help looking at my watch every now and then, but that was nothing to do with Mark. It was to do with Dad.

We'd come out of the concert in the middle so it was still only a little after ten when we'd finished eating. That gave us nice time to get home before the deadline. Mark paid the enormous bill, I put my arms back into my coatsleeves and off we went, back to where we'd left the bike.

It had gone.

At first we couldn't believe it. We thought we must have mistaken the street. But after a dazed moment we realized we couldn't have done. We'd left it right outside Soho Market in a proper motorbike-parking place. It had just vanished.

"It's been nicked," said Mark in a hollow voice.

Just at that moment a police-van came round the corner. Mark flung himself in its path, waving his arms, and it stopped.

When the policeman heard what had happened he asked for the number of the bike, and then rang through to some headquarters where they apparently have a computer which sorts out lost and found vehicles. He was able to tell us right away that it hadn't been found.

"How could it be? I'm only just reporting it lost," said Mark.

"Sometimes we find 'em obviously abandoned and take 'em in. It does happen."

"And if not?"

"Then you'll have to go into Vine Street and report it missing. We'll notify you when it turns up."

"*If*," said Mark bitterly.

"An awful lot of 'em do, sooner or later. Some yobbos probably took it for a joy-ride, or to get home."

Mark looked so glum the man took pity on him.

"Hop in. We're going that way, I'll give you a lift to the station."

We clambered in. Mark sat silent all the way, looking out of the window. There were other men in the van. One of them, not in uniform, leant forward and said, "Cheer up, mate, it'll turn up in a day or two." I wondered if he were a criminal being taken into custody, but it was probably a detective. Anyway he was trying to be nice, but Mark was just too depressed and furious to care.

When we arrived at Vine Street we had to wait quite a while because there were several other people before us who'd also come to report stolen vehicles. I thought there must have been a gang at work, but it turned out to be just a normal number.

At last it was Mark's turn and the policeman filled in a form very slowly with all the details. By this time I had realized that I was going to be late and a nasty fluttery sensation had begun in the pit of my stomach. I was tired and too full of food and my brain wasn't working very well, but I had a horrid feeling there was more to worry about at home than just being late.

By the time we came out of the police station I was afraid to look at my watch, but Mark looked at his.

"Crumbs, it's nearly eleven!" he said. "We'd better get a taxi."

Need I say we couldn't find one? Oh, there were plenty, but it was going-home time from the West End and every one was taken. We stood at the bus-stop near Green Park and Mark nearly went crazy trying to decide whether it would be quicker in the long run to go by tube or whether we should wait for a taxi or a bus. If we had gone by tube we'd have been home in half the time, but we didn't, and by the time a bus finally trundled along it was half past eleven and we rode home in a doomful silence.

"Your Dad'll have my head on a plate," Mark said grimly as we at last reached our stop and started to walk the last few blocks. It was after midnight.

"Mark, it wasn't your fault! You couldn't help it if the bike was—"

Then it struck me. It struck both of us. Our excuse—our water-tight, cast-iron excuse—was bound to backfire. It was worse than the crime. It meant admitting that I had gone on the bike—that Mark had taken me on the bike. And that meant—

"What shall we say, what shall we say!" I began to moan. I'd never felt so sick in my life.

Mark cuddled me comfortingly. "Oh come on, it's not so bad! You're a big girl now. You haven't done anything wrong."

"I have, I have! I lied to them! They're sure to ask me if I've ever been on the bike before, and when they find out—"

"Listen, let's go in and face the music. It won't make it any better to stay out here."

I could hardly get my key into the door I was in such a state.

"Here, give it to me," said Mark impatiently. Poor Mark! He'd had an awful night, and now this! I felt an impulse to tell him to go home and let me cope on my own, but I couldn't face it. Anyway he wouldn't have gone.

We went in to the living-room together. I had had a faint hope that Mum at least would have gone to bed, but she hadn't. They were both there. Heads turned, eyes fixed on the door as it opened. Mum's eyes were filled with reproach. Dad's—well, I'd have been quite glad to see anything as mild as reproach in his.

"And where have you been?" he asked instantly.

Mark did the explaining. He did it without any finesse, just the bald words. He wasn't going to humble himself.

"The concert turned out to be the wrong one. We went in and then came out again half-way through. Then we went to dinner in the West End. And when we came out—" he hesitated a fraction of a second, and I saw his throat-muscles move—"my motorbike had been stolen."

I quailed at the word "motorbike". Mum sat forward and her mouth opened.

"What motorbike?" she asked.

"Mine."

"You took Kate out on your motorbike?" she asked incredulously.

Now Mark looked at me—a helpless look. He didn't know how to answer without getting me into trouble. I had to take over.

"We always go on it," I said. "We have for ages. I'm sorry, Mum."

Mum looked at Dad. Dad stood up. He was looking at Mark, not me.

"I don't remember giving permission for Kate to travel round London on a motorbike," he said, quietly but dangerously.

"We knew you didn't agree. We just started it one day and kept on. It's not a risk, I'm always very careful."

"Not a risk!" Mum cried out sharply. "Of course it's a risk! Don't you know that hundreds of young people every year—"

"Mrs Dunhill, I'm sorry. We try to keep your rules. But we're not always able to."

"You don't always want to, you mean!"

"Yes. That is what I mean."

And now Dad started to come to the boil.

"Well, Mark, you've been admirably frank with me and now I'm going to be frank with you. We've let Kate go out with you because we thought you *were* keeping our rules. God knows we don't make many, only those we consider necessary to keep Kate safe. Your rules—if you have any in life—are probably concerned more with your own pleasure and convenience than Kate's wellbeing, but you must allow me to insist that mine have precedence over yours as long as Kate is living with us."

Mark was standing very straight. I could see from his chest that he was breathing hard.

"What you say about my rules isn't fair. I wouldn't do anything to hurt Kate or get her into trouble if I could help it—" Dad raised his eyebrows, but Mark went on, "You know what I mean! Trouble with her parents. We had a bit of rotten luck this evening, it could have happened to anyone, otherwise I'd have had her home on time like always."

"So that's your morality! Anything goes so long as you're not found out!"

"My morality's my own business."

"Not when you take my daughter out! Then you're responsible for her."

"Yes, and I never forget it for a moment."

"And yet you'll take a chance on injuring or killing her—"

"You take that chance every time you put her in your car, every time she crosses a road to get to school—"

"That's nonsense! It's not the same thing—"

"Life's full of risks. Riding pillion with me's no worse than—"

"Mark, will you listen to me? I—"

"I've listened enough! She's sixteen. You've kept hold of her conscience too long and too tight. Look at her! Crying and shaking as if she'd come in here to confess to some crime or something. She hasn't done anything except give you a couple of hours' worry, which is no more than any parents have to expect once in a while!"

There was a shocked silence. Dad wasn't used to that sort of back-answer from people outside the family. Mum said shakily, "You might at least have phoned—"

"Yes, Mark, we should have phoned!" I said.

But Mark was as angry as Dad by now, and not about to see reason.

"Maybe we should, but we were too busy trying to get home as quick as possible. We did our best. We're sorry we're late, and I for one am sorry we weren't more open about the bike from the beginning. I didn't want to interfere. Come to think of it, I think I advised Kate not to tell you. But—"

Dad pounced on this. "So you advised her to deceive us!"

"Oh come on!" said Mark impatiently. "Deceive you! It's against nature to tell your parents every little step you take towards growing up, they never understand. Sooner or later you have to start making your own decisions."

"It seems you think us very fussy," said Dad tightly.

"Yeah. I suppose I do."

"Well so we are. And so we should be. She's our daughter and we love her and taking good care of her is part of that. Which is something that *you* may never understand."

"Oh I understand that all right!" said Mark. Which was the nearest he'd ever come to saying that he loved me.

Mum stood up and came over to us. "I think it's time we stopped this discussion and let Kate go to bed," she said. And before I'd had time to think, I'd let her slip off my coat.

I heard her gasp behind me. "Kate! What on earth's happened to your dress?"

Mark closed his eyes. "Oh, bloody hell," he said under his breath. "That's all it needs."

It was well after one-thirty by the time the "discussion" finally ended. It was the worst hour of my life till then. I was crying, Mark and Dad were shouting, Mum kept telling everyone to keep their voices down but every now and then she shouted herself. The trouble was, they couldn't understand how we could have been so daft as to go into a Bo Janglies concert.

"Don't you read the papers? Don't you *know* what happens at those damnable things? A little girl was suffocated a couple of months ago, and there are never fewer than half-a-dozen carried off to hospital afterwards—"

We had no answer to that. Neither of us had known. Maybe we should have. Dad always says I don't read the papers enough, but I never thought he meant that sort of news.

In the end the "discussion" really deteriorated into an outright row, and that was the worst part of course. Dad, who had always been so polite to Mark, let his true feelings break out. He said he was a young ruffian with no proper standards or sense of values. I knew what he really meant, and that pushed me over the brink. I began to shout too.

"You've never liked him! You think he's not good enough!"

"I think he's irresponsible, and tonight proves it," Dad yelled.

Mark had gone oddly quiet. "What does that mean, exactly?"

"That I don't want you taking her out any more!"

"I thought we'd come to that. Well," said Mark, turning to me, and he seemed very calm now that I'd blown my top, "I think that's up to Kate."

"Oh no, it's not!" said Dad.

"It is. She's sixteen. That happens to be the age of consent."

"*Consent*?" roared Dad. "Consent to *what*, for God's sake? I tell you as long as she's living under my roof—"

He really was beginning to sound like a sort of Mr Barrett character. I wanted suddenly to cool everything before it got any worse.

"Shh, Dad, it's all right." I turned to Mark. "Mark, it'll seem different tomorrow. Please let's stop this now. I'll talk to you in the morning."

But Mark was too far gone. That stubborn look he sometimes got had his face in a stiff, tortured grip, so that suddenly I remembered the Hunchback of Notre Dame.

"You'll decide right now! Do you want to see me again or not? Because if not there'll be no talking to me tomorrow or any other time. I'll go back to my *own class*,"—he shot this at Dad quite viciously—"down among the other ruffians or yobs or whatever you'd really like to call us—and find myself a girl whose parents won't be ashamed to have their daughter go out with me, who aren't just waiting for the first excuse they get to make me feel I'm not bloody well good enough!"

He grabbed hold of me and pulled me out into the hall and slammed the living-room door almost in Dad's face.

"Now then Kate," he said fiercely. "This is between you and me. Quick. What's it to be?"

"What do you mean? You can't ask me to choose between—"

"I mean, are you going to go on seeing me despite them, or am I going to walk out of here?"

"Oh Mark, don't ask me *now*! I'm so tired and miserable!"

He let me go.

"You shouldn't have to think about it," he said flatly. "You ought to just know."

He walked straight out of the front door. I grabbed it just as it was going to slam.

"Mark! How are you going to get home?"

He turned at the gate. His teeth were locked. He looked *terrible*, like a gargoyle.

"I'm going to walk," he almost spat out. "Every bloody step. Now go to bed and forget me."

I went to bed. There was no question of Mum sitting with me that night. She didn't even speak to me. I crawled into my bunk, leaving my ruined dress in a heap on the floor. I lay there sobbing my eyes out. *Love*? You can keep it! I thought. If this is love, I'd rather be dead.

22

It must have been three in the morning when the door opened. I hadn't been exactly muffling my sobs; I suppose in the back of my mind I'd been hoping Mum or even Dad might take pity on me and come and comfort me. But it was Alastair, in his dressing-gown.

"What's up with you?" he asked, sounding kind but rather peeved.

"Oh God! I'm so unhappy!" I sobbed.

He switched on the light by my bed. His hair was on end and he looked sleepy and a bit fed-up, as well he might. But when he saw my face he seemed to wake up a bit.

"You look a right mess," he said. Then he stepped aside rather quickly. "Yukh! What on earth's this?"

I'd taken a whole box of tissues to bed with me and had just been throwing them into a soggy heap on the floor below my bunk as I finished with them. Alastair had trodden on the pile in his bare feet.

"Sorry," I said with a hiccuping gasp. "I'll get rid of them." I came down the ladder and gathered the revolting things up and stuffed them in the waste-paper basket, which they filled to overflowing.

"Come on down to the kitchen and let's have something to drink," said Alastair. "You can't carry on like this all night."

I put on my dressing-gown and we tiptoed downstairs. The kitchen was nice and warm and friendly and made a change of scene from the dreary dark loneliness of my bedroom. Alastair poured some milk into a saucepan.

"Cocoa or Horlicks?"

"Coffee."

"You're not having *coffee*, you nutter, you're supposed to get to sleep some time tonight." He made me Horlicks and put it before me. He hadn't mixed it properly and the blobs of powder were floating thickly on the top but I like it like that and skimmed them all off greedily with my spoon. An hour ago it had crossed my mind I would never want to eat again and that I might as well just let myself waste away. Now my after-sobs were dying down and I thought I might even be able to face some bread and butter or a biscuit. But it was only because I was cried out. I wasn't any less miserable and I still thought death would be quite a good alternative to facing up to things tomorrow morning.

Alastair sat opposite me. "Let's be having it," he said.

I drew a deep sigh which shook.

"Didn't you hear the row?"

"Yeah, not being stone deaf I did. What was it all about?"

"Oh . . . being late home . . . and me having been riding on Mark's motorbike when Mum said I mustn't . . . but mainly it was about class."

"Huh?"

"Yes. When you get right down to it. It was about—Mark being working-class and Dad having just waited for an excuse to get rid of him. Tonight he had it. He said the most awful things—and Mark did too—" Maybe I wasn't quite cried out, after all. I put my face in my hands. It felt all hot and damp and strange. I got up quickly and went to the sink, found a dish-towel, dipped it in cold water and held it to my eyes. Alastair waited. At last I went on, "Mark said I should defy them and go on seeing him. He said, if I loved him I wouldn't have to even think about it."

"Well that's silly for a start. Where there's a conflict of loyalties you always have to think."

"Anyway he's gone. He went off and said he was going to walk home. It's *miles*—through the cold—" The image of him tramping home alone and furious haunted me, even though he must be there by now. I felt so sorry for him. "I failed him," I said shakily. "I should have stood up for him, even if they threw me out—"

"Kate, sit down." I did, not looking at him. "Will you listen to me? You're being a bit silly about this. You've got it out of proportion. You're overdramatizing. They wouldn't 'throw you out' and you know it. You haven't 'failed' Mark. Now *listen*, will you? Calmly. What exactly has happened? Dad and Mum have come out into the open with their disapproval of Mark. Like Dad finally came out and told me, what I knew quite well already, that he didn't want me to carry on indefinitely at the garage. Well, that's *good.* It's cleared the air. You know where you stand. Mark knows where *he* stands. Dad's said what was lurking in his mind and he'll be feeling better. You and Mark have got the bike business off your consciences and no harm's done. You're sixteen and Mark's your boy-friend and if you decide to go on seeing him Dad will have to accept it. You may have him grumping around the place, or shouting at you, but he's not going to forbid Mark the house or anything, he wouldn't be so daft. He knows that would only lead to secret meetings and so forth which is the last thing he wants."

"But Mark expected me to—"

"Mark had no right to expect you to do anything on the spur of the moment. And he's quite bright enough to have realized that, probably by the time he reached home tonight. The whole thing's actually up to you. You've *got* to have a good think. You talk about class, which incidentally I bet Dad didn't. I've often thought you're a bit obsessed on that subject. What you'll have to ask yourself is, not so much whether Mark's accent and background and so on bother Dad and Mum, but whether, deep down, they bother you."

I stared at him with my mouth open.

"*Me*?" I said at last.

"Yes, you."

"How on earth would *I* get like that?"

"How could you hope not to? In this house?"

"What do you *mean*?"

"Look, what do you think class-consciousness *is*, or racialism, or sexism, or any of the other prejudices? They're things you drink in from your environment when you're a child, and they grow up with you and probably get passed on to *your* kids, if you're not damn careful."

"But we're not racialist or—what *is* sexist, anyway?"

"Thinking women are inferior. No, of course we're not, and we don't deserve any credit for it because there's no trace of that sort of thing in our family. But if we manage to grow up free of class prejudices then we *can* give ourselves a pat on the back, because both our parents, in their very different ways, are snobs."

I stared at him.

"We needn't love them any less for it," said Alastair, "but we have to recognize it. I did, a long time ago, when Dad was forcing me through that crammer course to get me into Burnfield Court. I made up my mind then to break free of all that and—"

"Shut up a sec, let me think."

He obligingly shut up and drank his Horlicks, looking at me over the rim. After a few minutes I said, "All right, I agree Mum's a snob. She couldn't not be, with Grandad going on about oafs and looking down his colonel's nose at nearly everybody—"

"That just proves my point—"

"But she fights against it. Not like Auntie Gerry, who glories in it. She does fight. I've only *sensed* her feelings about Mark, she's never *said* a word till tonight."

"Well, Mum's aware of it, you see. She doesn't like being that way. With Dad it's different."

"I just don't see how Dad can be a snob if it comes from families. He's got a working-class background himself."

Alastair dropped his eyes and was silent for a while.

"He's got a different brand of snobbery," he said at last. "He isn't prejudiced. He knows the working class from the inside, and he's deliberately rejected it and come away from it. He's more middle than the middles now, like a convert to a religion is always hotter on it and more bigoted than people who were born into it. Mum can take her middle-classness for granted and, as you said, fight against the side of it she hates in herself; but Dad can't. Dad's split. The thing Dad has to fight is a desire to be disloyal to his background, to deny it altogether. That's why he shouts so much about socialism. He's got a foot in both camps. That's very uncomfortable for anyone. But he feels deep down that being middle-class, living the way we do, is basically better than what his family had and *were* in Lancashire. That we're better than Uncle Steve for instance. That's why it bugs him so badly that I want to be a manual worker, and why it bugs him that you're attracted to a boy like Mark instead of a middle-class boy. He's hiked us up on to what he believes is a higher level of society, and he wants us to stay there and not—well, slip back, if you like."

Now it was my turn to be quiet. At last I said, "But I am attracted to Mark. He makes all the boys around here look like drips. What am I to do?"

"If you really like and admire him—I mean, it could be just physical attraction, only you can judge—then you've got to fight the class-thing that's been bred into you like it was into me. You've got to say, he's for me, for the time being anyway, and anyone who doesn't like him can lump him. On the other hand . . ." He looked at me very straight. "You mustn't keep on with him just as a reaction to Dad's snobbery. That would be stupid. Just as stupid as if I'd said to myself, 'I'd rather go back to school, but I'm going to stay on at the garage just to show Dad what I think of his wrong ideas.' Do you see what I'm getting at?"

I saw. Oh, I saw all right! I never saw anything clearer in my life.

"Al," I said slowly, "you're brilliant."

"So I keep telling everybody, only I never get credit for it. Now go to bed and let me get some sleep."

I came down to lunch next day (not breakfast you notice; the Horlicks, lumps and all, had done its work too well) feeling calm and clear-headed. I knew exactly what I felt, what I thought and what I was going to do.

We ate lunch in such subdued silence that Bruce finally asked, "What's going on around here? Has there been a family fracas?" He pronounced it "frackus".

"Frackah," said Dad irritably.

"Well, has there been one?" persisted Bruce.

"*Yes*, if you must know," growled Dad.

"Oh bloody hell," Bruce groaned through his Yorkshire pudding.

"Leave the table!"

"Why should I?"

"Because I tell you to!"

"But I'm hungry," said Bruce reasonably. "I've been playing tennis all the morning."

"LEAVE THE TABLE!" roared Dad.

Bruce heaved a martyred sigh. "Can I take my dinner at least?"

Dad rose menacingly to his feet.

"Oh all right, all right!" said Bruce hastily. "Mum, could you put it back in the oven till the *frackah* is over?" Dad lifted his hand, and Bruce, exaggeratedly shielding his head, dashed out of the back door. A moment later we heard the gate to Number Eight clash to.

Dad leapt to the door. "If he's gone next door to beg some food—" he began.

"Reg, will you kindly sit down?" said Mum in a voice she reserves for Dad's more unreasonable moments. He returned, reluctant and muttering, to the table. Mum got up and put Bruce's plate in the oven. Her lips were drawn tight.

As soon as we'd finished eating, Alastair retired to the living-room with one bit of the Sunday paper, and Dad hid behind the other. Mum started to clear, and after a few trips to the sink said to me, "What about a bit of help, seeing you slept all morning?"

"I'll do all that, but first I've got something I want to say."

Mum at once sat down again. The paper quivered slightly but stayed up.

"Dad? Will you please listen?"

"I'm listening."

"You can't listen and read." He's often said that to us. He lowered the paper.

"Well, madam?"

"It's about Mark. You said I wasn't to go out with him any more. You also said a few other things that could mean he won't want to take me out any more, but in case he does, I've decided that I want to go. I'm not going to do anything more behind your backs—like the bike business, I mean—so I'm telling you now. I'm very sorry if you don't like him, but I do, too much to give him up, and I don't think you should be able to tell me to or even ask me to."

"So you think you should be allowed to live in our house, at our expense, and do as you like at the same time?"

"Yes," I said, "when 'doing as I like' doesn't involve doing anything wrong." I looked quickly at Mum, who was staring at Dad. "Anyway I've always considered this my house as well as yours."

"Of course it is," said Mum. "It would be a tragedy if you ever thought of it in any other way." Dad looked at her and they exchanged a few remarks with their eyes which I couldn't interpret.

"So you think you're now grown up enough to make your own decisions," said Dad at the end of this silent conversation. "And it seems your mother agrees with you."

"I don't see how I can accept your decision about a thing like this."

"If I actually forbade you to see him, what would happen?"

I looked at him. I thought of all the lovely, sweet things he had done for me, and of how much I loved him and how much I knew he loved me. Was this threat just stubbornness, or did he feel that strongly about it? Was it to protect me that he wanted to ban Mark from my life, or was it some kind of warp in himself? After all, he must know more about life than I did. I was used to taking his advice. It's not easy to dismiss the habit of a lifetime. Maybe he *did* know best. I remembered the crowd Mark had gone around with at Willcox, about the scene in the pub, about *his* family and their prejudices which must have rubbed off on him . . . Maybe we were too different. Maybe I was just being carried away by physical attraction . . .

But then I thought of other things. How Mark looked after me and protected me, even from myself. How clever and sensible he was, and how honest and strong, despite his strange anger and stubbornness. I thought of his behaviour about Leo, his wisdom which was as deep in its way as the wisdom I had seen last night in my brother. All his "bad" experiences—drug-taking, nearly getting that girl into trouble and so on—he had learnt from, they had all made him grow. He was a man, not a boy, and I respected him. *That* wasn't just physical.

"Dad," I said, "you wouldn't, would you? Not really. You can't dislike him that much. Besides . . ."

"Besides," said Dad, still looking into my eyes, "if I did, you'd see him anyway. Is that it?"

"I'm afraid so. I think I'd have to."

"You're that keen."

"It's not only that. I can't let you decide for me. If it's a mistake, I have to find it out for myself."

Dad sighed and leant back, looking at Mum. "That's it, you see," he said, as if continuing a conversation with her. "That's what's wrong with mankind. That's why we never learn. Because every generation insists on making its own mistakes. The same old ones. Over and over and over again."

I phoned Mark as soon as I'd done the dishes.

His mother answered the phone. She sounded even less friendly than the last time, and I realized that she, too, must have been worried last night when he didn't come home until so late, and that she probably blamed me. She might even have got quite the wrong idea.

"He's not here," she said shortly. "He's gone for his bike."

"What do you mean, Mrs Collins?"

"They rung up this morning from the police. They found it."

"Oh, that's marvellous! He'll be so pleased."

She grunted.

"Where was it?"

"Right the other side of London somewhere. Sidcup, I think he said. He said he wouldn't be back for a few hours."

"Oh—I see. Well—could you please tell him I phoned?"

"I always give him his messages," she said.

I dashed out to the car to get the Street Finder and looked up Sidcup. It really was the other end of the world. It would take him hours to get there by public transport on a Sunday. Or maybe Walter might have driven him there? I wished I'd asked. I wanted to figure out how long it would be before I could hope to hear from him.

I sat around all afternoon, getting more and more restless. Mum and Dad worked in the garden, doing the spring digging. I thought I ought to go and help them, considering Alastair's total disinterest in gardening, but although I already sensed an easing of the tension I somehow couldn't bring myself to join them. Instead I made the time pass slower by doing nothing. I thought of phoning Emma—a good way to pass an hour or so—but I knew if I did I'd tell her everything and I didn't want to, not yet. Not till Mark phoned and we made it up.

I kept remembering the last big bust-up when I'd written and phoned and he hadn't responded and I'd had to go and find him. I prayed that wouldn't happen this time. I thought it wouldn't. He *did* learn. Mad as he'd been last night, the hours between then and now must have calmed him down. He would phone me tonight. I was sure of it.

But six o'clock came and—nothing. Seven o'clock. I began to feel desperate, but I realized I was being silly and tried to control myself. After all, why should he come straight home when he'd collected the bike? He might have gone off somewhere and not be back till late. The more he didn't phone, the more I longed to hear his voice. It was the old, old story. Ring, telephone, ring. But like the watched pot, it didn't.

About eight-thirty I belatedly realized I had homework to do and tried to get down to it. Hopeless. For discipline I started with French. I couldn't get to grips with it at all. I tried to get into the mood by reading a few of Jammy's poems. They *all* seemed to be about star-crossed love. Trust the French. And it sounds sadder in French as well. I gave it up and turned to maths, but that wasn't much better. By the time the hands on my purple clock had dragged themselves round to bed-time I was just like a lump of jelly, I couldn't do a thing with myself. I didn't even feel tired enough to sleep. But Mum wasn't to know that, and at nine o'clock she came banging on my door.

"Kate, are you ready for bed?"

I slowly undressed and lay in my bunk in the dark, straining my ears. The phone did ring once, and I leapt up and raced to the top of the stairs, but it wasn't for me. I crept back to bed again. I'm ashamed to admit there was yet another disgusting little heap of multi-coloured damp tissues beside my bunk before I finally fell asleep around midnight.

By the next day I was hating him.

I knew he must have got my message. He had deliberately decided to keep me in this agony. Of course he couldn't know what a giant step I'd taken in defying Dad's wishes and deciding to go on seeing him, but he might at least have given me a chance. Awful words like "stubborn pig" were seething in my mind all day at school. I'd never had bad thoughts about him before, and they made me feel sick at my stomach.

As going-home time drew near, I began to have hopes that he might be waiting outside for me. I always discouraged this because he couldn't get to my school in time without missing his last lesson, but today I was prepared to overlook this. If only he'd come—if only we could talk! I felt frantic. The bad thoughts would get worse and worse if he let much more time go by. And I was powerless—I couldn't phone him again, or seek him out this time. I felt how frightful it is to be a girl and to have to leave everything to the man when the real crunch comes.

School ended and I ran out. There was no one by the gate. My heart ached—really ached, with a true, physical pain. I could hardly breathe. But there was one more hope—that he would meet me at our bus-stop. I sat absolutely still on the bus all the way home, my whole mind concentrated on willing him to be there. But he wasn't.

When I got home I found I couldn't bear to go in. Mum would know at once how upset I was, and why. She wouldn't say anything; she would be kind to me, and I couldn't bear that somehow. But where could I go? Home wasn't home at that moment. I went to Number Eight.

Rebecca was there, absolutely glowing with happiness. She'd been out with Peter and everything was lovely and perfect again. She was full of talk about him, how marvellous he was, how much in love with her; she even said she wasn't so sure any more that she was such miles away from getting married. She was so bubbly and excited she never noticed how quiet I was. After a while her raptures got too much, and home seemed preferable. Besides, Mark would be back from school by now and—who knew? The phone might be ringing at this very moment.

I fell over myself getting home.

The phone was ringing!

I rushed to answer it. A familiar voice—but not Mark's—asked after a moment or two if Mr Dunhill was at home. I laid the phone down, horribly disappointed but also puzzled. Who was it? It was a voice I vaguely knew, a voice not unlike Mark's, the same accent. I called Dad to the phone and hung around while he picked it up.

"Hallo . . . yes . . . yes . . ."

A very long pause followed. I could hear the voice at the other end going on and on. Dad had his back to me. I'm not a very intuitive person usually, I mean I don't get "feelings", but something about Dad's back—its stillness, I think—suddenly struck absolute terror into my heart. I stood there as if I were frozen. There came a moment when the voice at the other end stopped speaking and still Dad didn't say anything. After an endless silence he drew a sharp, deep breath and said, in a voice I didn't recognize, "I see. Thank you for phoning. I'll attend to it." He put the phone down and turned to me.

I knew at once. From his eyes. I didn't cry out. I just stood there. I screwed my eyes shut. I pressed my hands to them. I felt Dad come up to me and put his arms round me.

"Kate—"

"No!" I gasped. "Don't tell me—don't—"

We stood still for a long time, with me rigid in his arms, my head trembling with stiffness from my clenched teeth and tight-shut eyes.

"Kate—" Dad began again.

I forced myself to come back, to look at him. I think I looked at him beggingly. As if he could change it. He suddenly pressed my face to his chest.

"He's not dead," he said in that queer, strangled voice he had used on the phone.

I pulled away, ill with sudden hope.

"But he's hurt. Badly. He crashed the bike coming back from Kent. Skidded on a patch of oil."

Mum had come out of the kitchen and was standing behind me. She and Dad held me between them. The three of us clung together. I felt we were part of each other. Mum was trying to hold back sobs, but I felt absolutely numb and empty.

At last I said, "Can I see him?"

"Yes," said Dad. "That was Walter on the phone. He says I should bring you to the hospital—right away."

He didn't need to tell me what that meant. Mark wasn't expected to live very long.

23

The hospital was a long way away. We seemed to drive for hours. Alastair came with us—Dad stopped off at the garage to pick him up and he came as he was, in his oily overalls. Dad drove and Al and Mum sat in the back seat with me between them, each holding one of my hands.

I didn't feel anything. Not anything. Except perhaps fear of what I would feel when feeling came.

At last we got there. We went up a long flight of stone steps into a big old-fashioned building. Dad motioned us to stop and he went to the reception desk and spoke to the woman there. After a while he came back and led us down a corridor and up three more flights of stairs. At last we came to a ward marked "Intensive Care Unit".

There was a nurse sitting at a table outside the double doors, and after Dad had spoken to her she went through them. I caught a glimpse of cubicles. We stood there waiting. After a short time she came back with Walter. He came straight up to me and put his arm round me.

"This is her," he said to the Sister, "the one he's been asking for."

"Very well then," she said, "but not too long. And only one. The rest of you must wait here." She looked at me over her glasses. "No fuss now. Brave girl."

It was only when Mum and Alastair let me go that I realized they'd been holding my hands all the time.

Walter took me slowly along the aisle between the rows of little closed-off rooms with glass windows in their doors. I knew that in each of them was some dangerously ill person. I was trying to get myself ready and Walter seemed to know it, because he put his head down to me.

"They've bandaged him up, girl," he whispered. "So don't get a shock. But don't you worry, he's not a goner yet. Putting up a right fight. The doctors say he's got a chance if he can keep it up."

I braced myself as Walter stopped by the last door. "Brave girl," the Sister had said. She wasn't saying I *was* brave, she was saying I ought to be—that I had to be. But how can anyone be brave when they see a person they love with his chest all bandaged, and his arms and legs plastered and hung up on pulleys, with wires and tubes going into him and a look of death on his poor shadowed face?

The numbness which had been so kind suddenly went away and the most horrible wave of feeling broke over me. His body had been all broken like a doll's. He was going to die! I wanted to scream, to fall down on my knees, to beat my head on the wall or tear my hair and clothes the way primitive women do. I felt quite crazy. If it hadn't been for Walter holding me tightly I think I would have gone completely to pieces.

"Shh, girl, shh, hang on, he needs you," he kept saying under his breath while his big hands gripped me so hard they hurt. I needed that pain. I wanted it. It held me to myself, to reality. After a little while I was able to say, "It's all right, Walter. Let me go to him."

As I moved to the side of the bed I noticed for the first time that Mr and Mrs Collins were sitting there on either side of him on chairs. Mr Collins was on my side of the bed and he stood up and moved away so that I could sit in his place. I couldn't hold Mark's hand because it was in splints and bandages, but I put my face down close to his.

"Mark . . . Mark . . ."

He opened his eyes. His face hadn't been hurt, nor his head I noticed now. That was something. Do you die from broken arms and legs? But perhaps he'd been injured inside . . . his chest was in plaster too . . . The thought nearly made me faint.

"Hallo, love," he whispered. He'd never called me love before.

"You poor thing," I managed to say, choking with tears.

"Not—so bad—" he whispered. "I keep thinking—if you'd

been—on the back . . ." He closed his eyes and turned his head slightly away. After a second he turned back. "Tell your Mum—she was dead right—never again . . ." His mouth twisted into its crooked smile.

"Mark . . . I told Dad yesterday morning I want to go on seeing you. That it's my decision."

"I said you were a—big girl."

"That's if you want to go on seeing me."

He smiled and flicked his eyes down at himself. "The chance'd be a fine thing," he said very faintly.

"Here! None of that," said Mr Collins from behind me. "It's up to you."

There was a black nurse sitting at the foot of his bed. "You'll have to go now," she said to me.

Mark made a little movement. We all fell back as the nurse rustled to his side and bent over him. After a moment she straightened up.

"Well," she said, "some of you will have to go. I can't have such a crowd."

"What do you say, Mother?" said Mr Collins. "We'll go and have a cup of tea and leave young Kate with him for a bit."

"Will you tell my family?" I said. "They're waiting for me."

Mrs Collins, who hadn't spoken yet and whose face was set like marble, unexpectedly said, "We'll *all* go and have some tea. Come along, Walter." She hurried out first without looking back. Walter patted my shoulder.

"Keep your kisser up," he said.

Then he and Mr Collins followed Mrs Collins out and the glass door closed.

I sat down again and stroked Mark's face and hair very gently. My tears had stopped and I felt a little calmer. He just lay looking at me with that crooked smile on his face. The shadows round his eyes weren't grey, they were a sort of reddish colour; actors call it "crimson lake" but I'd never seen it on a real face before. I tried not to let my eyes wander to his chest. The sheet was turned down and there seemed to be such an awful lot of plaster and wires and bandages there. But the tube going up his nose I couldn't help seeing. I longed to just keep saying, "I love you, I love you," over and over again. I said it in my mind.

After a while Mark's eyes closed.

I called him softly but he didn't stir. I turned wildly. The nurse was sitting there writing something.

"Nurse! He's—"

She jumped up at once and bent over him. My heart seemed to stop. Then she straightened up.

"Fast asleep," she said. "Now don't you go getting yourself into a state. Just sit with him quietly. I am here all the time."

I sank into the chair, shaking all over. "He looks so—"

"He had a major operation twenty-four hours ago. It's a wonder he can recognize anyone, let alone talk. He has plenty of strength in him, this boy of yours. Now sit there goodly and think all the time he will get well."

I stayed an hour. Then the Collinses took over and I kissed Mark and went home with my family. Walter promised to ring me that night. Instead he came round. I'd been put to bed with some sleeping-tablets, but Dad came up before I was quite asleep to bring me down to see him.

"He's holding his own," said Walter. "That's what I come to tell you. He's still on the danger list, I'd be telling a lie if I said he wasn't, but the doctors haven't given up hope. My belief is that seeing Kate did him good. Of course they're doping him pretty heavy so he don't feel nothing." I was feeling rather dopey myself, but Walter's words, and his honest, down-to-earth manner, somehow loosened some of the tightness round my heart. Dad offered Walter a drink and when Mum led me up to bed again they were sitting talking.

I was allowed to stay away from school for a week, and I spent most of it at the hospital. Sometimes Mum would take me, sometimes Dad; when neither of them was free, one of the Collinses would meet me and take me with them. Once it was Brendan and Linda. Linda talked all the way as if she couldn't stop. "I always knew something would happen, he's so reckless, and he gets these moods, just like Brendan, when you can't do a thing with him, he just has to bash his way through them and out the other side . . . I'm never easy a minute when Brendan's out of my sight, never know what he'll get up to, when someone'll give him a wrong word that'll end up in a fight, or him coming home itching to let it all out on me and Sharon—" "Will you shut up, Linda?" Brendan would interrupt every few minutes in a weary tone. "She don't want to hear our troubles." "Why not? Take her mind off her own, poor kid," retorted Linda.

Mrs Collins was nearly always at the hospital. I think she was allowed to sleep there. We often sat opposite each other. We didn't talk much, but every now and then our eyes would meet across Mark's bed. There was no feeling of unfriendliness now. She and I were sharing something very deep. Whether we liked each other or not, that brought us together.

She wasn't a woman who could cry easily or let her feelings out, but I knew how badly she was taking it inside. One day I came into the cubicle when she wasn't expecting me. Her face, so like Mark's, was all screwed up and she was tearing her handkerchief into little shreds. She put it quickly in her handbag when she saw me, but I could see she was in a dreadful state. I wished I could think of anything comforting to say to her.

"You must be missing a lot of school," she said in a high voice as I sat down.

"I'm going back next week."

"That's right. You should. No sense falling behind. Give you something to take your mind off. Not healthy for you, sitting here day after day."

"Do you mind my being here, Mrs Collins?"

"No," she said quickly. "I don't mind. I'd be foolish to mind, when it's helped him to have you. Young people. They're more important to each other than anything or anyone. It's not they don't love us. We just haven't got power to help them after a certain age. It's only natural."

"How is he today?"

"Well I thought he looked worse but they say he's better. They ought to know. I've been here most of the night so perhaps I'm not fit to judge. They're trying to ease off the drugs a bit and he's feeling the pain from time to time. Moaning and that." Her face was blank but she was twisting her wedding ring round and round and round her finger.

Suddenly I heard myself ask the question I hadn't dared ask anyone since it happened.

"He won't die *now* will he?"

Her fingers stopped moving and she fixed her eyes on me. Despite the way she was holding herself in, her eyes were red and wild. No wonder she scarcely ever looked straight at anyone.

"He might," she said.

"But after all this time—"

"They won't say he's going to live. So I don't see no point in getting too hopeful."

How could she say that so calmly? I burst into tears. She made no move to comfort me but let me cry for a while and then said, "It's better to face it in advance than have the shock if it happens. I never hope for anything. Then if the worst don't come, you can enjoy your relief."

"But when will we know?"

She didn't say anything for a while, but then she said, "You know what's the trouble with him, don't you?" I shook my head. "It's not his arms and his leg. Those'll mend. It's inside. He smashed his ribs and some of 'em stuck into him. If that gets infected he'll die. They'll know in a couple of weeks. If he can hold out till then, he may be all right. But he'll never be the boy he was. That's another thing you have to face up to."

There were long hours when I was there alone. I had some funny thoughts. I would remember all the times we had been together, especially towards the time of the accident. Like touching a sore place I would force myself to go over and over the scene in the hall when he had asked me to commit myself to him despite Dad, and his awful look as he set out to walk home. It was as if, by re-living it enough times, I could take the sting out of it, but I never could.

I thought about the moment when he had pulled up at the kerb and insisted on going into the West End for dinner. There had been a Kentucky Chicken place right beside us. What if I had said I wanted a box of fried chicken and chips, and refused to let him take me to the fancy place? Then we wouldn't have left the bike, it wouldn't have been stolen, he wouldn't have had to go to Kent to fetch it—none of this awfulness would have happened. I'd begun to realize that even if he didn't die, it would take him a long, long time to get better. If he ever did . . . I tried to take Mrs Collins' advice, and face up to the thought that he might be a cripple.

Several times I thought about the thieves who'd taken the bike. Would they feel anything if they knew what it had led to? It was hard to imagine what sort of men they must be. It was hard not to hate them. Religion crept into these mixed-up thoughts sometimes. A good Christian would find it easy to forgive them—perhaps. A person who believed God takes care of all of us would be able to pray for Mark's recovery. Sometimes I had a yearning to pray, but I refused to let myself. It would be dishonest when I didn't believe at other times. Besides, I'd never understood why, if God intended someone to die, he might be persuaded to change his mind if you prayed hard enough. If I did believe in a God, it wouldn't be one who couldn't make his mind up.

Still, I remembered the black nurse saying, "Think about him getting well." *She* obviously believed in the power of thoughts. The doctors had said several times that it was Mark's will to live that was keeping him alive. And those were scientists. So it was worth *willing* him to live, thinking hopefully and positively. I tried to stop myself thinking the dark thoughts about the thieves, and about my last evening with Mark.

He slept a lot of the time, but sometimes he would wake up and sometimes he would even be able to talk a bit.

"Bloody fool me," he said one day. His voice was still terribly weak, but, I thought, a little stronger than at first.

"You couldn't help it," I said.

"I was so happy to get the thing back. And yet I was still angry. I was going too fast. Didn't see that patch of oil till I was flying through the air . . ." I knew about all that. An oncoming car had hit him as he came down. The thought of it made me feel sick.

Another time he opened his eyes and immediately said, "Bike's a write-off."

"Are you sure?"

"Walt wouldn't tell me, so it must be."

"You're insured. You can buy a new one."

He moved his head in a faint shake. "Uh-uh. Enough. I'm not a nutter. Car for me next time."

I remembered he'd been due to take his test again round about now.

"I'll miss the old bike," I said.

"I'd never have taken you on it again anyhow."

Once he said, "Give us a kiss." And when I kissed his forehead he said, "No, a good one." I kissed him very carefully on the lips. His breath had a bad smell which frightened me—I knew it came from his internal injuries. "Am I horrible?" he asked me.

"You're lovely," I said.

"I bet. I must look a wreck."

"You do, but you're lovely just the same."

The weeks went by. The strain was really awful sometimes, and I didn't always behave well. There were days when I even felt I couldn't go to the hospital. I wanted to forget all about it, to get away from it, to go back to being carefree and happy. But if I missed more than one day, I couldn't bear it, and would go straight from school on the bus the day after, aching with guilt for being a coward and a traitor. As soon as I saw him again, as soon as he looked up at me and I saw how glad he was to see me, I felt sick with shame at having been able to think about anything but him, even for a few minutes.

My family and friends, and even my teachers, gave me the most terrific moral support. Rebecca was too happy to be much use to me, though she did her best; but Emma was wonderful. Sometimes, when I had no lift to the hospital, she would come with me, and sit in the waiting-room, patiently getting on with her homework or reading, for hours so as to be able to come home with me on the bus and cheer me up if I felt low.

Another tower of strength was Leo.

He used to come round uninvited two or three times a week, just to sit and talk to me, and he never once said or did anything which made me feel it was disloyal of me to be glad of his grown-up company. Once Mark asked me, "How's your other boy-friend?" and I was able to say, "He's just a friend now." And so he was, a true friend. I was really glad when he met a girl of his own age and started taking her out.

That awful time had one good result. It brought our families together.

To start with there were phone-calls nearly every day between us, and we saw a lot of each other at the hospital. That third-floor waiting room came to seem as familiar to us all as our living-rooms. Then it seemed sensible to combine transport when we could, so there were calls at each other's homes to pick people up and drop them after hospital visits, which often led to cups of tea or beers round the kitchen table. Pretty soon everyone knew everyone.

I can't really say Mum and Mrs Collins found much in common, but when they were thrown together they could always discuss their children. I think it helped Mrs Collins, at the worst times, to have her attention pulled on to her other sons. Once she asked if she could leave Derek with us while she went to the hospital because Gran was poorly. Bruce was put in charge of him, and despite a few fights they got on so well that Derek didn't want to go home. After that they stayed an occasional night with each other. I must say, if there *is* any built-in snobbery in our family it passed Bruce over. He thought the Collins household was great. He said our place was like a tomb by comparison, and he was especially impressed by the food—all those chips and chocolate biscuits and fizzy drinks, and no undercooked greens, smelly cheese or "mucked-about foreign messes".

Alastair and Walter had got on from their first meeting, and Dad had soon come to see Walter's worth. I'll say that for Dad—snob or no snob he recognizes a real person like Walter, and all barriers disappear. The same went for Mr Collins. Dad said a funny thing about him, that he reminded him of his own father. They found a lot of interests and even opinions in common.

A conversation between Dad and Mr Collins is one of my most vivid memories of that time.

One evening I was having a nap in the waiting-room while Mrs Collins and Gran were sitting with Mark. Mr Collins and Dad were there, talking in low voices so as not to disturb me. Suddenly Mr Collins seemed to burst out, though keeping his voice down, "Young hooligan! Mad as a perishing March hare—always was."

I came fully awake but I didn't move. Could he mean Mark?

"Beats me," Mr Collins went on in a strained undertone, "how you ever let your girl go out with him. If I had a daughter, believe me I wouldn't let the likes of our Mark anywhere near her. What if she'd been on that bloody bike with him?"

Dad didn't answer at once, but then he said, "He may be a bit wild, and I won't say he hasn't given us some bad moments. But he's a marvellous lad. I can't really blame Kate for falling for him."

"She needs her head looking at if you ask me," muttered Mr Collins. "A girl like that. Oh he's bright enough I grant you, and not bad-looking in a poor light, but he's a terror. The worries he's given his mother and me! And yet he's her favourite. It'll kill her if we lose him. Who can figure women out? And your Kate, who could pick and choose—she has to pick him. Someone ought to tell her. He's nothing but trouble. Nothing but trouble."

I lay on the padded bench with my eyes shut. I didn't want to see Mr Collins crying.

In books and films there's always a moment when the doctor says something like, "He's over the crisis," and everyone smiles and relaxes while the patient slips into a peaceful sleep. It wasn't like that with Mark. There wasn't one big crisis, there were a lot of them. About a month after the first operation, to straighten out his ribs and sew up the damage inside his chest, he had a relapse. But they operated again at once and took out his spleen, and after that he had to start getting better all over again. So it was weeks before we gradually became sure that he wasn't going to die. I only knew it for certain when I arrived at the hospital, one lovely day in early May, and found he'd been moved into a public ward.

By the time he was finally discharged from hospital the Dunhills and the Collinses were more like one big family than two. We all arrived together to take him home.

The nurses who'd looked after him escorted him down the wide stone steps to where we were all waiting in a crowd. He still needed a stick to walk with. His arms had healed almost completely, but he hadn't got back the full use of his right hand; the physiotherapist said it would come with exercise. As to what had happened to his insides, that had healed too, but as his mother had warned me he would never be as strong and healthy as he had been. After injuries like that, you always have to be careful.

His mother was the first to hug him. They're not at all a kissy family, and it was a very short, sharp sort of hug. He put his free arm round her, then handed his stick to Derek (who immediately began hobbling about on it) while he shook hands with the nurses. Then he put his right arm round me and gave me a kiss.

I looked up into his face. The dark shadows were still faintly there, but they would go when he put on a bit of weight and got some sun. Whole and healed or not, he would be my Mark again.

We had no fewer than four cars between us—Walter's old banger, Alastair's brand-new old banger, Brendan's Ford and our Renault. Mark was to ride in the Renault because it was the smoothest. We helped him into the back. I stood aside to let his mother get in beside him, but after a moment she said, "You sit with him, he'd like that best." So I did.

Walter came to the window.

"See you back at our dump for tea," he said to Dad, and then, stepping back, added to Mark, "All right, mate?"

"Yeah, fine," said Mark. "Hey, Walt—"

"What?"

"When did you say they postponed my test till?"

"What, your A-levels? You'll have to do those next year—"

"*No*, not them! I can do those any time. My driving test I mean."

"Oh, that! Twelfth of September."

"That gives me just nice time," said Mark, settling back comfortably and putting his arm round me. I saw Dad and Walter exchange looks. Then Dad heaved a deep sigh and we drove off, leading the convoy.